The huge bulk of the lead rig materialized in the mist

The Executioner held his ground, the road beneath his boots vibrating as the monster rig with its savage cargo grew, closing.

He waited, then lifted the HK-33, sighted at the engine housing and squeezed the M-203's trigger. A muffled pop, and the hellbomb streaked on. Rubber squealed as the driver stood on the brakes, as if slowing the truck would save him and his load of terrorists.

The 40mm grenade impacted, detonated, hurling up sheared debris, the fireball and wreckage blowing in the cab's window, the driver's face of shock and horror lost to sight.

The Executioner had officially declared war.

DON PENDLETON's
MACK BOLAN®
Deep Treachery

A GOLD EAGLE BOOK FROM
WORLDWIDE®

TORONTO • NEW YORK • LONDON
AMSTERDAM • PARIS • SYDNEY • HAMBURG
STOCKHOLM • ATHENS • TOKYO • MILAN
MADRID • WARSAW • BUDAPEST • AUCKLAND

First edition November 2001

ISBN 0-373-61481-0

Special thanks and acknowledgment to
Dan Schmidt for his contribution to this work.

DEEP TREACHERY

Printed in U.S.A.

A God all mercy is a God unjust.

                                        —Edward Young,
                                          1683–1765

Funny how the savage calls out to God for mercy
when his number comes up, the same savage who
would snuff out the lives of innocents with calculated
coldness. They will get no mercy from me.

                                        —Mack Bolan

For the men and women of the FBI

PROLOGUE

Adim Sayal feared he was about to finally pay for his role in the rape of Kuwait. It wasn't anything he could outright explain, at least not in rational terms that wouldn't betray a superstitious impulse. There was the sudden knotting in his bowels, an inexplicable swelling of coldness in the chest. It left him wondering if he was the right man for the job, chosen as he was out of nowhere in the desert village by the one who called himself the Messenger. Incredible, he thought. There he was, maybe less than twenty-four hours away from tasting ultimate revenge, and the fear was threatening to eat him alive.

Pull it together, he told himself. It was just a routine border check. So why was he so riddled with doubt and anxiety?

"Hope for the best, but prepare for the worst," the Messenger had told him, before he was swallowed up by the night as suddenly as he had appeared before Sayal. In other words, Sayal thought, no sacrifice for the jihad was too small in the eyes of God. Perhaps all sacrifices, whether great or small, simply had humble origins in a man's personal commitment to truth and righteousness.

Sayal shut his eyes to the customs agents, thinking he could will them through and on their way before he looked again at their grim searching faces, the holstered side arms.

Something like six months ago his own search for sacrifice to truth and jihad began when the Messenger had come to him out of the dark, this nameless shadow man with all the answers, it seemed, to help see his dream of vengeance come true. A true blessing from God himself, this man handed off the necessary visas and passports, assuring him of a new identity, a concrete background cover to safely land and plant himself and two fellow Iraqis in Montreal, family in tow. Not to mention enough cash was waiting for them on the other end to get the ruse started in earnest. They were instructed to build a life as a family of rug weavers and pottery makers, he briefly recalled, run their own shop, blend into the urban scenery. In short, remain quiet, all humility and gratitude for the world to nod and smile down on, see they could go along with the Western flow—until the time when they were called upon to act. And, if they had to, they were to sacrifice their own women and children.

No exceptions, this was war.

The Messenger had made it sound so easy, so simple, so right. Vengeance for all the wrongs and injustices inflicted on Islamic peoples the world over was theirs for the taking, if they wanted it bad enough. In fact, the Messenger seemed to know so much about the former Republican Guard colonel that, even though he was Sunni Muslim, Sayal began to think of the Messenger as the twelfth imam, just like a

Shiite believing in one holy descendant of Mohammed who had never died, only remaining hidden in
the world until the time of the great calling for all
Islamic peoples. Well, Sayal believed himself called
by the Messenger, whoever he really was, but who
had personally sought him out to lead holy warriors
in glorious battle against the infidels, and on their own
soil. And the Messenger had stated it was long since
time for all Muslims to put aside their personal and
ideological differences. Only in unity could they survive, triumph over the Great Satan, find themselves
returned to glory.

Perhaps the time for action would come sooner for
Sayal than he wanted. Then again, there was God's
will to consider. What would be…

Sayal drew a deep breath, decided he was momentarily afflicted by a simple case of jumpy nerves,
chided himself then for even daring to think he might
not have the brazen resolve to get past them, clear
and free, and away on the journey to do what must
be done.

He opened his eyes, and of course, it was all just
the same. Feeding some gas to the engine, he slowly
rolled ahead, cutting the gap to the next vehicle in
line. He braked the minivan behind a red Toyota with
New York plates, then began waiting in the dark
again, his mind once more wanting to scream at him
with any one of a dozen worst-case scenarios, all of
them ending in his own violent death. Try as he
might, he couldn't deny the fear.

The first indication it might all go to hell, end here
and now on the border between Quebec and New
York, was the three state police cruisers parked on

the American side. Number-two bad omen was rolling into sight up ahead, the shadowy forms of three customs agents marching in lockstep with a uniformed cop framed in the headlights, the foursome having angled away from one of the booths, now eyeballing his vehicle and passengers from the distance. Sayal felt his fingers curl around the steering wheel, heart pounding out a few more jackhammer beats than moments ago. If he was prepared to silently will himself into calm and reason, his brothers-in-jihad began voicing their concerns, thus bringing his disturbance roaring back to the surface.

Beside him, Sayal glimpsed Ali Basrat giving his jaw a nervous massage. "This is not good, Adim. I do not like this. It feels wrong, I tell you.

"The policeman, see how he is staring at us? I count three cruisers. Where are the other policemen? As soon as they looked at us, I swear I could already hear their minds raging with their bigoted American thoughts."

From directly behind him, Sayal heard the older brother, Abdul Basrat, speak in a voice loud and clear with venom toward all things West. They spoke in Arabic, as Sayal had earlier instructed. Call him paranoid to a fault, but Sayal was suddenly imagining parabolic mikes aimed their way from the dark wooded hill country along the border. Perhaps a helicopter even hovered somewhere in the vicinity, a sophisticated listening device picking up their conversation through the roof, an interpreter onboard, wired in to a platoon of subgun-toting FBI agents, ready to give the green light to kick some Arab ass.

Sayal looked into the rearview mirror, searching for

the right words to tell them all there was nothing to
fear, even though everyone in the van knew that was
as far from the truth as they were from Baghdad. It
was difficult to stay calm, he knew, when fifty-
some pounds of plastic explosive was spread around,
packed inside the door panels. Even more nerve-
racking for Sayal, since he had the hell box in his
coat pocket, the C-4 wired up to one radio frequency,
ready to blow away whatever their target along with
themselves to Paradise, leave behind nothing but a
smoking crater.

There was Abdul's wife, Sisara, and their two teenage sons, Naim and Jabal, squeezed in beside the former tank commander of the First Republican Guard
Brigade. Sisara was a dark-haired beauty, and as instructed by the Messenger she had forsaken the tra-
ditional black veil and *abaaya*. Instead she'd gone for
white blouse, blue jeans, suede jacket, with her hair
tied back in a ponytail to reveal stunning beauty that
made Sayal think it was a sin alone for her to even
consider ever wearing a veil. While both sons were
outfitted in baggy pants and Montreal Expos baseball
caps—worn backward, of course, as seemed the con-
temporary uniform of the day for the rebellious young
Westerner—the men were clean shaven, short hair,
windbreakers and jeans. No beards, beads or kaffi-
yehs, nothing at all that would point to their roots.
But if Sayal was under the illusion that foreigners
could fade in among the West by miming their fashion apparel alone, it was quickly becoming dashed the
longer the trooper stood and stared at them. Sayal was
thinking the cop was perhaps memorizing the license
plate, about to run it down. A moment later, he was

sure of it, as the trooper wheeled with two of the customs agents beside him, the trio disappearing inside one of the guard booths.

Ali kept rubbing his face. "See how the customs man simply waves the other vehicles through. A quick look inside, no search, no examination of any bags. Smiling, waving. I see an old man and woman in the headlights. I see some young guy in a business suit. All American or Canadian, Western faces. I can read his lips, that customs agent. Have a nice day, welcome to America, he says. He will look at us hard, I tell you. He will ask us questions."

Sayal was growing angry and more nervous. He wanted them to shut up, to simply get this whole border check over, no fuss, but sure enough Abdul had to keep the anxiety ball rolling. "I heard on some news program, one of their live police shows, the ones where they film people being arrested, how American police engage in profiling of drivers down here. You drive up I-95 from Florida, you are black or Hispanic, you must have drugs, just like that. These people, they do not like the way you look, they stop you, harass you, do not even need a reason, they think they are God because they are on the side of their so-called law. They may even detain us, they have that power. One look," he said, snapping his fingers, "we are Arab, our passports say, we must be terrorists."

Sayal moved his right hand up and down, palm facing toward the floor. It was the body language of their native custom for silence.

"They have computers inside those booths," Ali went on. "They are sure to be hooked into INS."

"Pray to God our new identities hold," Abdul said. "If not..."

Stifling the urge to lash out and tell them to stop braying like old women, Sayal watched on as the customs agent went through the motions with the Toyota. Something, though, didn't feel right where the trooper was concerned.

On the ride down from Montreal the former Iraqi Republican Guard colonel had expected little if any traffic going into America from Canada's largest province at that early-morning hour. He was right on that count, with only three vehicles ahead of them, free to drive on after the American customs man gave the visas, driver's licenses and registrations a cursory exam before waving them through. No search of the interiors, no malingering, everything looking quick and routine to Sayal.

Just like the Messenger's contact promised.

They were next, and Sayal's gut told them it was all about to change.

Just like that, Sayal was seeing the future, and somewhere in his heart he believed it was linked to the past.

It was easy enough to rationalize the plunder, considering war was war, and the vanquished simply deserved what they got since they weren't strong enough to keep it in the first place. At the time of the invasion, Sayal knew oil-soaked Kuwait was declared the richest country on earth per capita by the World Bank, pumping out something like a billion barrels of petrol a year. Why would a bunch of pampered, rich, lazy Arabs have any right to whine and dare miss all the booty Sayal and other Republican Guard units hauled off in trucks?

Hypocrisy, and cowardice, had been the order of the day for Kuwaitis as far as he was concerned, when he had led the rolling waves of Soviet T-72 tanks into Kuwait City. Abusive Kuwaitis had grown rich, fat and soft while they were protected by the Great Satan simply because they were sitting on a bunch of dead dinosaurs, all that fossil fuel. Land that rightfully belonged to Iraq anyway, he thought.

Still, it wasn't the spoils of war that wished to unchain the howling ghosts of the past. No, it was the blood on his hands.

How many Kuwaitis had he tortured during the seven months of occupation? Hung them, naked and upside down in the police headquarters he'd taken over as his command central. How many genitals had he burned off with either cigarettes, lighters or electrical wires? How many times had he sneered at an old Kuwaiti man, "Tell me, what does your Emir do for you? He marries several hundred of your women and takes all of your money. True?" They tended to agree with Sayal when he put the flame to their testicles. Another glance at Sisara, and he wondered if she knew the truth about her husband. How many Kuwaiti women had Abdul raped, then mutilated and decapitated, hanging their heads from lampposts for their husbands, brothers and sons to see? And brother Ali? Well, the stories about him were nothing short of legendary, if not revolting. Ali seemed to enjoy unvaunting Kuwaiti skulls, literally cutting out their brains...

The customs man was knocking on the window.

"Everyone give me your passports," Sayal said, and lowered the window. He put on his best kiss-up smile. "Good morning, sir. How are you this morning?"

"Looks like you know the drill," the customs man said, accepting all the passports and visas.

"The drill?"

"Never mind."

Sayal saw the customs man look past him toward the glove compartment. Sayal felt his heart lurch. If the American looked close enough, he might be able to see the false compartment fixed beneath the glove box. Hidden inside was an Italian Spectre submachine gun, a 50-round box of 9 mm Parabellum rounds up the snout. Sayal saw the man studying the glove box, then felt his own hand twitching. At the first sign he might reach for his holstered side arm, Sayal determined he would haul out the Belgian BDA 9 double-action pistol, fixed in a makeshift frame under his seat. Likewise Abdul would go for his own BDA, ready to go the grim distance.

"I also need to see your driver's license and the vehicle's registration, sir."

Ali opened the glove box, and Sayal thought he would scream in horror when one edge of the false compartment gave way. Thinking quickly, Ali gently cupped the palm of his hand beneath the edge, somehow quietly fastened it back on the plastic blot.

"No luggage, sir?"

Good. The customs man had been too busy looking around the interior, studying faces, actually smiling like some fool at Sisara.

"My sister-in-law's mother. She lives in Albany. She has fallen ill and we left in a hurry."

"Uh-huh. I thought you people all lived under one roof, one big happy family."

Sayal managed a patronizing smile, choked down what he really wanted to say, which was, "And don't forget the camel."

"Just joking. Give me a few minutes, sir."

The customs man started to walk away, inspecting the passports, when Ali said, "They know. Has someone tipped them off?"

And everything changed forever in the next heartbeat.

It was as if a dark cloud dropped over the customs agent's face as he wheeled, hand falling over his pistol.

"Know what? Who would tip us off about what?"

Sayal was stunned. It was so silent in the van, he believed he could hear the collective beating of hearts.

"Yeah, that's right, I understand Arabic," the customs agent said. "I'm a Gulf War vet. All of you get out of the—"

Bragging killed the customs agent, giving Sayal enough time to snap up the Belgian BDA, thrust it out the window. A quick tap of the trigger, the early-morning quiet shattered by a resounding peal of thunder, and Sayal blew half the man's face off behind a scarlet cloud.

"Go with God!" Sayal roared at all of them, then barged out the door. The sons were screaming for their father to stay put, Sisara shrieking for him to come back, something about just driving on. Was the woman a fool? Sayal thought, sighting down the pistol as the trooper came out of the booth, his own pistol out and barking.

There was no turning back, no driving on. It was time to go to Paradise, take as many of the infidels with them as they could.

It was little more than a flash in the corner of his eye, but Sayal caught Ali cutting loose with the Italian SMG, then the younger of the Basrat brothers was falling.

Sayal marched ahead, indeed prepared for the worst. Shouting "God is Great," he pumped out round after round, believed it was the fourth shot that slammed through the trooper's forehead and sent him toppling back into the booth, legs folding under him like rubber.

Sayal heard the repeating thunder of Abdul's BDA in his ears. It ended, though, as quickly as it began.

Two shotguns began splitting the darkness beside the booth with flaming tongues. Sayal was vaguely aware of the cracking din of pistols to their other side, since suddenly he found himself falling, his right arm flying away as the combined force of 12-gauge buckshot ripped the appendage off at the shoulder. Funny how he felt no pain as he found himself staring at the stars before he knew it, someone bellowing at him from a great distance, "Don't move, asshole!"

It was awkward, reaching across his body, delving into his pocket. Something like fiery needles began digging into his legs and stomach, causing him to flinch and twitch. They were shooting him up, he realized, as he felt the warm stickiness of his life's juices hitting him in the face. Shadow figures rolled his way.

Good. A little closer now, he thought, flicked the switch to activate the radio signal. He smiled at their snarling faces, heard one of them say, ''What the hell's he smiling about?''

''I am smiling…infidels…because I am about…to B-52 all of you straight to hell…''

Sayal thumbed the button, prepared to discover the final truth, accept his ultimate sacrifice. A roar, then a sensation of fire consuming and lifting him up for the heavens, toward Paradise, the screams of a mother and her children lost in the din, and Sayal saw the lights go out.

THE ROAR and the thunder above made him flinch in his seat. They were on simple nighttime maneuvers over the Chesapeake Bay, screaming inland over Norfolk for any one of the many naval and air bases in what the infidels called the Hampton Roads area. But that hellish shriek of turbofan engines had been causing him nightmares for a solid two months, reminding him of a day he so desperately wished to forget.

They had been holed up in a motel in Virginia Beach since landing in America, waiting for their contact to give them further instructions. For two months he'd endured the near around-the-clock shriek and thunder of the fighter jets. Two months of recurring nightmares, where he saw winged lions, roaring out of black clouds parting on mighty trumpet peals of thunder, the beasts surging out of jagged fingers of lightning. He heard himself screaming in the nightmares as the winged beasts descended on him, but just before they clamped their jaws over his legs and arms he always jolted awake, thrashing…

A vision of the future? he wondered. A warning from God? Or guilt over having been one of the few survivors that day? Had he been left questioning his own bravery all those years?

Whatever, more than a decade later, and Hafiq Muswat could still see the highway of death. The Iraqi could still hear the terrible thunder of the B-52s, the snarling of the 30 mm chain guns on the Apache gunships, the hideous wailing of men burned alive in the cabs of fuel tankers or torched inside the hulls of T-72s, the buses and vans stuffed with plunder lifted and hurled for hundreds of yards across the desert by the American air attack. Such a vision of hell on earth had remained so branded in his mind, it could have all happened a mere five minutes ago.

Soon enough, at least one marker for the grave injustice done to them, their country would get called in, even if it proved a far cry from evening the score in the final analysis.

As they drove for the gate to the new VEPCO plant, he may be reliving the horror again, but this time there would be permanent closure. No ensuing nightmares, no jolting awake in a cold sweat. The van's wheelman, Fariq, had been there, also, and Muswat looked over, hoping his brother-in-jihad had not seen the fear and doubt on his face, relieved to find his comrade focused on the gate ahead.

Brothers in Holy War, he thought, it had, indeed, been a long and frightful journey just to arrive at this point. They were two of a mere handful of survivors of that day when the retreat from Kuwait City had been ordered by Saddam, when the sky had rained fire and death on the road to Basra. Somehow they

crawled off, left the dying to countless others. Somehow—call it God's will—they eluded the Marines
and the roving fighter jets during the long weeks
when they had trekked back to Baghdad, only to find
a city in ruins. And, worse, discovered their immediate families had perished during the bombing by the
infidels. With nothing left to lose, searching for something, anything to give their pitiful post-Great Patriotic War existence meaning, they had moved far away
from demolished Baghdad. The next stop was the desert village of Al Buswaj to the north, settling in with
relatives, the two of them eventually finding work for
the execution squads. Thirty dinar per Kurdish head
wasn't much, but it went a little ways in dulling the
edge of their rage and hate.

Until the nameless shadow man came to them that
night, just over two months ago. Paperwork, instructions, cash enough left behind to insure their relatives
were comfortable, that the younger cousins wouldn't
have to stalk the dangerous and cunning Kurds for
blood money.

Gone to America then, in search of taking two eyes
for one, having found meaning to go on with life,
even when they knew they would sacrifice their own.

"There it is," Fariq said.

Muswat spotted the skeletal towers, the superconductor high-tension wires that made up the electrical
power grid. All things considered, it seemed an un-
likely target. He would have preferred to stroll into
one of the hotels, even a crowded restaurant in Virginia Beach, cut loose with the compact Ingram
MAC-10 now in his lap, just start spraying lead, killing as many infidels as possible before he committed

martyrdom by cop. Orders were orders, though, and someone else was footing the tab for their ticket to Paradise. And since it was the off-season down there on the beach, with nothing but a smattering of drug dealers, derelicts and fugitives as far as he could tell, he couldn't imagine giving it all up to God on a nearly deserted resort town of penniless drifters and bums no would ever miss.

A glance over his shoulder into the shadowy hull of the van, and he gazed at the two fifty-five-gallon drums, the universal sign for radiation staring him back. The lids were ajar, but since both of them were going to perish when he touched off the wired-up three hundred pounds of plastic explosive beneath the tarp, there was nothing to fear from exposure to radioactive waste. With any luck, the waste would take to the air on the fireball, quickly dumped into the reservoir the power plant used to pipe in the water to the superheating chambers belowground. And if God was truly smiling on them that early-morning hour, maybe the Chesapeake Bay itself would become a vast body of poisoned water.

In his final few moments on Earth, he figured he might as well spend them in hope.

A number of questions wanted to leap to Muswat's mind. Who, exactly, was the Messenger? Who was the contact in America? And how did he get his hands on radioactive waste? Why a power plant? If the idea was to knock out power to Norfolk or points beyond, well, there might be a transformer or two in the power grid, but the guts of the power station were belowground.

Well, if they were being used as a statement, so be

it. He had been informed there were many others out
there right now, doing what they were about to do.
Ultimate sacrifice was the order of the day.

War had been declared on the Great Satan, and that
was good enough for him.

A lone security guard stepped out into the light
washing over the booth.

"Go with God," Fariq said.

"Go with God."

And Fariq floored it, the van's nose aimed at the
chain-link fence. Framed like some frightened animal
in the headlights, the guard froze, then dived off to
the side as Fariq crashed through the gate. Even
though the power plant had to stay open around the
clock, there were only a few vehicles in the sprawling
lot, a line of vans with VEPCO painted on the side.
Not much by way of personnel, but the living here
would be left with their own vision of hell for some
time to come. He wished them many nightmares.

Fariq whipped the wheel hard to the left, barreling
straight for the razor-topped chain-link fence of the
power grid.

Muswat glanced into the sideview mirror. He saw
the security guard running after them in vain, his
mouth working frantically over his handheld radio,
arms flapping, the man looking to him like some flailing chicken in a suit. The steel skeletons loomed as
Fariq roared ahead. Twenty meters, ten…

This was it, a few more heartbeats and they would
sail to Paradise.

Fariq bellowed an obscenity, seemed to vent every

last bit of rage and hate he felt toward this country. Pulling out the detonator box, Muswat lit up the red light and thumbed the doomsday button.

CHAPTER ONE

Boston

Boston was familiar turf for Mack Bolan, some of the old hunting grounds where a Green Beret sergeant had cut his teeth on Mafia blood, what now felt like a hundred lifetimes, a thousand battlefields since to the soldier.

Memories, indeed, buried beneath the waking conscious, but which would haunt the dreams at night of any sane man, no matter what his level of combat expertise, or how much blood of bad men stained his hands, or how many times he took down his enemies and came out the other side, walking on to fight another day.

Maybe it was the predawn hour, not much by way of traffic flooding into the city yet, the soldier alone behind the wheel of his rented sedan, stared down by the glass and steel monoliths of the new and improved downtown Boston, the skyline shrouded in what struck him as a pall of ghostly light. Maybe it was lack of sleep for the past twenty-something hours, senses and instincts jacked up on adrenaline ever since he had started the watch-and-wait phase at Logan International's Terminal E, the international arrivals building, waiting on Flight 346 from Heathrow to touch down. Perhaps it was the rumblings of fear echoing out of the State Department, the CIA, the NSA, that the borders of America were being poked and prodded by suspected terrorists as they searched for any opening to slip into the country...and do what? One arrest along the Canadian border with Vermont some two weeks ago, an Arab man of undetermined origin found with a van loaded to the gills with C-4, a crate of AK-47s, all told enough plastique and bullets to blow away every resident inside three square city blocks.

Connection to a larger, more insidious scheme in the wings? Armies of international terrorists sweeping into America, armed to the teeth, prepared to commit suicide just so they could blow up some landmark, slaughter untold innocent citizens before checking out in their twisted blaze of glory? No one could say for certain, but the cyber wizards at Stony Man Farm, Bolan knew, were hard at work seeking out some answers to get him steered in a solid direction.

Times may change, and the more something stayed the same...well, it may be a slightly different game now—new angles for the new millennium with nuclear blackmail, industrial espionage, shaky alliances with old foes who were now skipping off with all manner of classified intelligence tossed onto the plate—always another mission, for sure, since those early days in his war of retribution against the Mafia. The faces of the savages changed, Bolan thought, but the cannibals marched on, every day, all day, without letup, still doing what they did best. Which was kill, oppress, terrorize, rape the innocent in all ways savage and inhuman to place themselves alone among their gods of power and money. The memories of his own baptism by fire wanted to come back, all the way, as alive as if it was only minutes ago, but the soldier shelved it to the deepest corners of the mind, where it all belonged anyway.

What was done was done, gone forever like all the dead, both the bad and the good, strewed behind him. And whatever had happened to create the man they now called the Executioner was, indeed, ancient history.

They knew they were made, fidgeting in the front seat of the Lincoln Town Car, a shadow head turning back every few blocks. The soldier had followed Habib Najim right out of the terminal where a cabbie, whose attention had been caught by Bolan's Justice Department credentials identifying him as Special Agent Mike Belasko and whose help had been assured by a twenty spot, waited by his sedan. From there, Najim, masquerading as an Lebanese jeweler, had climbed into the waiting Town Car. Two men in that vehicle now, having just shot out of the Callahan Tunnel, heading south on Washington Street. Destination unknown. Intent—yet to be determined.

Bolan gave his talk with Hal Brognola, the Justice Department liaison to the President of the United States and who ran the Sensitive Operations Group out of the supersecret Stony Man Farm, some brief recall. The rumor mill had churned Brognola's way since the arrest of Mr. Mystery Arab who had promptly clammed up, stonewalling all attempts to get him to see reason unless he wanted to spend the

rest of his life as someone's girlfriend in the peniten-
tiary. Brognola had worked his contacts inside the
FBI and the CIA but come up with more questions
than answers. Najim had been tracked clear from Beirut to London, where the FBI and Interpol had him
under surveillance in both countries. Najim was a suspected bagman for various Islamic fundamentalist
groups. The identity of Najim's lord and master unknown, the Lebanese provided cash, contacts and
phony passports for a few of the more militant Muslims so they could move freely about to scheme, kill
and blow things up. Brognola had ordered the FBI
team on Najim to back off, ready to insert his own
man who would pick up the Lebanese once he hit
Boston.

And there Bolan was, sent out to get a few answers.
As usual, when embarking on a campaign where bad
questions demanded quick answers or else, something
told him the snatch and follow-up interrogation would
be done the hard way. Fair enough. In the event it
went to hell, meaning one or both of his quarry decided to stand and fight, the soldier had come prepared to take on any and all comers. No mistake, he
had commitments of his own. The standard hardware
was packed beneath his knee-length black leather
trench coat, the Beretta 93-R in shoulder rigging, the
mammoth .44 Magnum Desert Eagle autoloader riding on his hip. Stowed in the trunk, the nylon war
bag carried whatever he might need to stalk or mow
down any large herds of savages. Everything from
secured satlink with fax to a variety of grenades, skintight blacksuit and HK-33 assault rifle with modified
M-203 grenade launcher, the bag bulging with enough

spare clips, plus a mini-Uzi, two LAW rocket launchers and a stubby multiround projectile launcher, and
the soldier could drop one-man urban warfare on the
town at anytime.

Mr. Fidget Number One shot their tail another look
as the wheelman bored the Town Car down Washington. Bolan thought he saw Najim bend to reach for
something on the floorboard. Bolan's mental radar for
trouble began blipping overtime.

Chinatown was Boston's financial and retail district. Even with all the glitz and glitter of fashion and
money that would see the light of day, Bolan noted
the ever present shadows of the night denizens malingering or shuffling around, in search of God only
knew what at that hour when most people were either
asleep or waking up to go to work. The Executioner
put them out of mind when the luxury car's wheelman
started playing games with the traffic lights. Once,
then twice he slowed when the light flashed yellow,
then tapped the gas and blew through when it changed
to red. With no serious traffic to factor into his tail,
the soldier had no problem staying glued to their
bumper. They were running scared, most likely
pegged him for a Fed. Tweaked by fear or not, Bolan
wanted them to panic anyway, call the play, get the
ball rolling. At some point soon he believed they'd
make a stand.

When the Town Car swung onto Essex, barreled a
block or so along, then tore deep into a vacant lot,
they didn't disappoint Bolan. Clearly their nerves
were shot, indicating they had something to hide.

The wheelman was barreling out the door, bringing
into Bolan's line of sight a compact SMG, looked like

an Ingram MAC-10. Hard to say, since the wheelman suddenly cut loose with the weapon, gouging webbed holes across the windshield.

Game time.

The Executioner ducked beneath the steering wheel, floored the gas. A mental calculation of range and position of target, and the soldier aimed the grille of the big sedan straight for the subgunner, ready to squash the guy into roadkill.

WHATEVER SILLY BASTARD coined Boston the cradle of American Independence, he thought, the heart and soul of all things New England and civilized should see it today, the way he saw it.

The way it was.

It was a freak show out there, a frigging psycho circus once a man crossed the imaginary boundaries of the city and took a stroll—or, rather, ran through Roxbury, Dorchester, Jamaica Plain, fearing for his life unless he was armed with nothing short of a full-auto assault rifle, preferably one with attached grenade launcher. No, Delta Force Colonel Bob Powers didn't think Paul Revere would rein in his horse and salute the crack dealers, pimps and prostitutes, tip the hat to all the addicts, petty thieves and gangbangers in do-rags that, in the colonel's mind, had sent decent law-abiding folks fleeing for the outer suburbs long ago. Well, these days Boston was pretty much just like any other city in America he'd seen, except he just couldn't tolerate the phony, staid, upper-crust face the town's self-proclaimed upstanding old-guard elite put on for the country at large. Bah-ston, Beantown, he thought, kiss my... Hell, Sam Adams had his name and face plastered on a beer, of all damn things, and the ghost of John Hancock headed up an insurance company.

Well, in short order, he'd take another little sojourn for justice, once more do his own part to make "Bahston" a kinder and gentler place for the town's elite.

Right then, Powers hauled his focus back to the moment, a fleeting chill hitting him just the same, but he cut off the angry memory before it took shape in his mind. Those late night jaunts through the city's mean streets...

Stow it. If this didn't go down right, by the numbers, he knew, he was finished, facing perhaps a fate worse than death.

The alleged targets were Palestinian terrorists, four in all, holed up in a bowfront Victorian in the South End. The house was empty, of course, the Palestinians gone two hours ago to hunker down in a safer haven, but only Powers knew that.

A silent shadow, Powers led his four-man team, one hand on the rail of the low chain-link fence, up and over, movement so swift and effortless they could have shamed any Gold Medal winner to ever come out of the Olympics. God, they were good, he thought, all of them landing on their rubber-soled boots. Down the side of the house, crouched, full body armor, balaclava helmets, HK MP-5 subguns leading the way. Powers gave the hand signal to hold up at the back edge, hit a button on his chronometer to light up the time. Fifty seconds and counting, the FBI men were now moving in, ready to crash the front door. As co-commander of this joint FBI-Delta Force Counterterrorist Unit, it was his show here in Boston.

The FBI special agent, his partner of sorts—it some-times galled him to even think of his name—was right then in Detroit, doing the same thing, the same way, with the same expected results. A glance over his shoulder and Powers found Jameson giving him a look, the young commando wanting to say it again, no doubt. Before moving in, Jameson had voiced the one question Powers would be later called on to an-swer. No sweat, he already had a litany of reasons and rationales to hand off to the head honchos, hope-fully shut their cake holes before they dug too deep. Even still, he could almost hear Jameson's mind churning with the Big One. "Why was the surveil-lance team called off two hours ago, sir? During that time, the tangos could have cleared out."

If the kid only knew. Well, there would be an an-swer to that one, Powers thought, thirty seconds and counting down, in fact, but the real truth could never be known, not to Jameson or anyone else.

Powers put a finger to his lips, shook his head at the young commando. They were up and moving, gaining speed as Powers led the way up the back steps. They split up, two ready to go high left, two low to the right once the door was crashed. They flanked the door, listened to the silence around them. Just as Michaels slipped the battering ram off his shoulder, Powers found it, exactly where it should be. Waving Michaels off, he took his miniflashlight, shone the beam on the thin red cord curling out be-tween the jamb and the door.

"Fall back!" Powers shouted. He gave it a few more seconds, glancing at the time, knew it had to go down in perfect sync, aware his own butt was in the pan and about to get fried. War, though, always called for men to sacrifice their lives, and this raid, as bogus as it was, was no exception. Only he didn't think he could look himself in the mirror if he gave up his own men to further his personal agenda, but figured the world wouldn't miss a few overpaid Feds who probably would have never cut the mustard at Bragg anyway, much less come out the other side in Panama or Iraq where the men were separated from the wannabes. He also didn't care to check out before he saw through what he was helping to engineer, reap the rewards while smearing it in their faces from a great and safe distance.

Some Feds cut down, or in this case blown all to hell and back in the line of duty, just another statement, he hoped, to the ones who thought they had the power, believed they were in control of something and somebody.

Powers was bounding down the steps, tapping the button of his com link, raising Supervisory Special Agent Jordan, when he saw the doomsday numbers ticking off to four, three...

His men were already vaulting over the low fence, scrambling for deeper cover behind a vehicle parked in the alley. "Jordan, it's a trap, the house is wired."

"What the—"

Jordan's bleating of alarm was cut short by the explosion. Powers was sailing over the fence when the world erupted in fire and thunder behind him. He landed hard on his helmet, senses pulverized by the roar of the blast, the superheated windstorm of the explosion racing up his rear. Even as the wreckage rained around him, the sky above lit up like the

Fourth of July, Powers felt extremely pleased with himself. He'd put on a good front for the troops, but the best was yet to come.

Detroit

DETROIT WAS nothing but a vast sewer, human or otherwise, as far as he was concerned. It was an industrial apocalypse at best, from what he could tell, spewing clouds of noxious gas from factory smokestacks so thick they blotted out the sun even at midday, while pumping out poisonous sludge into lakes Saint Clair, Huron, Erie, even Lake Michigan clear across to the western edge of the state. At worst it was a savage wasteland of crime, corruption and drugs, not too unlike most big U.S. cities anymore.

Special Agent Paul Grevey had spent all of two days in the town made famous by the automobile, and already he couldn't wait to get the hell out of there. He could only imagine the hunting expeditions his partner could undertake here, scouring these dangerous, crime-infested streets late at night, indulging his killer instincts, some rage at the world being vented when he would lure...

Back to business, he chided himself. He was pretty sure his partner had already paid Motown a visit sometime in the past.

"We haven't seen the first sign they're even still inside, sir. Before, they left at least one light on in the living room, a man posted to watch the street. The lights are out, the place looks deserted."

"Your point?"

"I don't understand why you ordered the surveillance team pulled off the block two hours ago."

Grevey knew the doubting Thomas routine would come crying his way sooner or later, expected as much. The big SAC hoisted the weight of his Kevlar vest with a shrug of his shoulders, cradling the HK MP-5 subgun in massive hands, which were scarred and battered along the knuckles from the giving end of more than a few barroom brawls. Their black van had just come to a stop on Michigan Avenue, west off Vernor Highway. Behind Grevey, the worrywart, Agent Klieger, looked to him like some pink-faced scrubby kid as he stared out from beneath a balaclava helmet that appeared a half size too large. Two more agents, Chalmers and Bitsdale, were hunched, eyes shining in the soft overhead light with either fear or precombat nerves, Grevey couldn't say. Another van of agents was one block north, ready to go as soon as he gave the word to move in over his com link.

"Take a look at where we are, son," Grevey told the baby-faced kid, who wasn't even a full year out of Quantico but who'd been handpicked by the SAC when the special counterterrorist unit had been approved and funded by Congress some ten months back.

Even before the dickless wonders in Washington saw the need to somehow put together and finance a formidable, experienced and skilled counterterrorist unit that would prove up to snuff if and when a bunch of foreign thugs with more grim determination than sense infiltrated America with guns and bombs galore, Grevey knew he'd need to offer up cannon fodder at some point if he was to pull off his own agenda, show the other side he was playing ball. Too bad, he decided in a rare moment of regret, this kid, Klieger, had placed at the top of his class all around, especially out on the firing range. Young wife, a baby on the way... Well, he may or may not live out the next minutes. Fate was a fickle bitch.

"Sir?"

The kid still didn't get it. Maybe he wasn't all that smart, after all, he thought, maybe Quantico had lowered the standards these days, grade curves, all that, supercomputers and DNA doing what basic fieldwork and ass-kicking used to do. Obviously, the old-school guys had gone the way of the dinosaur.

"Son, this is crack central. No one sleeps in these neighborhoods. They're so wired here, you might say even the trees have eyes and ears. Now, since I can tell you're still having difficulty following me, what I'm saying, I didn't want a van or an unmarked hawk-eyed by some twelve-year-old lookout for the home-boys. Sounding the alarm all over this godforsaken hellhole, our three Palestinian friends just sashaying out the door, driving off to wherever. Gone for good, maybe another week or so, if we're lucky, before we can pick up the scent again."

"Yes, sir, I...understand, sir."

"Good. Any more questions, gentlemen?"

That was that, God had spoken, as far as he was concerned. Knuckles started popping as fists tightened around the subguns. Time to do it.

Grevey tapped the button on his com link. "Front-side Bogeymen to Backdoor Tigers, come in."

Agent Jackson's voice patched through. "Backdoor

Tigers, all looks quiet on the northern front, sir. We're ready when you are.''

"Synchronize now. Thirty seconds and counting to reach your positions. I'll give the word to slam and wham. Go!''

Grevey led the charge out the side door. They were running shadows, dashing across Michigan, Grevey watching the redbrick house that was dark and looked as abandoned as he knew it was. Sure enough, a shadow, here and there, broke into a dash down the sidewalk. FBI was stenciled on their jackets, and Grevey knew there were at least five, maybe more major crackhouses operating on that one block alone. Of course, the human watchdogs had no idea he could care less if their homies and their whores smoked themselves into the ER.

Something far more serious than a simple drug raid was going down.

He had just about reached the front sidewalk when Grevey heard the staccato chattering of autofire behind the house.

"Sir, we're under fire!"

Grevey hit a crouch, adjusting his throat mike as he waved his team past. "Go, go! Crash the door and go in shooting!''

"Sir, I've got two hostiles—''

Grevey heard a scream over the com link.

"Shit, Miller's down, sir!''

Something had gone terribly wrong, and Grevey's mind seethed with a slew of questions that would probably never get answered to his satisfaction. This was his puppy, one he had elected a week ago to give away to the opposition, show them he could play ball, fair and square. Now his man on the other side had decided, for whatever reason, to muck up his play, make it all into some grandstand showdown.

Grevey watched his troops storm the front steps, one of them moving on the front door with a battering ram. A part of him wanted to feel shame over what he was about to do, but another voice told him he'd come too far to turn back now. He pulled out the small box. If his boy had decided to snip the wires...

Only one way to find out how screwed up things were about to get.

And Grevey depressed the button, hit the deck and heard the house go up in a peal of thunder, whole sections of the structure taking to the sky, lifted on a volcano of fire, consuming, he knew, the young, the brave, but the unaware and the very much dead.

Boston

THE CYCLIC RATE of any machine gun, Bolan knew, tended to ride the barrel high. Whether it was panic, lack of experience or simply haste to get the job done, the shooter started high, his first line of slugs wasted on the top half of the windshield, a few more rounds rising to slash off the edge of the roof when Bolan ended the hardman's stand before he could correct his error and try again. It was merely a glimpse, a sound of brutal contact, as the Executioner hit the brakes, shot the sedan's nose on a lurching skid that delivered the expected result of breaking bone, a scream of agony and a flying body. The Town Car's door absorbed the weight of the shooter on the launch, glass blasting over his sailing form, the severed door spinning away.

In the heat of combat, Bolan caught a fleeting blur of the hardman slamming into a dark wall beyond, pinned there in a sloppy crucifixion for a couple of eyeblinks before he slid to ground.

The Beretta 93-R was out and tracking, the Executioner shouldering his way out the door.

Najim was also getting it together right then, the Lebanese shouting obscenities in his native tongue, hauling into Bolan's view an Ingram MAC-10. Down but not out, the fallen shadow ahead of Bolan was stirring to life on a hideous groan of pain. Folding at the knees, as Najim burst out the passenger door of the Town Car, came up over the roof firing, and Bolan cracked out a 9 mm Parabellum round. A dark red hole blossomed between the wheelman's eyes, his face appearing stark white, etched in a permanent scowl as it was framed in the Town Car's headlights.

"Death to America! This is holy war!"

Najim was going all the way, hell-bent on taking whatever his sojourn to America was all about to the next world as he held back on the trigger, sweeping the barrel, clearly spraying and praying he'd score flesh. Bolan, crouched and scuttling for the rear of his rental, was more than willing to oblige the Arab's death wish. Behind him, Bolan heard the storm of bullets spanging off the roof, drilling into doors, glass blown out as the Lebanese bagman kept pouring on the lead.

"You will not take me alive! We are at war with you! You will take no prisoners!" Najim roared, blasting away, peppering the sedan front to back. "This is only the beginning!"

Enough. Bolan knew the magazine would burn out,

and a split second of an echo of the din in a sudden silence was all he needed.

He got it.

The problem was Najim was there and ready with a pistol as Bolan rose. The Arab's shot went high and wide, a slipstream of hot lead grazing Bolan's earlobe. The Executioner made certain he got it right the first time, tapping the Beretta's trigger twice, delivering a facial to Najim's expression of rage that no mortician could hope to fix up. His head snapping back as if he'd been kicked in the jaw, eyes going wide in a blank stare skyward, and Najim toppled out of sight.

Bolan knew it was pointless to search the dead, confiscate any passports, any other ID. Even Stony Man Farm, he suspected, would hit a dead end if they went into cyberspace, hoping some detective work would track down the source of their phony credentials.

The game here was as dead as Najim and his wheelman. Bolan didn't see the point in getting bogged down by Boston's finest, corralled while Brognola went to the red tape mat to get him free and moving. ˙

The soldier was sweeping the glass off his seat when his cell phone with its secured line trilled. There was only one frequency, tied into a series of cutout numbers. Brognola either wanted a sitrep, or the Man from Justice had some news.

Bolan punched Send, settled in behind the wheel, checking the dark stillness of the empty lot, listening to the silence.

"Striker."

Brognola's tone and hesitation on the other end didn't inspire Bolan with confidence he was about to hear good news. "I'm here."

"It's already started."

CHAPTER TWO

Atlanta

Happiness was a vast sea of slaughtered infidels.

Nassir Abdil's search for his own version of true rapture, though, was right then stalled by a traffic jam on Interstate 75. He bit down a vicious curse over what he perceived as another slap in the face by fate. But maybe not, he thought. Perhaps he could work this snarl of metallic shells and their hapless occupants to his advantage, create the kind of carnage he'd craved to wreak all of his life.

Still, thirty-three years of hardship and disappointment seemed to have trailed him to America, and he couldn't help but wonder if this was just another Zionist dagger in his side. Or was God merely testing his resolve, his courage to do what he'd been called upon to do? Either way, he would decide the issue in a few short minutes. He had come too far, suffered too much to let this opportunity escape, find himself denied martyrdom along with his rightful seat in Paradise.

Before now, he'd only ever dreamed of a defining moment like this, where glory would be handed over to God in the last millisecond of his life. Certain of his reward in Paradise, faith bolstered by the mere thought alone that his suffering had been worthwhile, he gave silent praise to God for seeing fit to at long last bless his struggle.

It hadn't always felt this good. For as long as he could remember he had wondered if his life—half of which had been spent languishing in the squalor and filth of the refugee camps on the West Bank, watching in helpless rage while his brothers and sisters starved to death—was just a sad joke of circumstance, years of loud desperation sticking in his craw, that his lot was all nothing but a wasted and empty existence of poverty and bitterness. Even though he'd struck out on his own years later—a car bombing now and then, a skirmish with Israeli soldiers maybe once a year— it had all felt more of the same endless angry running in circles, searching for some grand way to fight back against the oppressors of his people.

Denied, somehow, that brass ring of glory, no matter how hard he tried, his Palestinian blood always suffering on.

Funny, though, how all that changed, overnight, in fact, when the Palestinian had finally caught the break of a lifetime seven months ago. It seemed he was chosen for greatness, after all. He was going to be shipped off to America, driven to and flown straight out of Beirut, handed a student visa by the man who had come out of the night, the one who called himself the Messenger. Abdil remembered the mystery man, experienced a moment of deep gratitude toward the one who had made all of this possible. He would go to America, he had been told, where an established

Palestinian family would take him into their home in a suburb north of Atlanta. Do not worry about the finer details, he'd been told, it was all taken care of, have faith, go with God. He would find work in America, green card waiting for him, sit tight until he received further instructions. He would find glory in America, he was finally told, but it would come at the ultimate cost of his own life. Since his wife and four children would be provided for by the Messenger, given enough money, with Palestinians in Beirut prepared to receive his family into their home to build a new life, Abdil figured he had nothing to lose and everything to gain by striking his own major blow against the Great Satan.

The previous night the call had come in, the unfamiliar voice telling him simply, "The time is here." The voice told him he was to go to a bakery owned by Palestinians, given directions to their place of business. There, he picked up the package, received his instructions—in writing, of course, since it was a well-known fact the American FBI was everywhere—returned to his temporary home, putting the match to his written jihad orders. Sleep never came. Visions of his final day on Earth, going to Paradise on a blast of glory that would send countless infidels to hell, fueled a living fire in his belly the entire night.

Tomorrow was here, and it was a good day to go to God.

"I'm sorry, buddy, but if we sit, I gotta run the meter."

Abdil caught the surly tone, the challenging look the cabbie threw him in the rearview mirror, the Palestinian certain the American was wondering whether he could afford the fare. The American was shrugging, shaking his head, trying to act apologetic as he turned on the time meter and the numbers began clicking off every few seconds.

"Happens twice a week, freakin' Atlanta traffic. It's some of the worst in the country, I know that. All you need is a fender bender and we could be stuck here an hour, maybe more. The sun won't even be up for another fifteen, twenty minutes. I swear, I don't know where all these people come from anyway. Whole town's just one huge parking lot."

The cabbie was squishing tobacco juice into a coffee cup, scratching his beard, wiggling around in his seat, eyeing the frozen lines of cars in all lanes of the highway, grumbling about something he had no control over. The American talking just to hear himself talk stoked Abdil's rage.

Abdil saw brand-new minivans, Porsches, a Jaguar. There was one American to a car for the most part, space and privacy a luxury every single American appeared to enjoy. Burning with resentment, he eyed a couple of fresh-scrubbed men in fancy suits yammering away on cell phones, winding up for a big day, no doubt, making deals, fattening up personal bank accounts. Americans, he thought. How could they have so much when he had so little? He was a man, a holy warrior in the eyes of God. He should have been blessed with the wealth and all the creature comforts and pleasures they seemed to take for granted.

The cabbie didn't know it yet, but his passenger was in charge of the immediate destinies of everyone around them, was about to invade their personal space forever. And even with the Atlanta skyline no less than a mile ahead, Abdil so close to his objective, he decided an abrupt change in plans was in order. He'd been instructed to find a crowded street corner, even a deli, someplace where a throng was gathered. He searched the faces in the cars beside them again. Beyond the obvious irritation on their faces of being forced to sit in traffic, they looked lifeless to the Palestinian, as good as dead, he thought.

Abdil cursed them in Arabic.

"You say somethin', buddy?"

The Palestinian found the cabbie running what he believed was contempt over his long tattered green raincoat, eyeing his scraggly mane of curly black hair, the unkempt beard the manager at the restaurant where he'd worked—no, slaved as a busboy—had always insisted he cut, and under threat of termination.

Terminate this, he thought, feeling the weight beneath his coat, wrapped around his torso, all of it wired up and ready to blow with one touch of his finger on the button.

From his coat pocket, he took a hundred-dollar bill. Leaning forward, he let it slip from his hand, flutter to the seat beside the cabbie.

"What's that for?"

"Your silence."

"You some kind of smart-ass? You sittin' there thinkin' maybe I'm thinkin' you can't pay?"

"Were you?" Before he could prattle on and spit more of the vile brown substance into his coffee cup, Abdil made his final decision. This was as good a place as any. "I have been in this country, my first time, for seven months now. I look around, I see a few who have much and too many who have nothing. They take, they want, they whine if they can't have it. I watch your abominable talk shows, the ones where so-called guests boast about their indiscretions and marital infidelities, your own children even bragging about their disobedience and rebellion.''

''What the—''

''You people disgust me. You are like nothing more than animals to me. Here, if you do not have money, you have no fame, you are looked down upon, if you are even noticed at all. You even turn your women into whores and you wonder why your families fall apart.''

''What the hell you talkin' about? You some kinda Commie religious nut? Where you from, anyway?''

''Spring Hill.''

''I know where I picked you up!''

''I am from Palestine.''

''Where?''

''You wouldn't understand. What I believe, what I feel in my heart, is beyond you.''

''You know somethin', I'm of a mind to tell you to take that hundred and stick it, kick you the hell out.''

Abdil produced the small box from his coat pocket, held it up for the cabbie to see, the American's gaze frozen in the rearview glass.

''This is a detonator box,'' Abdil said.

Opening his coat, he smiled as the American's eyes widened in horror at the sight of the red wires lacing the bundles of white bricks, the cabbie's lip quivering, coffee cup disappearing as he snatched at the door handle.

"If you wish to kick me out, after you," Abdil said, hitting the button and launching both of them on the final ride.

Boston

"IT JUST GOT even worse, Striker. One or two more like this... I don't even want to say the words 'martial law,' but we're getting close. I'll know just how close after I talk to the Man."

After what little Brognola had filled him in on, Bolan didn't see how it could get any worse than what he'd already heard. But if the Congress, Senate and the President approved and ordered the military to seize control of certain cities, roll in the troops and the tanks, the soldier knew it could prove a giant and fatal first step toward anarchy. It would be a first in American history, could well signal the beginning of the end for democracy if military law was imposed. The big Fed had already informed the soldier that a van carrying three men, a woman and two teenage boys had gone up in a fireball at a border crossing between New York and Quebec not more than two hours ago. For reasons unknown, the van's driver had shot a U.S. Customs agent to get the killing started. The facts were sketchy, but first reports Brognola had gleaned from his sources at the FBI indicated the customs agents and three New York State Troopers might have been prepared to search the van, the FBI now hunting through the cyberspace that linked the border crossing with the State Police barracks in the county and the INS office in Manhattan. A gun battle erupted, a man with a machine gun cut down by shotguns, before the driver, wounded during the exchange, had touched off what amounted to a suicide bomb, the van apparently rigged with so much high explosive only a single witness was left alive near the crossing. A Canadian man, who'd seen the whole incident unfold as he approached the border, apparently hadn't been off the cable-news TV cameras even long enough to take a leak, telling and retelling this tale of horror to an entire nation now just waking up. At almost the same time the U.S.-Canadian border was shattered by violence, another suicide van had crashed the gate at the Virginia Electric and Power Company plant in Norfolk. In the process of blowing them halfway across the Chesapeake Bay, the tremendous explosion touched off by the fanatics had demolished enough aboveground transformers, sheared enough high-tension superconductor cables nearly a quarter million people in the Hampton Roads area were without power.

Before he learned any more, Bolan had cut Brognola short, telling him to call back in fifteen minutes, quickly filling in the big Fed about his terminal encounter. The Executioner needed to put distance to the two dead Arabs, find some private space where he could talk to Brognola without having to worry about Boston cops. The dark alley between the red brick tenement buildings in the Old West End now appeared to give Bolan the best temporary sanctuary he could find on short notice. A quick search of his surroundings, and Bolan found he was alone with just the grim disembodied voice of Brognola on the secured cell phone, coming from the big Fed's office at the Justice Department in Washington.

"Breaking news on CNN," Brognola said. "A taxicab just went up in a fireball on the expressway going into Atlanta. Seems whoever touched off the blast got sick of sitting in a traffic jam, decided to take out fifteen people, two to three times that many wounded, a number of them critical to serious."

The soldier felt the familiar cold rage knotting up his gut over the senseless slaughter of innocents.

"The FBI, choppered in from downtown Atlanta, were on the scene, it sounds like, before the wreckage even stopped falling. Dexter Cab Company's log for pickup fares that morning was rifled through by the FBI who promptly traced the suicide cab bomber back to a quiet little suburban home outside Atlanta. The passenger in question was Nassir Abdil, Palestinian, here on a student visa. They know he's been in Atlanta seven months, worked as a busboy in some steak house, thirty-three years old, which kind of puts him a little beyond the tender age of your average freshman. Naturally, the family he lived with knew nothing about the sleeping monster they had under their roof, but that particular investigation has only begun. If there's anything the family's hiding, I'll bet my pension they'll find it. Striker, I take it your silence has you, like me, wondering just what the hell is going on."

"Someone has declared war on America, Hal. They're sparing no expense, no amount of killing power either in the form of men and matériel to make it happen. Three separate attacks, three different locations. You don't need to be a whiz number cruncher to add two and two on this one. A sophisticated network has been set up, and someone on the home team is pulling the strings to make it happen. You don't get into this country with a suspicious background, stay here, melt into the scenery like the new millennium version of Ozzie and Harriet, get your hands on what I have to assume is plastique—military ordnance—and just walk around until you decide to set it off. They're well-organized, financed, backed, entrenched. It's a safe and scary bet there are plenty more of these fanatics out there, loading up, as we speak. Probably waiting on their marching orders from whoever got them into the country.''

"Not trying to sound flip in the least, but I didn't see Scully or Mulder out in the hallway, Striker. Am I hearing the makings of some vast conspiracy theory? Trust no one?''

"I can't say one hundred percent, not now, but I saw Najim and his buddy. I understand. You want proof. Hunches, that's what I'm playing. But Najim stated war has been declared on the Great Satan. He wasn't just coming to America to see himself get killed. He was on a mission.''

Brognola heaved a breath. "Fanatics shooting up state cops and customs agents, suicide bombers blowing themselves up, killing innocent people in the process. What the hell goes through the minds of people like that? Murder women and children, men with families, noncombatants, who, for God's sake, wouldn't know a Shiite from a Sunni, an imam from a sheikh if you drew a picture. And they believe God is going to welcome them straight to his open arms if they slaughter the innocent?''

"I don't need to walk through their heads. I just need to see this stopped before it gets worse.''

"And it's only just begun."

"It damn sure reads that way."

"Well, you haven't heard what could be the worst of it yet, Striker. My sources are telling me the VEPCO plant was, somehow, contaminated by radioactive waste. The area has been quarantined by a special Navy HAZMAT unit. A Pentagon source of mine has also been burning my ear that either uranium or plutonium dust or irradiated water taken from most likely a light-water reactor was among the big bang delivered by the suicide bombers. They could be looking at an ecological nightmare down there in Hampton Roads. So far, they know the reservoir has been poisoned by radioactive waste, they're not sure about the Chesapeake Bay yet. Either way, that power plant looks to be on long-term shutdown, if it's ever even again fit to power up. I know, the big questions keep piling. You're wondering where to go from here, now that Najim chose martyrdom. I'm way ahead of you. It's called SCTU—Special Counterterrorist Unit."

Bolan listened as Brognola explained. The funding for this unit was approved by Congress in these times when the threat of international terrorists doing exactly what they were now doing might come to pass. When he heard it was a joint FBI-Delta Force operation Bolan had trouble buying the concept that some of the best commandos around would team up with Feds in the spirit of patriotic cooperation, but shrugged it off as simply that. Or maybe not. SCTU had been active and operational for ten months. The President of the United States had approved the Congressional bill and funding to originally cut SCTU loose. Of course, the President knew all about the covert Stony Man Farm operations, privately sanctioned its own top-secret war against criminals and terrorists, homegrown or overseas. Bolan couldn't be certain what the Man was thinking, chalked it up to politics as usual, his thoughts echoing Brognola's opinion. Perhaps the Oval Office wanted to show the American public it heard the cries of alarm about terrorists charging onto U.S. soil, guns blazing, grenades hurled about in shopping malls, schools and city streets.

"Any home runs hit by this SCTU?" Bolan asked.

"I know you don't have much idle time to channel surf the cable-news stations, but about two weeks ago SCTU tracked down and took out a major cell of Arab terrorists in Chicago. Burned down another cell in Cleveland. The terrorists went down shooting to a man. Some intense digging and backtracking by the FBI and a team here at the Justice Department under my direction, and it turned out they were small-time Yemeni terrorists. How they finagled their way into the country, or were slipped in, where the visas and passports originated—counterfeit paperwork, is my guess—we've hit a dead end."

"Yemenis, Palestinians. It looks like someone has marshaled the Arab world together."

"Right, a worst-case 'we are the terrorist Arab World' scenario, hear us roar. Someone, as you alluded, has made them see the light, stop killing one another, turn a blind eye to their own personal differences. One saber, one jihad, one common enemy. Us, as in U.S."

"Just what the Arab World needs. Another Mahdi

promising them paradise if they march out there and slay the infidel, paradise guaranteed if you kill a bunch of innocent people. What else do you have on this SCTU?''

''I hear a plan of action?''

''I'm working on it as we speak.''

''Well, it's pretty much need-to-know, and I've had to twist a few earlobes just to scratch the surface. Even the media is screaming all over the place about black ops in our backyard, and they don't have much more than speculation and rumors at this point. Talking heads, doing what they do best. Talk. Government conspiracies, spooks with guns, black helicopters over the suburbs.''

''Extreme measures for extreme times.''

''Gotcha, and they should walk five feet in our shoes. Well, a memo just came across my desk. I put in a call to the commander of this SCTU to confirm it. About the same time VEPCO was going up in flames and that van went up at the border two simultaneous raids by SCTU in Detroit and your neck of the woods went to hell. Both targeted safehouses went up in flames, blown to the sky, someone from the inside touching off the blasts. Eight dead FBI agents, two more clinging to their last breath.''

''Sound to you like the bad guys knew the opposition was coming?''

''Right now, nothing would surprise me.''

''What have our own people come up with?'' Bolan asked, referring to the cyber wizards at Stony Man Farm.

''I've got the Farm working up the background on the two men who run SCTU in the field. With Able and Phoenix in the field and presently under the gun, they're pulling triple duty but I've shoved this one to the top of the priority list. They're hacking through the files over at the State Department on all known terrorists, big, small, in-between. Kurtzman and the others will also comb through Interpol, CIA, NSA files. If I can get concrete identities on the fanatics gone to hell so far, they'll run a background check, organizations, movements, associates, the whole nine yards. If there's something that might smell about either man who heads up SCTU, you'll also be the first to know. But I was thinking. Since you're in the neighborhood of one Delta Force Colonel Bob Powers, I'm going to pull some strings on my end to see you pay the man a little visit.''

"I'd like more than a handshake on this one, Hal."

"I'll see what I can do to get you onboard."

"We know about Bin Laden and his global reach,'' Bolan said, referring to the Saudi billionaire hiding out in Afghanistan, who was suspected of being the muscle behind a worldwide terrorist machine. "Any others like him out there who have the connections, the money and the men to mount a terrorist offensive like we're seeing now?''

"Funny you should ask. Another item Kurtzman and company are working on is an Omani sheikh, Ahman Nafud. Seems he was third in line to be the next sultan until he got antsy to take the throne. Rumor is he murdered his brother in some fit of rage. He's known to be in exile in Sudan.''

Bolan grunted, a grim smile cutting his lips. "Nice place for a killer to hole up, especially one with a few bucks to grease the locals.''

"Yeah, Sudan, a real land of enchantment. It's at the top of my list for vacation spots for me and the wife. Anyway, a CIA contract agent working out of Khartoum has been keeping his ear to the ground about Nafud. The word is that a lot of weapons are moving in and out of the country, with sightings a few of the more well-known faces in the fanatic Islamic world tasting the nightlife around Khartoum lately. One thing I've learned is this sheikh is protected by the military junta over there. Get this, the so-called elected president—you want to talk about election fraud—he heads up what they call the fifteen-member National Salvation Revolutionary Council. Translation—a bunch of thugs with guns. He has publicly listed an address for the People's Palace where his friend the sheikh can get his fan mail, money, guns or whatever. Only the scuttlebutt from Langley is the sheikh has female, uh, groupies imported from all over the world. Almost all of which, you can imagine, are dumped, kicking and screaming, into the sheikh's lap."

"Sounds like one big party."

"And the Khartoum government has no problem airing over their radio and television the sheikh's definite strong opinions about the West. It was one of several reasons the sultan, I'm told, had some problems with Nafud taking his place, meaning taking control of all the oil that comes out of Oman. Oman needs U.S. military bases over there…well, you know the situation. Anyway, I should know more on a number of fronts as soon as I touch base with the Farm."

Bolan's mind buzzing with questions, began seeing shadowy pieces of some dark puzzle wanting to come together. Lights strobed in his sideview mirror. A boost of adrenaline hit his veins, and he found the police cruiser already gone, shooting past the mouth of the alley. Dawn was breaking over Boston, and Bolan knew he needed to leave the shot-up rental behind, get moving.

"Get back to me in an hour, Hal, and get me that intro with the SCTU. I have something to run past you, but I want to get a read on this Delta colonel before I make a decision."

Brognola signed off to go work his usual magic to latch Bolan on to the scent of the enemy. Only this time out, the soldier heard the rumblings of the dark clouds of some conspiracy, every instinct he'd honed to perfection over the years warning him some deadly shadow game was just around the corner.

The Executioner hopped out of the rental, retrieved his war bag from the trunk and set off to acquire another set of wheels. He would search out a motel where he could set up his own one-man command central, wait on word from Brognola. A new day hadn't even quite dawned, and already the dead were piling up, a river of innocent blood already running across America. Unless he put himself on the right track and fast, the soldier feared the worst was yet to come.

The war had started, on American soil, no less, and that alone was bad enough. But the enemy, whoever it was, had yet to find out just what the Executioner was capable of.

CHAPTER THREE

Texas

She wasn't too shabby, he thought, a little too squeaky clean for his taste and not much behind the eyes, believing he saw something vacant in those baby blues, a naive PC view of the world, at best. When she carried her spiel over to the body count, upping it now by another two corpses since her last report, injecting what he decided was the sort of contrived horror reserved for just such newsworthy scenes of carnage and tragedy, making him wonder if that's how they taught it these days in Journalism 101, Buck McClintock hit the Mute button.

The opening shot had been fired, and that was pretty much all he needed to know. Actually, CNN was reporting three opening salvos had sounded, one-third of the nation, he knew, awake now and reeling in confusion and terror. Soon enough one mass echo of outrage and fear would be heard from coast to coast, Americans everywhere wondering if some apocalyptic doom was hanging over their heads, ready to fall from the sky and snuff them all out where they stood. Or drove, or shopped, or dined.

If they only knew, he thought. Hell, he didn't even know the full extent of the bigger picture, and he was on the inside.

McClintock unfolded his muscular six-three, two-twenty frame from behind the huge mahogany desk. With the sound off on the giant-screen TV, it seemed an even more impressive and ominous sight, truly a silent vision of hell on Earth. Morbid or terrified faces flashed by on the screen, lips moving, hands flapping at the horror, everyone confused and numb with shock, the masses and Uniformed Officialdom alike trying to make sense out of it, maybe searching for reason they would never find, nor least of all, he thought, could ever hope to understand. It looked as if at least a dozen or so vehicles were still burning shells on the Atlanta expressway, police choppers soaring over the light show of cop cars, fire trucks, EMT vehicles. An overhead shot from a news chopper, zooming in on the destruction, and he saw the first of many black bags getting zipped up, rolled on gurneys for the coroner's van.

So this was jihad, he thought.

"It's started," former FBI agent, Josh Monroe stated, matter-of-fact, his dark gaze taking in the slaughter zone with a fascination that made McClintock stop and pull up short beside the two men in the wing chairs.

"No shit," McClintock said, then studied the man closely, wondering just how insane Monroe was, but already knew the sudden violence and brutality the man was capable of, something that had seen him kicked out of the FBI with no pension, no future. Nothing but bad memories.

Such was their lot, but he'd always believed suffering did, indeed, build character.

The stocky, buzz-cut Sam Jansen cracked his knuckles, the ex-ATF man chain-smoking, as if the killer habit would pull his nerves together. "Now what? Where does it go from here, gentlemen? Could somebody in this room kindly define our role from here on?" he asked on the tail end of a boiling smoke cloud that nearly obliterated his worried expression.

Another glimpse at the big screen in the corner of his office, still more police cars and another ambulance slowly wending their way through the bottleneck of vehicles behind the police barricade, and McClintock moved to the bay window beside the wet bar.

"Buck?"

"I heard you, Sam."

"And?"

"Relax. Smoke another cigarette."

It was incredible, he thought, staring out at the thickets and scrub brush, the thinly wooded slopes of their valley in Brewster County, how what was promised was actually now in motion, delivered, no less, by a foreign enemy. Things were only heating up, though, he suspected, inside and beyond the walls of their compound. As if Mother Nature herself were angry at something or someone, he noted the sun was rising over the sawtooth ridges of Dove Mountain, and already the bright wash of light promised another unusually scorching day for that time of year. Even for the rugged, moonscaped wilderness of southwestern Texas it would be hotter than a furnace out there in a matter of hours.

McClintock clasped his hands behind his back, taking a long moment of silence, scouring through his thoughts to try and find an answer to the man's question.

What could he say? They knew the truth, had accepted their role in whatever the bigger scheme—as small and undefined at times as they might find their part—several years ago.

As unbelievable as he found it now, the present had its roots in a few angry remarks, the tongue loosened up over whiskey and beer in a yuppie pub that fateful day near Capitol Hill. Even though it eventually cost him his job guarding what the rest of the country might view as the most important and powerful man on the planet, the former Secret Service agent believed he had simply spoken the truth, drunk or sober. He'd seen, up-close and personal, all the perks, frills and special interests that came with being enshrined in the Oval Office. The previous administration, the one he was supposed to protect with his own life, had disgraced itself before an entire nation, but few knew just how far, wide and deep the real shame cut, how ugly and sordid was the whole truth and nothing but. Well, the whispered rumors of drug use, late-night orgies in the pool, talk coming through the grapevine about far-reaching conspiracies and cover-ups—even murder—were something he had originally wanted to believe were fabricated lies by the sore losers in that other party.

Not so. He'd seen a lot of it with his own eyes, soon found himself completely and permanently disgusted by the indulgences of prima donnas who said one thing but did another. Well, he hadn't signed on to be a pimp, look the other way, wink and grin as if boys will just be boys. Unfortunately, a few pairs of the more noticeable yuppie ears, their lips forever pressed to the buttocks of some congressman or senator they longed to impress in hopes of advancing some career, had overheard the indignant railings from a real man on the front lines. The young and the spineless had quickly gone scurrying to tell all to their idols, leaving him with the bitter taste in his mouth that told him he was finished as a Secret Service agent. Following that forced but quiet resignation, there were the follow-up anonymous phone calls in the middle of the night, the white envelopes with only his name typed on them stuffed into his mailbox. For months the voices and the mail kept coming out of nowhere, the threats implied—he was to keep his mouth shut about what he'd seen during his tour of duty—but the confidence loud and clear they could pull off his own vanishing act, no one the wiser, warning him it was best to see no evil...

As luck or fate had it—and often he wondered which it was—a few good men had come to offer him comfort, rallied around his plight back then. News, good or bad, fact or fiction, always traveled at light speed in Wonderland. They were law-enforcement officers for the most part, a high-ranking military man here and there, joining in the late-night clandestine bull sessions. Only they weren't just a bunch of good old boys slugging down Jack Daniel's whiskey and ranting about a changing world that no longer fit their ways and means.

These were men of power, and they could make things happen.

They had. It turned out a plan was in the works all along, and they were personally interested in seeing him survive getting bounced out of the Secret Service, and for just being a stand-up act, of all the injustice and hypocrisy. If he played ball, asked no questions, a donation would be placed in his bank account. If he was serious, he would move to Texas where a large compound was right then being erected, a private enclave where men of like vision would gather and discuss the future while awaiting their orders. If he looked at it now, heart free of anger and resentment, he might view it all as signing a pact with the devil.

He couldn't. The truth was, he'd been handpicked, just like the thirty-two other members of the group deemed worthy with a blessing from those shadow men, given a reason to live. The Man with the Plan, as he'd come to think of the FBI agent, had to have kept running files on the chosen ones, seeking them out when the time was right, meaning when they were all at their most vulnerable. To a man, McClintock knew they were all divorced, their children scattered across the country, living God only knew where, doing their own thing. Money, alcohol or legal problems had plagued them from their previous lives. All of them were retired or forced to quit from various law-enforcement agencies or different branches of the military, their lives holding some stench that told them they were destined for failure. Disillusionment, though, a collective force of being fed up with the decline of America across the board, one union of awareness there was corruption of every institution at every level, was the bond gluing them all together.

That, and looking forward to the day when they

could strike back. But hit back at who? Where? And when?

Turning, McClintock stared at his two most trusted comrades. He felt his stomach lurch for some strange reason at the mere sight of them, aware next in some hideous way he was looking at mirror images of himself. Buzz cuts could never hide the gray around the temples. The hot Texas sun could only further deepen the scowl lines around the mouth and eyes. They looked old, tired, the eyes still glowing some, thank God, with anger and determination about the only sign they shouldn't be put out to pasture yet and shot. He looked away, glanced at the phone on his desk, checked his watch, wanting to distract himself from their probing stares. The call should be coming through any minute.

Marching orders were on the way.

''The men should all be up by now,'' McClintock said, purposely evading the original question. ''I suggest we go have breakfast in the mess hall. Company is expected shortly.''

''Who?'' Jansen asked. ''Another nameless Arab with more orders for us to move their merchandise around the country?''

''We have enough helicopters and private jets out there now, Buck,'' Monroe said, ''to start lifting a few eyebrows should some rancher lose a head or two of cattle this way.''

McClintock ran a meaty hand over the bristles of his buzz cut. ''Do I hear in your voices, gentlemen, anxiety? Do I read in your faces you're losing your stomach?''

''Buck, let's face some facts here,'' Jansen said. ''I

don't care if our private airfield is FAA approved, how many people you've greased along the way, how much you pay the sheriff and his deputies to keep their eyes peeled for men in black. You've rounded up every member of our group from all parts of the country on short notice. Shabby as some of the lives of our members are, some of them still have jobs, people that might question their sudden disappearance."

"You are losing your nerve."

Jansen bared his teeth. "Not hardly, my friend. But after seeing that it's started, knowing what our part has been so far, any loose tongues start wagging out there and we might find ourselves going up in Waco, part two."

"You're worried about some Feds stumbling around out here, seeing some guys out on the range, firing away with handguns, all of which, I might add, are registered, hence legal to own. Or is it the stash?"

"It's not what's here that troubles me," Jansen said. "It's not the others that concern me."

"We're covered among ourselves," Monroe said, but he didn't need to point out the obvious to Mc-Clintock. "Hey, we're just a men's club, right?"

"Right. No attention drawn to us from locals or anyone on the outside. I don't even want us referring to ourselves beyond these walls as God's Crusaders. Okay, I see you both fidgeting, wondering, worrying about the future. All right, if you're looking for me to put your fears at rest, once more, the stash is buried so deep you'd need a corps of Army engineers with nuke-powered mountain diggers to unearth it. From the beginning I've been ordered to keep up and maintain a deceiving appearance. That's why one of my mandates is we never distribute literature, we stay off the Internet, we don't recruit. We don't get drunk in bars and sound off about Zionist conspiracies or hurl around racial epithets. We don't wear cowboy hats and boots or drive around in pickup trucks with rifle racks. We put on a legitimate face, we go on with quiet, law-abiding lives. On the face of all things visible, we are businessmen. We are tied in, thanks to the men in charge, to a legitimate trucking company, we own and operate our own airport, even though it's under another name. Yes, I know what we really do, what we really move around the country. You want answers…''

The phone rang, cutting off Jansen as the man opened his mouth to voice more concerns. McClintock scooped up the receiver, heard the familiar voice of the nameless Arab on the other end as he said, ''We will be landing soon.''

McClintock locked on to Jansen's stare. It was time, he decided on the spot, for him to step up, take charge and begin to find out exactly what was their role in the big scheme. ''I'll be waiting. You've seen the news?''

''Yes. And?''

''I think this would be a good time for us to have a talk about the future.''

Sudan

AHMAN NAFUD watched the feeding frenzy. From his position, standing on the parapet, looking out beyond the wall of the pool, he saw enough raw meat tossed into the pen, or hung out on poles by the more adventurous, the Omani figured the lieutenant general's soldiers could have fed half the population of Shilluks and Nuer in the south for an entire week.

But this was Sudan, he knew, a nation divided by the Arab north and the black south. Race relations, though, were probably the least of Sudan's woes. The largest country in Africa, plagued by mass starvation, genocide, long periods of searing drought and never-ending civil war, Sudan was one of the most dangerous places on Earth, where life wasn't even weighed on the cheap scale of things. If there was any question about that, all he needed was to sit through one more of Sayid's "public screenings." Almost every night, he recalled, Sayid would order all the men, including the thirty-odd force of soldiers guarding the People's Palace, into the sprawling living room. While Sayid drank cognac, chortled, toyed with the vast array of medals on his uniform, he gave a blow-by-blow narrative for each killing, every gruesome torture inflicted on the rebels of the Sudanese People's Liberation Army.

Knowing the kick Sayid derived from his snuff films, it only made sense to Nafud that the lieutenant general, who headed up both the National Salvation Revolutionary Council and the National Islamic Front, would take care of his pet crocodiles better than most men might treat their wives. Last count on that score, it was believed the man had, in addition to his four wives, at least two dozen concubines and mistresses at his beck and call. With something like over a hundred bedrooms in the palace, the sex play, both marital and otherwise, went on almost around the clock.

Nafud found himself wishing Sayid at least had the decency to move the crocodile pen farther from the pool.

It wasn't so much the ferocious sight of gaping jaws flashing out of the muddy water, clamping with terrible force over the slabs of red meat. Rather it was the live chickens tossed by the neck into the thrashing red soup. A desperate flap of wings, a massive scaly torpedo head shooting up through the churning surface and a hideous shriek, lasting all of one split second for the most part, would rend the air. Several of the soldiers began laughing as one of them held out a pole with a squealing chicken impaled on the steel tip. Nafud turned away before a croc boiled out of the water to make quick work of the squalling bird. How many men Sayid believed had double-crossed him, he wondered, or needed intensified persuasion during an interrogation, had been thrown into that pit?

He shuddered, cutting off the mental image before it took root, ruined what had been a pleasant afternoon of indulging himself with several of the imported beauties. Europeans, no less, a rare treat, indeed, Swedish to be exact, he recalled.

As he tried to put a deaf ear to that awful deep-throated roar-growl from the crocodiles, he looked out over the arid plain beyond the front palace gate. It was desolate, barren country for the most part, but there were points of tropical vegetation beyond the high granite razor-topped wall ringing the complex. Nafud couldn't be sure if the palm trees were transplanted here but knew they were close enough to the banks of the Nile River to grow and sustain those oasis pockets.

"My good friend Ahman. Enjoying the view?"

He was about to step off the parapet but already the massive shape, most of the bulk and girth confined to the belly, tromped up the steps, cutting off any retreat from the sight of the raging mass of reptiles.

The lieutenant general fingered his goatee, adjusted the bill of his cap, smiling toward the pen. He was shorter than Nafud's five-six, his blubbery mass seeming to want to pop any number of medals and ribbons pinned to his brown uniform. Why was Nafud reminded of some cartoon character whenever he looked at this short, enormously fat man?

Oh, well, he decided. Conspiracies and duplicity had a way of bringing together the unlikeliest of bedfellows. If he thought about it, he should count his blessings he was far removed from Oman, where his father, he understood, was still raging about the palace, screaming for the head of the son who had murdered Shiraq, the beloved eldest who would have been first in line to claim sultanate status.

Count his good fortune, indeed, that he still had untraceable and huge sums of money stashed in several accounts across Europe. Indulge his feeling of luck that the CIA man had whisked him out of the country, dumped him off in Sayid's lap. The lieutenant general was more than happy to see his Omani guest fed, housed and pleasured, as long he kept the money wired along from a Swiss account to the Bank of Khartoum. And Sayid, he knew, had proved invaluable in helping to launch the mother of all jihads. It was a well-known fact the CIA trained and armed the SPLA rebels, but they used mercenaries for the real dirty work. And it was a rare dog of war that wouldn't eat from the hand that fed it best.

And Nafud and Sayid were feeding their CIA mercenary war hounds filet. Without them, Nafud knew the merchandise, along with the holy warriors, would have never made it into America.

"Admiring my beauties, I see?" Sayid asked, still grinning at his reptilian pets. "They say next to the Australian saltwater crocodile, the Nile croc is the largest and most aggressive. Three of them are close to twenty feet. Look! There is Mohammed Ali!" Sayid was pointing, laughing. Sure enough, Nafud spotted the monster in question. Mohammed Ali was impossible to miss. The crocodile thrashed over several of his smaller cousins, the beast's raging bulk driving a few of the reptiles down the bank before it rose up and tore a hunk of beef in two. "Once they get the smell of blood, have a taste of raw red meat, they will become man-eaters, spoiled, in fact, for everything but human flesh. Perhaps you were wondering if I have proof of that? A special viewing one night?" Laughing, he added, "The night I break out the good French wine and you see them serving the casino stuffed shrimp, you will know you are in a for a rare treat."

Nafud decided he'd make himself scarce on that evening, beg off, a stomach virus, any excuse no matter how offended Sayid would be. "What we have engineered has already begun."

Sayid nodded, the smile fading. "Yes. The American news station I have piped in by satellite does not even bother to go to commercial, dare interrupt their constant parade of coverage. The infidels are blaming all Muslims from Pakistan to Morocco. They want revenge. Only we know the truth, my good friend. But the game is entering into its most dangerous phase—dangerous, perhaps, for the two of us, that is.''

Nafud had long since weighed the risks, knew he'd get shoved to the top of the list as the most wanted international criminal since Bin Laden. If he was brought to light, he knew the Americans wouldn't rest until he was hunted down, arrested or worse.

''You have assured me I am safe.''

''As long as you remain in Sudan,'' Sayid told him. ''I do not think you will be spending some romantic weekend in Paris any time soon.''

''I have been here for almost one year now. Have you heard me complain?''

''No, of course not. This is our joint endeavor, and I wish for my esteemed friend to remain here as long as he wishes. You might never see the American military kicked out of the Middle East, as you so passionately demanded when you were living in Oman, but your desire to strike a major blow for all Muslim peoples against the Western oppressors looks, as they might say, a dream coming true.'' A pause, then Sayid went on. ''I saw you looking out beyond the walls. Perhaps wondering how such a barren, inhospitable landscape may hold vast oil reserves that would rival those of Saudi Arabia or even your Oman?''

''Not quite, although I am aware of your agenda to see your country become a major oil power.''

"All I need is money, the men, the expertise and I could begin drilling tomorrow."

"My money, you mean."

"It certainly helps."

Nafud read something he didn't quite trust in Sayid's voice and look. "I have already placed a small fortune into your account. The way you just said that...is it not enough?"

Sayid seemed to weigh his next words carefully. "Understand, my good friend the sheikh, I have considerable expenses. There are my associates in the NSRC who must be compensated for their continued silence and cooperation. I have my own soldiers I must pay, having promised them more money as their duties multiply for not only myself but you. There are all these beautiful women I have my traders from Khartoum bring to us from all over the world, expensive women, young, drug-free, some of them even virgins. Do you realize how much it costs for one woman of European blood alone? Then there are my own perks, such as the crocodile hunters to pay for risking life and limb in the Nile. We have our friends in the CIA who have helped us establish a safe pipeline to smuggle both weapons and men into America. You have alluded to contacts the CIA uses as the overseas architects and guardians of your holy war, Americans, I am sure, who have their own agendas. I assume whoever is on the receiving end in America is getting a hefty sum of money."

"So, we are negotiating a new price?"

"Something to think about. I have just received word from our CIA friend he and two others are on the way."

"Why?" Nafud asked, but already suspected the answer.

"From what I could understand, reading between the lines of their usual double-talk, they, also, wish to negotiate a new price."

Nafud softly shook his head. Everybody always wanted more money, his money. "They have been paid well enough already."

"They are the ones who share most of the greater risk. No CIA mercenaries, no explosives, no pipeline for all the weapons that were delivered to America. You would also not have the benefit of their intelligence-gathering resources."

"All of what you have just said is true enough… but if I keep having to renegotiate everyone's price, I am going to start wondering if perhaps blackmail is in my near future."

"No, no, fear not. No one, I assure you, is going to hand you over to be returned to your father for certain beheading."

Nafud grimaced. "Please, spare me the melodramatic images."

"And no one will look your way for the jihad that has erupted on American soil."

Nafud snorted. "I only wish I could share your confidence. You seem to have all the right answers, but all it would take is for one of the CIA mercenaries to take my money then suddenly decide it's in his interest to become a patriot or a hero." He was about to pursue his fears and worries when a cry of alarm hit the air.

And Nafud found one of the soldiers had somehow been pulled over the steel-mesh fencing, the feeding pole snapped in two, his frantic shouting for help nearly drowned by a renewed chorus of reptile roaring. Nafud froze, felt his spine tightening as the horror unfolded down there. He started to look at the lieutenant general, urge the man to pull his revolver and shoot at the beast—Mohammed Ali, no less—who came whipping out of the water on a great spume. Nafud nearly retched, revolted next as he found Sayid actually smiling over the spectacle of one of his own men about to get gobbled up as live croc bait. He didn't want to look, but some gripping sense of morbid dread forced him to turn his attention to the pit. Mohammed Ali was roaring up the bank, the soldier slipping in the thick sludge, scrambling and wailing for the outstretched arms of his comrades on the other side of the fence. The crocodile's jaws parted in what struck Nafud as some ghoulish showing off of the rows of razor-sharp teeth. Somehow the soldier found his footing, nearly slipped again, before he hurled himself at the fence. Mohammed Ali snapped his jaws shut on empty air as the soldier was yanked over the fence. For escaping his near brush as croc food, the soldiers began laughing, whooping it up, slapping the man on the shoulders and about the head as if the whole thing had been nothing more than slapstick comedy.

Nafud heard Sayid chuckle. "That was close."

CHAPTER FOUR

"You want to tell me why your sudden calling off previous twenty-four-seven surveillance on both targets was not run by this office? You want to tell me where in this operation's manual it states you two are the voice of God and can add the eleventh commandment and send eight, now nine—yeah, count them—nine FBI agents marching straight to their deaths? You want to tell me how it looks our terrorists-in-question even knew we were coming, time enough to rig up both safehouses with enough explosives to blow themselves and our people to kingdom fucking come?"

It wasn't any stretch for either Powers or Grevey to see the FBI commander of SCTU was merely getting warmed up, the dressing down having clearly only just begun in full swing, the two of them having marched through the doors, all of two seconds ago. The rise in angry bass volume with each passing word, coupled with the curtains to the conference room already drawn to the sunshine and the jostling of downtown vehicular and pedestrian traffic below, were just two indicators this was primed to be the mother of all tongue-lashings. And, as if insult was meant to be dumped on top of injury, Powers saw the television, mounted in the wall, was playing his own disaster drama right then. The word Mute was framed just over CNN, he noted, a woman reporter taking center stage, with the taped-off background of smoking black wreckage being sifted through by firefighters, paramedics and a swarm of jackets with FBI stenciled across their backs.

Now that he'd arrived at some crossroads of fate, the colonel suspected it was going to be worse than anticipated during the drive here. In fact, he suddenly imagined the words "relieved of duty" were in the near future, but that could eventually prove the least of worries. It was going to take some serious tap-dancing over the land mines, he decided, to finagle his way out of this encounter of the red-tape kind.

Time to take it on the chin like a warrior.

Powers was about to claim a seat at the long table, empty except for the hulking, seething mass of Luther Jeffries at the opposite end, when the commander growled, "Don't bother to sit, Colonel. This won't take long."

Grevey had made a beeline for the coffeepot, was pouring himself a cup when Jeffries, loosening his red tie another inch, dropping it farther down over a barrel chest that looked set to pop chiseled pecs through his rumpled white shirt, snarled, "Put the coffee down, turn around and face me this instant, mister."

Powers glanced at Grevey who did as he was ordered. To the SAC's credit, Grevey didn't turn surly or betray the nerves he'd been chewing on since Powers had met him at Logan on the end of the red-eye flight from Detroit. During the drive to the SCTU's command center in downtown Boston, they'd hashed over their cover stories, hoping they'd nailed down all the "whys" and "what-ifs," making sure all the excuses meshed for their twin-bill fiasco. They only hoped it was enough to snow the commander, keep their own agenda shadowed and skirting along.

Commander Jeffries paused, snorting like some enraged leviathan, the veins on the sides of his shaved black skull pulsing. "What I'm asking, gentlemen, does either one of you have an answer for how the hell everything got all screwed up! Can either one of you give me a reason right this second why I shouldn't launch a full-scale, in-your-face, up-your-sphincter, around-the-clock investigation before I yank you both off this operation and send you packing? Somebody want to tell me just what the fuck happened out there this morning?"

Grevey squared his shoulders, face hardening with a determination that told Powers the SAC thought he'd found an opening to launch his spiel when the commander fell silent, waiting to hear it. "Uh, sir, both the colonel and myself..."

Jeffries smiled, but the expression struck Powers like some shark ready to tear into bloody chum. "Skip it. Truth is, I don't want to know, not at this time. Maybe never. Maybe I just wanted to see if you sweat, have blood in your veins and not ice water."

"Sir?" Grevey said, confused. One second Jeffries was bellowing for answers, and in the next breath he was prepared to sweep it under the rug. Curious. Psy-war tactics? Powers wondered. Did the commander suspect, even know something about them? Worse, was he just holding out the rope, waiting for one or both of them to slip their heads through the noose, cinch it on their own?

"The whole program has just been changed, gentlemen. Congratulations. I have just been hit by lightning, thanks to the both of you."

"Sir?"

"Don't say that again, Grevey, you're starting to really bug me, and the baffled face doesn't wash. Listen up very carefully. In case you don't remember, we still work for the Justice Department, under that department. I know, we have been classified independent operators, thanks to Congress—and, by the way, because we are funded by Congress and the Senate, elected by the people, meaning we do work for the American people, just to remind you cowboys of that little fact next time you mount up an operation to kick ass and take names or get your butts handed to you and I'm left fielding phone calls from my irate superiors yelling so loud in my ear I can't even hear myself fart for a month to come. What I'm telling you, because of this towering inferno you two dropped over our heads, I received a phone call from a man at Justice name of Hal Brognola who, I hear, wields some mighty clout, the kind you hear when Godzilla's tearing up half a city and coming to step you into a slick red ooze on the sidewalk. Didn't ask a lot of questions, this Brognola, didn't seem even to want to come up here and grab the reins out of our hands, take a close-up look at my heroes. Found myself wondering why he didn't ask a bunch of questions. At any rate, seems Brognola has already sent some guy who, I'm ordered from up top and clear down to your country—Fort Bragg, Colonel—is to be attached to your hips. Fact, he's already here and waiting to see SCTU's finest. Why my own search for facts has been ordered stifled.''

Powers exchanged a look with Grevey.

"Special Agent Mike Belasko is downstairs in Interrogation Room B, even as both of you stand there and give yourselves all that what-the-hell eyeballing. I understand he's already questioned a few of your people, Colonel, trying to separate fact from any fiction you might sling his way. You know, any excuses for this class-A fiasco. If I were you, I'd look alive, be ready with solid answers, not some bullshit you think you were ready to feed me.''

Powers didn't like where any of this appeared headed, the least of which was some clown suit from Justice standing watch over his shoulder. "Sir, I'm not in the habit of making excuses, never have been, never will be. Just so we're clear, I hold myself personally responsible for what happened to those men out there this morning, and I believe I share the same sentiments as Agent Grevey.''

"I see, well, that's good to hear.'' He nodded at the television screen, where a camera was showing the body of a fallen FBI agent zipped up in a rubber bag. "You might get the opportunity to show somebody—maybe even down at the Hill—just how far you're willing to accept your role in that mess. It all boils down to someone else's call right now, gentlemen—meaning if our funding is yanked, the plug is pulled, SCTU goes swirling down the drain.'' The commander's fleeting smile, aloof shrug of his shoulders somehow didn't inspire confidence in Powers. "What do I know? Maybe Belasko is simply here to help see that doesn't happen, I can't say. Give him full cooperation, everything you've got on any and all ongoing operations, here and in other cities. Those are my orders. That's it. You're on notice. Dismissed. Now, get the hell outta my face.''

Powers trailed Grevey out into the corridor, resisting the urge to haul out his shoulder-holstered Beretta 92-F, blast a few rounds through the TV as Jeffries saw fit to hit the volume, the voice of some civilian fretting how something like this could happen in Boston cranking up a few decibels through the roaring in his ears. Man making a statement to him on the way out the door, no sweat. Powers decided to eat it for now, go kiss some clown suit butt, dance to the tune of the day, which was starting to sound like a death knell.

Grevey looked so steamed to Powers the colonel half-expected the SAC to burst into spontaneous combustion.

''Something feel real wrong here to you?'' Grevey asked, marching down the hallway, shouldering past a young FBI agent clutching a manila folder, the dark suit nearly dropping his package, scowling over his shoulder. ''I can't decide if that was too easy, or if we're getting set up as sacrificial lambs. You understand, Colonel, if Commander Jeffries has the first inkling…''

''Not here. Me and you,'' Powers said, rolling for the bank of elevators, ignoring the suits and skirts throwing them curious looks, ''need to have lunch later. Alone.''

''Right. But, first, we need to go under the microscope of this wonder boy from Justice.''

Powers jabbed the button as they reached the elevator. "Pull it together. Hey, I'm the one who has the real problem here, considering how you brought me into the bigger picture. So our futures look to be riding on what does or doesn't happen this next day or so."

"All things considered, you sound pretty damn cocksure, Colonel."

"We're still in the game, mister."

"For now."

Powers smiled, but the feeling didn't warm anything inside, where it all felt colder than a Siberian wind. "What are you worried about?"

"The Justice Department, for starters. Some guy waiting downstairs to give us a measuring, maybe start digging around, thinking there's two and two walking right behind us."

Powers snorted. "The Justice Department can kiss my Delta butt from here to hell. I'm a goddamned hero, in case you've forgotten. I've paid my dues to this country in a whole lotta enemy blood."

"And your point, Colonel?"

"My point is I've walked many a time through the valley of death, and I fear no man. My point is I'm sure this Belasko's just another chicken suit pulled desk duty his whole career. End of discussion."

Texas

MCCLINTOCK WANTED to slap the smug look off the Arab's face. Twenty minutes he'd been standing with Monroe and Jansen, sweating it out under the broiling sun at the north end of the runway, having waited it out before the sleek executive jet finally showed as a distant white smudge on the burning azure sky to the east. The Learjet had touched down, taxied, had then finally dropped into a long agonizing slow roll. Another five or so minutes they had stood their ground, maybe shuffling from foot to foot to work out the nerves and agitation, the turbofan jets kept running hot, gusting fumes and grit in their faces, the storm of noise and wind having forced them to backstep to other side of the runway. Before showing themselves the Arabs had taken their sweet time, maybe enjoying from behind drawn cabin curtains the Americans standing there, sweating and wondering when they'd make their grand appearance.

Brazen bastards. How much weight did they really pull? McClintock found himself wondering. It was time to find out.

McClintock had only met the nameless Arab once, some six months ago, same spot. The call from his own sponsor had come in during the dead of night on the secured line, arrangements then made over the fax, with orders handed down by paper he was instructed to shred as soon as his eyes only perused and memorized the details.

Now this shit again, playing lackey to some guy he didn't even have a name for. The short Arab's strange smile made McClintock wonder if he was destined somehow to become human meat on the hook. If his chain was getting jerked by this guy, for whatever purpose, he'd learn soon enough. If he was forced to, by God, he'd jam a huge monkey wrench into the whole operation—whatever the hell it really was— and send them screaming his way for blood. Talk about an Alamo, some grand last stand, if someone was looking to grab him by the horns, they'd know a goring...

He caught himself, aware he was getting paranoid, imagination flaming up with all manner of doomsday scenarios. Maybe this was a straight deal, after all, money changing hands, orders going out so the grand shadow game could get launched in massive earnest. Whatever, the leader of God's Crusaders still felt his patience thinning to a dangerous snapping point. All this don't call us, we'll call you crap, he thought, all the cloak-and-dagger was about to force his hand either way.

He wanted some answers.

Standing there in their dark suit jackets and ties, crisp pressed slacks and Italian loafers, with their long black hair and various styles of facial growth, they looked more like foreign gangsters—Eurotrash to McClintock—than the businessmen they had alleged they were that one time they'd met on the runway. The bulges under the jackets of the two larger Arabs holding their ground behind the short one made McClintock glad he'd snugged the Glock 17 in his waistband, nestled against his spine. Monroe and Jansen were likewise carrying Glocks, good to go if things turned ugly.

"This will be our last meeting," the Arab said, and held out the aluminum briefcase, but maintained a firm grasp on the large black nylon bag bulging with what McClintock sure hoped was the payoff money.

McClintock took the briefcase. "I have some questions for you, my friend."

"No time. I have urgent business elsewhere."

"Make the time."

The Arab seemed ready to launch himself into some angry retort, then shrugged. "Quickly."

It galled McClintock to the bone to find himself in this subordinate role to a man he knew was helping to engineer the mass destruction he'd seen all over the news. Maybe, he decided, the whole world had simply gone nuts. No allegiance to blood anymore, no vision of a better tomorrow based on principles and virtue, things like honor and loyalty bonding together a once-great nation founded on life, liberty and the pursuit of happiness. Maybe it was all just about the money. If that was the case, he could play it that way, too, and better.

"I want to know precisely what is planned for myself and my men. I want to know what our role is, and what's in all of this for us on the other side when the dust settles. I want to know if myself and my men are in any danger here of being discovered by outsiders. I really don't think I need to spell out any number of initials where that is concerned."

"Your orders come directly from the one who recruited you," the Arab said. "I am simply a cutout."

"You're telling me you don't know shit?"

"I know much. I know your orders, and they are encrypted on the disk inside the briefcase. Same encryption as before. Once you have memorized the names, phone numbers and locations, have your men underway, you will delete the file as before. You have less than forty-eight hours to get your men into contact with the others. Further orders will be waiting those men. You will remain behind here with half of your force until the job is finished."

"How come I get the feeling someone somewhere doesn't trust us?"

"How you feel about it is your problem."

"Believe me, whatever problem I have because of this will become your problem."

"Do I hear a threat?"

"You hear a statement of fact."

"Is that all?"

McClintock nodded at the nylon bag.

The Arab looked on the verge of sneering, then tossed the bag at McClintock's feet. "That money, it comes from your true paymaster."

"Meaning one of you people."

"Meaning a man of vision far away from here and whose name will go down in Islamic glory forever."

McClintock muttered a curse. "Is that what this is all about? Killing a bunch of Americans in the name of jihad? You guys pissed because you need American engineers to keep the oil pumping and American guns to make sure you keep it?"

"You sound bitter and disillusioned, you sound like a man who has failed at many attempts to find his own glory."

McClintock took a step forward, then stopped. "You insolent little—"

"Have you and your people at this compound not turned your backs on your own? You want to judge me, but have you not accepted money previously from myself to deliver weapons and explosives by truck across this country? Knowing all along many will die in the name of our jihad?"

"I know what we've done."

"And now you're having second thoughts?"

The way the Arab said it, more sure of something than ever, threw McClintock a curve ball, made him rein in the hard approach. Was the guy probing, ready to scurry back to his own sponsor or this so-called paymaster with word that bringing their militant right-wing delivery boys into the fold was a colossal mistake? One that should be addressed right away, meaning send in the goon squads, raze their compound?

"That money," the Arab went on, "should cover any travel expenses, any necessary payoffs along the way. What will be left is enough for you to either carry on here..."

"Or?"

"Perhaps make your way across the border. Mexican authorities, I understand, are easily persuaded to help aid and abet fugitives if the price is right."

"So, you are saying trouble is headed this way?"

The Arab made a face, growing weary, getting bent out of shape. "We have been successful so far only because the real truth has been kept to a select few. At this juncture, too much knowledge would be a very dangerous thing."

"For whom?"

"For you, for starters."

"Now who's making the statement."

"I must go now. You have—how do you Americans say it—a nice day."

They wheeled, all smugness and grins.

"Hey!" McClintock called out, the short one stopping to look back. "Say there's a problem, just for the sake of chuckles. Who do I ask for?"

"I assume you are asking for my name?"

"If you're a straight shooter like you want me to believe, what would it hurt to give me your name."

The Arab considered it, nodding, looking away. "If you at some point find the need to pursue a foolish and most dangerous course of action, well, I have no name." He paused, took a step toward the Learjet. "But they call me the Messenger."

As they boarded the jet, McClintock felt the heat all around, the temperature rising, but more from the fear he smelled in the air than the wrath of Mother Nature.

"Have a nice day. That's it?" Jansen growled.

McClintock didn't know what to make of it all. "One of you grab the bag, count the money inside, then I'll put it in the safe. I intend to go ahead and play this out, guys."

"So, how come you're standing there, looking like you think someone's going to come here and break it off in our collective butts?" Monroe said.

McClintock swiveled his head, pinned each man in turn with an icy stare. "Let's get something straight. We were sought out, chosen, if you will. We took the money, asked no questions. I never meant to come here, hide out and play weekend warrior or start up some right-wing group of rifles and rednecks. If we have to play lackey for now, even though that sticks in my craw, I'll do it."

"You want the money, always have," Monroe said.

"I want to finish out my life like I always dreamed. I'll honor our commitment to disperse men, matériel, whatever." He heard the jet's turbofans shrieking in the distance as it tore down the runway. "If it looks like we're being sacrificed on the altar of some blood agenda, I'll let each man decide what it is he wants to do."

"Which is what?" Monroe asked.

"Simple. Stand their ground here and fight and die...or take their cut of the payoff and see just how friendly some corrupt greaseball across the border wants to be."

McClintock marched off.

Boston

THE INTERROGATION ROOM was a simple, private affair, built strictly for the sake of intimidation the way Bolan saw it. There was one table, two chairs. There was no one-way observation glass, but there was a small stand in the corner of the white-walled room, holding a full and steaming coffeepot, which told Bolan this wasn't meant to be one-hundred percent the loneliest corner of isolation in Boston. Bolan assumed one seat at the table was reserved for a suspect, the other chair for whomever played good cop maybe, while the bad cop roamed around, growling threats, muttering curses. Despite the austere simplicity of it all, the soldier could smell the stink of fear in that room, a lingering ghost of grillings past. After endless years in the hell grounds he needed only instinct anymore and not imagination to know more than just threats had been hurled around in this room.

While he waited for Colonel Powers and Special Agent Grevey to show, he helped himself to a cup of coffee. Before entering the renovated twelve-story building in downtown Boston, the command central for SCTU, according to Brognola, the soldier mentally walked through the steps leading to his next course of action. After abandoning his shot-up rental, Bolan had quickly acquired another set of wheels. He'd hauled the satlink out of the war bag once he'd established his own base of operations in a motel near the Charles River. The satlink's flashing red light indicated the Farm was ready to spill the fax, and the soldier had received the printouts he'd requested from Kurtzman. The jacket from Fort Bragg on Colonel Powers informed Bolan the man was a decorated war hero, but much of his service record was classified, spelling Black Ops to the soldier. Grevey, in turn, had made his own valiant climb to the top, medals out the wazoo, a field agent with an exemplary record.

Even with the obvious need-to-know, the whole picture was a little too Mr. Clean for Bolan. Given the double disaster the SCTU field commanders had witnessed dropped on their teams, a number of disturbing questions were left hanging in Bolan's mind. How could nine FBI agents go up in flames, storming different targeted terrorist safehouses in separate cities, while not one Delta commando suffered so much as a scratch? If Powers and Grevey had been leading the respective charge through the doors, how come they had managed to walk away with nothing more than egg on the face?

It was time to drop the ball—or the bombshell, in this case—into the laps of men he suspected looked too damn good to be true.

And the Executioner had received the intel he needed from the Farm to pursue the next and only logical plan of action. Depending on how Powers and

Grevey reacted to the news, he would determine whether his suspicions had merit.

The door opened. Bolan glanced at the two men through his dark aviator shades. It wasn't much, at first, but the soldier caught the whiff of corruption, instinct charged up, telling him he'd come to the right—or wrong—place. Something in the eyes, the way they carried themselves, examining the stranger who had summoned them to their own interrogation room.

Something reeked to the Executioner, all right, and it wasn't the bad coffee. It was the stink of rotting souls.

They rolled in, fanned out, as if they had the drill down, a form of silent intimidation meant to walk a chill down the other guy's spine. Brown leather bomber jacket was Powers, Grevey's muscled bulk filling out the black flight jacket.

They were dirty, and they had something to hide. The longer Bolan stood there in a silence that predators used to gauge the moment before pouncing, the more he was certain a dark truth was hanging in the room. More times than he cared to remember the soldier had seen the face of a cannibal, and these two wore it bad enough to leave him wondering just how far the stench traveled. They could try and mask their dark motives, could even spew out a slew of lies that would sound believable to anyone who had not stared into the face of evil, but Bolan had them pegged.

Savages. Traitors.

"You must be Belasko."

Powers spoke first, but it was Grevey who stepped forward and offered his hand.

"Special Agent Grevey."

The grip was a little too forced, hard and prolonged, the big SAC nodding, looking as if he wished to hell he could see the eyes behind the shades even as he worked up a polite tone.

Powers looked irritated as he followed Grevey's call to the introduction, pumping Bolan's hand, announcing himself.

"Understand you had some problems this morning," Bolan said, and sipped his coffee.

Grevey plucked up a foam cup, lifted the coffeepot. "It happened, don't ask me exactly how, we're still looking into it. We lost nine good men. Family men. I'm sick to my stomach about it."

"We'll find the SOBs behind it," Powers said.

"Behind what?" Bolan asked.

Powers balked. "Why, whoever figured out we were crashing the door, maybe gave the order to prime both targets."

"Sounds like you think it might be someone on the home team."

"Didn't say that," Grevey said, a little too quick for Bolan, as if the excuses and bullshit to steer him clear of any accusations had already been shaped up, ironed out.

"It's an ongoing investigation," Powers said, helping himself to a cup of coffee.

"I'm hearing need-to-know?"

"When we learn something, you'll be the first to know, Agent Belasko," Grevey stated.

Bolan had already decided against any dancing with these two. "Here it is. I'm not here to pick your brains about what went wrong. I'm sure it's something that will weigh on you both for a long time. I'm sure you'll find yourselves getting reamed for weeks to come about losing nine men. You don't need me pissing gas into the fire.'' Bolan drank some coffee, set the cup down on the table. ''I'm thinking you have leads on other suspected terrorist targets.''

Both men paused, working on their coffee.

''We do,'' Grevey finally said, as if it were some great chore.

''I'll want what you have in three hours,'' Bolan said, heading for the door. ''Just so we don't get our signals crossed, I'm not here to hammer down on your operation, tell you how to go about your business of hunting down terrorists.'' He showed them a graveyard smile, read the sudden change in their mood, both men looking for a second as if they'd just been kicked in the gut. ''I'm here to help.''

''That's it?'' Grevey wanted to know.

''Did you expect something else?'' Bolan paused, grasping the door handle.

The soldier watched them watching him, sizing him up, wondering what the hell was really going on. Time to chuck the live grenade into his play.

''His name is Abu Amman,'' Bolan told them.

''Who?'' Powers asked, playing it cute.

''The suspected terrorist who was grabbed up crossing into Vermont? The one, I'm told, SCTU has been sitting on for two weeks.''

Grevey tried to play it off, Mr. Baffled. ''Hell, how did you get that much? We haven't even been able to get a name out of him.''

Bolan grinned. ''Hey, I only work for the Justice Department, I'm a mere grunt.'' He laughed, trying to make it sound like he was just one of the boys. "Besides, if I told you how I came by my information…I'd have to kill you."

Grevey forced a sound that was between a grunt and a chuckle. Powers ran a hand over his buzz cut, eyes falling off Bolan.

"Anyway," Bolan said, "I've got an idea, but I want to see how it goes."

"How what goes? You care to fill us in," Powers said, "or would you have to shoot us?"

Bolan forced his own chuckle. "Fair enough. Amman is a former Iraqi Republican Guard. We learned this because UN weapons inspectors," Bolan said, giving them just enough of what he'd learned from the Farm's cyberspace detective work to mull over, "found military records Saddam tried to keep secret. Seems this Amman became a bounty hunter for Saddam. Maybe you've heard. Saddam doesn't particularly care for Kurds."

"So this Amman lopped Kurd heads for Saddam after the war?" Powers said. "Now he comes to America to do…what?"

"I'm not sure," Bolan said. "He's being arraigned this morning, but you already know that." The soldier made a show of checking his watch. "In about ten minutes actually. The U.S. Attorney, the D.A., they've already been spoken to and agreed to it."

Bolan let it hang, watched them grow dark with curiosity, anger wanting to flush itself out, blow up in an all-out tirade.

"Agreed to what?" Powers asked.

"Bond," Bolan said.

"Bond?" Grevey rasped. "The bastard's been denied bond. We saw to it ourselves."

"I know. Like I said, I have an idea."

"You're going to see he's cut loose," Powers said. "Then you're going to follow him, hope you can smoke out a few more tangos, maybe a big fish."

Bolan opened the door, let the smile fade, then put an edge into his next words. "I was thinking more along the lines of reeling in a shark."

And the Executioner left them alone and standing at the table. It was a judgment call, going in, hoping to feel out a viper or two hidden in the shadows, putting his play on the table for them to see. The soldier had just shown one trump card, but if it went down with the Iraqi the way he suspected, even hoped, a sinister and dangerous game was only just beginning.

A blood game the Executioner didn't intend to lose.

CHAPTER FIVE

Abu Amman couldn't believe his luck. Before arraignment at Suffolk County Courthouse, he would have never even dreamed it possible to walk, an Iraqi free again on infidel soil. Funny how life worked, he thought, feeling blessed, as light on his feet as a feather, wending his way through the suit and skirt traffic of the courthouse, homing in on the unoccupied pay phone.

The previous night in his cell, under heavy guard by the U.S. Marshals, he had hit his knees, prayed in silence imploring for some miracle to fall from heaven, unchain him from bondage at the hands of the infidels. Those prayers included an urgent call to God, a raging desire to see a full battalion of his brothers-in-jihad storming the courthouse, shooting up the place, grabbing hostages, dishing back to the Americans what they had done to his soldiers in Kuwait, to countless Iraqis on the road back to Baghdad. All that carnage just to find him free, one warrior, walking on, laughing even as he avoided slipping in the blood of dead and dying infidels.

For two weeks now he had suffered through the abuse of the FBI, seethed inside at their insults to his

Islamic heritage, choked off a cry of pain now and then when one of them slapped him in the face, calling him everything from a liar to a bastard son of a camel. He didn't think they tortured prisoners in America, but he wasn't surprised by their brutality and bigotry. War in and of itself—no mistake, he and whoever was calling the shots beyond him were at war—cried out for all manner of atrocities, meaning no one was exempt from pain and suffering, all the way down to the smallest infant. American FBI agents were truly barbarians, but he could appreciate their methods. Even when he'd been a colonel in his Republican Guard Special Unit he understood the power of fear, the prevailing might of one man's will to dominate others if he freely used the most horrible and shocking forms of violence. It seemed like only yesterday, but he could vividly detail in his recall all the *souks* in Kuwait he'd personally destroyed after, of course, pilfering what he wanted as booty.

The pleasant memories of better days rolled on as he shouldered through what he assumed were a couple of lawyers, ignored their bleating indignation hitting his backside.

He remembered how he'd helped shoot up the emir's palace, participating with a boyish enthusiasm in the mass raping of the wives and concubines after watching his own men shoot down the son, the idiot having chosen to stand his ground, he recalled, in a desperate fool's errand to save the Kuwaiti empire of oil and easy living. He could still remember—with fleeting pride—the brutal but necessary interrogations that went on in the palace his unit had occupied in the following months. Weeping women, bawling children and tired old men would come to him on bended knee, offer him bribes to return their men to them, safe, in one piece. He would take their money with a benevolent smile. He was a fair man, after all, he felt their pain. Then he would order them to return to whatever was left of their ruined homes before marching their men back to their waiting open arms. Smiling, he would force the men to their knees, shoot them in the head. The wails of the women still pierced his brain even then, as they watched the horror and he proclaimed the dead men free forever of their corrupt, self-indulgent emir. Rolling on then, pumping bullets into the faces of the women while the children shrieked...

A chill walked down his spine. He shrugged off the memories, shaking his head, as a sudden confusing stab of fear tore through his belly. It all left him wondering why those images wanted to sink down into some black mass of guilt. No time for a dark mood, triumph against his enemies, he was sure, was just around the corner, beyond the lobby doors of the courthouse.

First he needed a little help to get back on track.

He picked up the phone, used the calling card they'd returned with his passport and cash, punching in the number he was ordered to only use as a last resort. Waiting while the phone rang on the other end, Abu Amman hoped today was the first day of the rest of his life. Yes, a new beginning where he could carve out his own road to another jihad against the hated Americans. He felt a surge of hope at the image of himself as a warrior free and on the move once more. With sheer strength of will, he shelved all the faces

of his victims to some dark forgotten corner of yes-
teryear, grateful that he hadn't caved to the FBI's per-
sistent grilling. Somehow—call it grace from God to
endure—he'd summoned the courage to stay silent in
the face of their insults, bigotry and threats, not even
lash back with his lawyer vowing to see them wilt
and waffle under a dreaded visit from their ACLU,
nor had he whined about civil rights, which were
clearly denied him since he hadn't even been fed the
first three days of his incarceration. He hadn't even
given them his real name, simply stating that he was
Palestinian, Ali Fazzah, just like the passport said.

Idiots.

Soon he would shove all their threats and intimidation back down their throats.

Then again, he might simply want to count his
blessings, he decided.

The list of charges against him was so long he got
a headache just trying to rattle off the first three or
four. The FBI had told him he was looking at life in
prison if he didn't cooperate, start dancing to their
tune of cooperation, which meant naming names and
places where his co-conspirators were holed up. What
could he have possibly told them, anyway? That some
nameless shadow had boiled up in the dead of night
in his village in central Iraq, given him cash, passport
and new identity? Somehow had connections inside
Syria where he was choppered across the airspace of
that country to the Lebanese border. Driven then to
the airport in Beirut by another nameless man. Flown
to Canada. Given instructions over a pay phone there
by yet another man he'd never seen. Picked up the
explosives at a warehouse…

The arrest at the Vermont border was like the cling-ing shroud of some distant bad dream, and he was putting all that behind him anyway, praise God.

Amman, thanks to someone posting a half-million-dollar cash bond, was a free man. God had answered his prayers.

The voice on the other end said in English, "Yes?"

In Arabic, according to his instructions, he recited the password. "The *munazala* has only begun." He didn't find it the least strange he was echoing the call to arms by Saddam during the Great Patriotic War, *munazala* effectively meaning battle between us and the infidel evil-doers, he knew. Even in defeat, Sad-dam, he thought, lived on, larger and more powerful than ever, outlasting two American presidential ad-ministrations that had tried, and failed, to bomb his country off the face of the Earth. Surely God was reserving a special destiny for the Iraqi people.

"A moment."

The voice had switched to Arabic. "I see where you are calling from, I know who you are," the voice said, moments later, and Amman balked. How could... American technology, of course. Some form of caller ID, the voice checking the area code, a com-puter tracking down the number to its exact loca-tion...

"Quickly explain your situation, but be careful what you say."

Amman stated he was free on half-million-dollar bond.

"Who posted it?"

"I inquired, but the magistrate said he did not know. I assumed it was—"

The voice muttered a curse. "Silence! You do not know who set you free, put up that sort of money? You do not find that troublesome, or strange?"

Suddenly, the day didn't look as bright as it did a minute ago. What was wrong with this picture, all too promising before the voice started barking at him in anger, on the verge maybe of telling him he was the spawn of a goat, unworthy to live another hour. If one of his own people hadn't come to his rescue, he wondered, then who had put up that kind of money as secured bond?

A knot seized his gut. He didn't even want to think it, but couldn't help but suspect a trap was being laid.

"You will wait there in the lobby. I am sending someone with further instructions."

The dial tone buzzing in his ear left Amman feeling terribly alone and afraid. He looked around the bustling lobby, some hot rage he couldn't fathom welling up in his gut. The day had suddenly turned dark, would maybe even soon grow as black, he imagined, as the midday sky over Kuwait had turned, the sun itself obliterated as half of the emir's thousand oil wells of Burgan he'd helped torch spewed mountains of fire and smoke. He looked around the lobby, the infidels surging all over the place. He longed for an AK-47, a dozen banana clips, grenades. Better yet, he wished he had some of those shaped charges he'd fixed to several of the emir's wells, the ones that were packed with a germ Saddam had bred in one of his underground labs. The Americans, he believed, called it Gulf War Syndrome, but he knew different. If his luck was about to sour, his life would prove a dismal failure if he didn't find a way to at least go out as a glorious martyr.

Abu Amman felt his paranoia taking hold of his senses as he slowly melted into the swarming crowd. Silently he began to pray, instinctively aware he was still a long way from being a free man.

IT TOOK a good two hours, but Brognola had worked his usual magic to spring Amman. Bolan knew the clout the big Fed commanded, could only imagine the call, the exchange of dialogue as the judge and team of special prosecutors gathered in His Honor's chambers while Amman was shuffled into the courtroom by a full squad of U.S. Marshals. The fact was that Brognola was liaison to the President of the United States for Stony Man Farm's covert ops, and if the Man had to personally issue the order to set Amman free on bond, well, the judge might find himself looking for work the following day and a few up-and-coming prosecutors might never see their dream of a judgeship or holding down some political office come true.

The bond itself existed only on paper. No money or collateral found its way to the magistrate, and the order from Brognola's office was to inform Amman there was no known source for his sudden freedom, if he even bothered to ask. It was a last-minute abrupt change in plans for all concerned, from Brognola on down, the System getting manipulated by faceless shadows, and even maybe under the threat of a presidential directive. The special prosecutors and the judge would probably go scratch themselves and grumble over a martini lunch later about the legal rug getting snatched from under them by the Justice Department, but Bolan needed to make some noise.

Starting now.

The FBI agent Bolan had borrowed from the intel-gathering team at the SCTU command center had been sitting in the courtroom, then the magistrate's office while Amman was bonded out, finally lingering around the lobby, keeping the soldier posted on Amman's movements over a cell phone. It didn't matter to Bolan if word got back to Powers or Grevey about the soldier's next move. In fact, Bolan wanted them stomping around, nervous, sweating, thoughts ripped by questions with no clear-cut answers. Things were about to turn ugly. The heat was going to crank up to scorching.

And the soldier intended for the noise to find its bellowing way back to what he strongly suspected were two vipers in hiding.

Sitting behind the wheel of a Jeep Cherokee he'd purchased off a used-car lot with allotted war funds, Bolan dropped it into Drive when his target practically flew down the courthouse steps, hit Somerset, then proceeded south on foot. The FBI agent had informed Bolan of Amman's thirty-second encounter with another Arab who had left the building before Amman.

Driving through any big city was always tough, but Boston was some engineer's idea of a bad joke. The streets were a jumbled maze cutting through forty-story glass-and-steel leviathans, asphalt long since, of course, dumped over what used to be narrow village lanes during the days of Paul Revere. The way Amman was throwing looks over his shoulder told Bolan the suspected terrorist was searching for a tail. It wouldn't be difficult for the man to shake Bolan, but if he had to, the soldier would park in an alley, grab the war bag off the back seat and set off after the guy on foot.

One of two things, he knew, was going to happen. Amman was running to meet what Bolan thought of as unknown enemies. Whoever was on the other end to greet the man would either take him back into the fold or would persuade him somehow to tell them if he'd talked to the FBI, before, of course, they killed him.

The Executioner wanted to see Amman at least live out the day until he could pose a few choice questions.

"HOW THE HELL can you shovel food in your face at a time like this?"

According to Powers's watch, the calamari, oysters Rockefeller and seafood chowder arrived promptly at 1120 hours. Jumpy nerves, or that limbo period before the next engagement with an enemy, tended to make his belly rumble. He appreciated the swift service, so far, made a mental note to leave the waitress at least a twenty spot, depending on how things went from there. As for Grevey's reluctance to dive in and gorge, he couldn't expect the FBI man to understand the one basic working principle about food where a warrior was concerned. In the field, under combat conditions, soldiers went without eating for ungodly, subhuman stretches that would break the average man. And then what they ate wasn't worth feeding Aunt Judy's poodle. He didn't expect Grevey to appreciate the deprivation of creature comforts, the clock frozen while waiting in ambush, the concealed soldier maybe forced to piss himself because he didn't dare even breathe, in general, forsaking all the things the civilian world took for granted, the warrior out there stalking an enemy...

Screw it, why bother?

Behind Grevey's mask of worry and irritation, Powers saw what he'd long since come to think of as the glint. He took a sip of Heineken, holding the look, and wondered if the man was going back in time, calculating some new angle of threat and intimidation to keep him on the short leash. Like he could anyway.

Perhaps this was the perfect moment to clear up a few matters, Powers thought. The Italian restaurant, with its red-checkered matting, a crowd of suits, the roving leg show, he observed with admiration and subdued heat, was a sudden stark reminder of a mobbed-up joint he used to frequent in Brooklyn.

It was a time where the glint had first shone his way.

"I understand the veal here is some of the best in town. But I was thinking I'd order that scampi and mussels special..."

Grevey leaned up, glanced around, looked ready to leap out of his skin, terrified they'd been followed. They'd taken a corner booth, deep in the restaurant, close enough to the kitchen where the noise beyond the swing doors should help mute the discussion Powers knew was coming.

"Cut the crap, Colonel. I didn't come here for the veal, the specials or the joy of your company. We've got problems, and I suggest we begin addressing them or we may find ourselves in the proverbial world of shit. I smell something wrong with a capital W about this chicken suit, as you call Mr. Justice Department. You may think you know men, warriors, whatever, better than I do, but I've seen some killing in my day, too. And I've seen the face of a man who can dish out some ass-kicking, present company excluded, and I'm telling you, Belasko was fronting us off. He's more than just another desk jockey looking to impress his boss.''

''I thought we already discussed this.''

''Oh, excuse me, I thought you were the one so anxious to have this little powwow.''

''But I'd like to also eat. You can talk and eat at the same time, can't you?''

Grevey settled back, and Powers clearly spotted the glint. ''I'm going to be real frank.''

''Don't say it—'if I go down, you go down.'''

''Thank you. Took the words right out of my mouth. Good to hear we're still on the same page.''

Powers felt the anger suddenly boiling in his belly. ''I wasn't aware this had become a pissing contest. Is this where we go back to Brooklyn? Is this where you tell me about your one-man spy show, how you have the mother lode of all blackmail angles?''

''I'm hoping it doesn't get ugly between us.''

Powers snorted, chomped down on some calamari, talking around his food because he knew that would irk Grevey some more. ''You know, now that you mention it, I was thinking I could always pay you off to get those pics back. I'm even willing to negotiate on the negatives. Up to, say, thirty percent of my cut from our foreign friend on our final payment, guaranteed after their big jihad showdown with us hated infidels.''

"It's gone way too far for a simple cash transaction between us, much less a burning of the bridge.''

Powers grunted. "Funny you should say that. I mean, it's always been just about the money for you. Me, it was principle…''

Grevey waved that off, smirking. "I've heard the spiel plenty enough. Honor and duty and manhood, the savages are out there, devouring the American way of life. Spare me you wrapping yourself in the flag. I know you for what you are.''

"Do you now?''

"A stone-cold killing machine who wants the world to be the way he and he alone sees it and wants it, or else. What do you think would happen if somehow those pics found their way down to Bragg, Colonel?''

"I don't think I like what you're implying, friend.''

"Hey, you're the war hero, the ultimate tough guy. I'd think you'd be proud of your accomplishments. Want the whole world to know.''

"Yeah, I'll start writing books like that SEAL guy about my exploits, tell everyone how big my stones really are.''

A smile, the glint shining brighter in Powers's face. "You're the hunter, America's answer to street crime, the ACLU's poster child for their right-wing conspiracy and bigoted paranoia flap. There he is, our man, the hunter, out there, late at night, making America's city streets safer, wiping out the drug-dealing, pimping, whoring, thieving scum of the earth.''

Powers chuckled, found himself somehow enjoying

the imagery. "Which reminds me. I'm getting that itch again. All this anxiety you're throwing at me, I'm, uh, feeling that way. Need some release for all this testosterone buildup."

"We've got Belasko to deal with, Colonel, whether you think so or not. You need release that bad I'll hand you a *Playboy* and some soap. I can't spare any more peace of mind while you head out for Roxbury tonight and wax some do-rags."

Powers sported Grevey a mean grin, felt it heating up between them, good and fast, but he was ready to go the distance. "What about my peace of mind? Since we're being frank and all, why don't we talk about how you took that away from me when you were working the FBI's Special Task Force on Organized Crime in New York, or whatever the hell you called it."

"It was an accident." A shrug. "I put you under surveillance."

"So you've said. I just happened to look like one of the Don's button men. You were just tailing me."

"You're lucky I did it on my own, didn't assign a half-dozen agents to follow you around while you made New York a safer place to live."

"We'll have to disagree on our versions of luck."

Grevey went on as if he hadn't heard Powers. "I watched as you executed—what was it—six gang-bangers? Told them you were a cop, lined them up against the wall. Don't get me wrong, I don't really have a problem depriving this country of six potential future heart surgeons or nuclear physicists. It was the woman you shot in cold blood, that was wrong." Grevey paused, peering hard at Powers. "I always wondered why you did that. Remember how she begged for her life, screamed at you she had four children. She was just a user, no more, no less."

Powers couldn't bring himself to answer. When he'd done it, shot her down in that alley, one bullet to the back of her head, it felt like he was gripped by a force beyond his control and reason. The trigger finger had a life of its own, natural as breathing.

The colonel tried to justify it anyway. "She was just another crack whore. Kids half-starved, growing up wondering why they never had a father, probably abused when she's broke and her mind's screaming at her for dope. They're probably all dead by now, or strung out on dope, or in jail."

"How do you know all that? Maybe she would've been busted in time, forced to get help by the system, cleaned herself up. She works two jobs, kids get an education, grow up, make a contribution. Mom's proud, finds she really always had a reason to live— the children—just had to struggle through her own demons, get past all that pain and heartbreak."

"Aren't we Mr. Sensitive today," Powers growled, felt his stomach coil with rage, forced somehow the trembling out of his hand as he stabbed at the calamari.

Grevey turned smug, seemed to alternate his moods as easy as hitting a light switch. "The great colonel, the hunter, I can't believe it. He sees a truth and turns a blind eye."

"You're really starting to irk me, friend. Not just that, but I can't believe I'm hearing what I am out of your mouth, of all people."

"Why? Because I say some things once in a while

that maybe move in sync with part of your darker perspective of the world? Who can say, but you're right about one thing. I want our foreign friend's money, and it's always been about that. No matter what I say, or really think, it certainly doesn't mean I change course." Grevey watched Powers squeeze lemon over the calamari, chomp down angrily, then work on the soup. "You know, Colonel, I'm thinking you brought me here just so you could hint you're on the verge of bailing, keep me guessing about this thing of ours, where we stand. I'm thinking you believe you can outcon the con. I'm thinking you want to take what you have squirreled away and boogie."

"Now you're a mind reader?"

"Am I right?"

Powers spooned some more soup, took his time responding. "The answers are yes, no, and maybe."

"My ass is the one over the fire, Colonel."

"But you're the homegrown genius, helped set in motion what's already happening. You were the one used a couple of disgruntled CIA types stationed overseas to get the ball rolling. You think it was just coincidence you were sucking down booze one night in a bar they happened to frequent? I can see it all now, the three great minds of the new millennium, talking about how the world as we know it is going all to hell, what can you do to fight back in this age of political correctness and Jerry Springer. Hatching up a conspiracy so vast and buried so deep, hell, it should be a script for the *X-Files*."

"I put in the time, I invested the money, I took the initial risk, all right, I got it started, with a little outside help. Just so happened a few easy pieces fell into place.''

''Such as the source for our money forced to flee his own country and hole up in the asshole of the world. Allah just so happened to be smiling your way, that it?''

''Now our way.''

''How about our next payment? You check the wire transfers to our bank down there?''

''I'll know something by the end of day's business.''

Powers chewed, stabbed some more calamari and bit down. ''Does it bother you we had to sacrifice those men?''

''Only if I think about it.''

''But we showed we could play ball, huh? We're a couple of straight shooters, bad guys believe in us now.''

''The cutout for our overseas source wanted to show his master we were on the level. Since we took out a few of theirs to put up the smoke screen and make SCTU look legit, he wanted us to prove we're willing to offer up a few sacrificial lambs on our side. Hey, what are you crying about, anyway? You didn't lose a single Delta shooter.''

''You see me crying?''

Grevey paused, a dark expression clouding his face. ''When I went to the can, I called about Amman while you were ordering your starters. He's been freed on bond. Half mil, cash. No name for the bondee. Kind of strange, huh, especially after our encounter of the Justice Department kind.''

''So, you're thinking Belasko's boss pulled some

strings to set him free. What about it? This would have gone federal anyway, it falls under the jurisdiction of the Justice Department, given the scope of it, shades of domestic terrorism, all that. On the upshot, we finagled getting Amman handed over to us, sat on him these past two weeks, made sure he didn't start singing the Islamic blues.''

"Well, Colonel, if Amman is picked up by the cell here in town, and Belasko's on hand to sniff them out...ask yourself what might happen if the Justice Department raids their hellhole by the river, rounds them up, puts the squeeze to them. Are you aware how much damaging intelligence about the operation they have stored on disk? Names of contacts, even phone numbers and locations of safehouses in other cities.''

"Encrypted.''

"I've seen their so-called encryption. Any hacking Internet wannabe superstar could break it down by the time you finish your soup.''

"And you're thinking somewhere in cyberspace our names will pop up?''

"It's a possibility.''

"So,'' Powers said, "let's throw Belasko a bone. Keep him busy. Say you take him on a little detour tonight. Pick out one of the remaining three safehouses you know of here in town. Have him maybe lead the charge. Who knows? We might get lucky. Chicken suit has to get his hands dirty if he wants in on a raid, might even catch a bullet.''

"Why does it sound like I'm going to pull a solo act for this little sideshow?''

Powers stopped eating, put some edge in his voice.

"I'm getting tired of having to repeat myself. To-night, I'm unavailable. End of story."

Grevey grunted. "Telling me you want to stretch your legs, take a stroll through Roxbury."

"A most pleasant way for me to spend the evening, unwind, get myself refocused. You want, I'll take a few pictures so you can fatten up your portfolio on the hunter."

"You're going bring us down."

"The hell I am. We'll brief at eight p.m. I'll even run this one by Luther."

"And how are you going to make yourself scarce?"

"I'll think of something. Got a tip about another safehouse, struck out on my own, last-second thing. Too dangerous to bring on the team, wanted to check it myself first."

Grevey stood, scowling as Powers worked on an oyster dripping with hollandaise. "You've got all the answers, don't you, Colonel?"

"Where you going?"

"You'll have to excuse me. One of us needs to take care of business. For some reason, I've lost any appetite I might have had."

"Suit yourself. But while you whirl around, all jacked up about Belasko and Luther, find out about our money." Powers stopped eating, eyed Grevey for a long moment, trying to get a fix on where it all stood. He never liked Grevey's smug attitude, all the arrogance he'd endured from this guy who thought he had the upper hand, something like two years now since Brooklyn. Even worse, as a warrior, he could never feel at ease when he knew his own destiny was

beyond his control. Well, perhaps he was overdue to
take a hard stand, force the whole issue, and starting
tonight. Going out for a hunt was strictly an in-your-
face message, let the SAC know Colonel Powers was
still his own man, didn't jump through hoops for anybody. He knew Grevey believed he held his fate in
his hands with the blackmail, but if he did pack up
and boogie, well, life on the run, in hiding at that
point, looking over his shoulder, was better than life
in D Block at Leavenworth.

Still, he had to wonder how the hell it had all come
down to the implied threats, the raw nerves between
them, some Justice guy showing up out of nowhere,
looking at them funny from behind his aviator shades.
Shit did happen, perhaps, but Powers had always been
the guy who made the feces fly and smear the other
face. Now he was starting to see the fan turning his
way. What could he do but ride it out? From the beginning Powers had agreed to go along with the conspiracy to help the man slip terrorists into the country,
stay in loose contact over secured lines or pay phones,
shipments of weapons and explosives moved through
a legit trucking company, setting the table with the
help of their shaky allies in Texas, guys who used to
be on the other side of the law but who'd wised up
and gone for themselves. If it was just about the
money, then so be it, getting rich was a program he
could go with, no matter how much blood got shed,
as long as it wasn't his own. Powers could see the
future, all right, white sandy beaches, the booze flowing, young women paid to do whatever he wanted.
He'd paid his dues to man, God and country, and he
figured it was now shaping up to be the right time to

look out for Number One. The problem, the way Powers saw it now, was that too many people knew too much. At some point a link in the chain was going to get broken. When that happened and the winds of suspicion began blowing his way, he would be prepared, make sure his bank account was fat enough to carry him away, gone for good, an angry memory that would leave everyone seething for his head. Good luck finding him. Luckily that slice of beachfront paradise was already bought and paid for, ready to take him to a new home, some heaven on Earth where he could live out his golden years in pleasure, somehow secure that elusive peace of mind when he left the coming Armageddon in his wake.

"Enjoy your lunch, Colonel," Grevey said with all the sincerity of some bitter ex-felon.

Powers watched him march off, the guy fuming in silence, nothing settled in the SAC's mind. The colonel went back to work on his soup, then hailed his waitress to the table. With a full belly, he thought, he shouldn't have any problem out there tonight, doing what had to be done, making America a little safer, kinder and gentler place. He damn near felt sorry for whoever turned up in his path tonight.

CHAPTER SIX

After someone bounced his potential songbird from pay phone to pay phone, a black Lincoln Continental had finally picked up Amman several blocks from the Charles River, according to Bolan's mental map of the town. With dark-tinted windows obscuring any head count inside the luxury vehicle, Bolan maintained his tail, roughly five car lengths behind as they rolled down Beacon Street. Vehicular congestion would either hinder the soldier's progress—maybe cost him his pursuit—or it would lend his SUV the appearance of just another link in the traffic chain. If he'd been made, his quarry gave no sign they had him under paranoid scrutiny, ready to rabbit with the stop-and-jerk traffic through changing lights like the now-extinct Najim and his wheelman had earlier performed.

Another ten minutes of holding his course, turning north toward the river, and he saw the Lincoln cruise through the open yawn to what looked to the soldier like some abandoned industrial complex, deserted warehouses. In the neighborhood of a hundred yards deep into the no-man's-land, he saw the Lincoln brake near a concrete loading dock running behind a three-story redbrick warehouse. Doors flew open, a driver in a dark suit jacket disgorging while another swarthy man similarly dressed in expensive threads hopped out the passenger side. Bolan was cutting the wheel, spying a gap between two grimy blocklike structures at two o'clock, when he saw the passenger fling open the back door, haul out Amman while eyeing the SUV beyond the chain link fence. To the suspicious credit of Amman's handler the man didn't shout, point, throw off any indication he was set to panic, call out any guns on-site.

The Executioner didn't care, either way. The soldier was primed for a straight-on bull charge. He was going in, blind, of course, no solid read on numbers, what manner of hardware poised to greet him on the other end, the layout of the building. Sometimes the hard way was the best approach, rolling the dice, catching whatever turned up in the gunsights. Experience had long since showed Bolan a blitz was only as good as the man on the razing end.

More times than he could count, Bolan had proved a master at dishing out wholesale slaughter. Daring in the form of sheer guts and will, seizing the initiative during the opening rounds and a simple show of overwhelming force flung in the face of an enemy usually shaved the odds in his rapid favor. Of course, once the bullets started flying and guys were bleeding and checking out, all bets were off.

SUV parked, engine killed and keys slipped into his pants pocket, Bolan shed the topcoat. War bag opened, and he was ready to blitz on after a few quick deft moves. The sleeveless nylon vest was the next best thing to combat harness under impromptu con-

ditions. Slots, pouches and webbing were filled and
fitted with a mix of flash-bang and high explosive
grenades, spare clips for the HK-33 and side arms,
two 40 mm grenades as backup for the M-203, which
was already stuffed with a high explosive round. No
sense in getting caught short on firepower. Two sets
of plastic cuffs, and Bolan was out the door to go in
search of enemy blood.

Leaving the war bag behind was a risk he'd have
to take, but there didn't seem much by way of wandering human traffic in the area, not even the sound
of machinery grinding at work to indicate some work-
force in the vicinity. It was as if this chunk of turf by
the river was an eyesore the city planners wanted
tucked away, forgotten. When the noise of the shooting started it would, he hoped, confine itself to this
deserted wasteland.

Near perfect striking ground, good as it got.

Locking the doors, the soldier headed out, rounded
the corner of the building, found they had disappeared
inside the warehouse, if that's what it even was. On
the move, aware eyes could be watching from the
building or cameras could be hidden somewhere in
the vicinity, the soldier made swift tracks through the
open gate. On the way in, he glimpsed a sign that
read Leland Trucking. Mentally he filed that away for
the Farm to check into, get a fix on who owned the
property. The place was an obvious haven, maybe
some staging point for a terrorist attack. This was
merely his own beginning, Bolan suspected, a launching point for total war against some shadow army of
terrorists and conspirators.

The Executioner was stepping up to the plate to swing for the fences.

Slinging the assault rifle around his shoulder, the Executioner palmed the Beretta 93-R, the sound suppressor already threaded in place, the selector mode set for single shot. At the deepest north end a minivan was parked near a garbage Dumpster. Figure four, maybe five beyond the two he'd counted, inside the building. Then there was Amman.

The soldier was hoping to take a live one, maybe bag two songbirds. With any luck he might strike a mother lode of intelligence, from the mouths of savages, on paper or on disk.

Only one way to find out if he was about to strike gold.

The first savage nearly flew out through the open rolling door. The SMG tracking Bolan's way, as the soldier hit the loading dock, told him they were geared up, waiting for the mystery invader to make his move in. The shooter was quick, opening up with a lightning stammer of subgun fire, nearly caught the big intruder out in the open. The gods of war chose that moment to smile on the soldier, offering up a steel support beam in his path. On the fly, Bolan was shielded a heartbeat later by the beam, the tracking line of steel-jacketed hornets screaming off the post. The soldier went low, thrust himself around the opposite corner of the beam and tapped off a 9 mm Parabellum round. Downrange, the slug blasted through the shooter's teeth, muzzling on like some bolt of steel lightning, puking out a pink-gray cloud on its way out of the target's skull, the hardman's legs whipsawed out from under him.

One down and out of play.

Beretta stowed, Bolan took the assault rifle, bored ahead, ready to cut down any hardmen who might surge into view. They were shouting from beyond the doorway in their native tongue. Bolan had a working knowledge of Arabic and in the frenzy of bellowed demands he heard someone give the order, a warning that told the soldier his gold mine was just around the corner: "Delete the files."

Gauging the distance to the voices, the sounds of men scuffling around, barking in Arabic, Bolan primed a flash-bang grenade. Crouched by the open doorway, he chanced a look around the corner. Another hardman, charging toward the doorway, made eye contact with Bolan for a heartbeat, bringing his stubby Ingram MAC-10 to bear. The Executioner hosed him down with a one-handed figure eight from the chattering HK-33. A flash of frantic activity, guys wheeling his way, and Bolan saw the swarthy passenger from the Lincoln grab Amman by the shoulder. Another hardman was charging past the group, cutting a beeline straight for a set of stairs. Doomsday numbers ticking off in Bolan's head, he lobbed the steel egg with a sideways whipping motion, glimpsed it bouncing up, dead center in a group of four, maybe five. It was hard to tell since he was driven to cover. Autofire tracked his way, slugs tattooing the door frame, shrieking off concrete, a lot of spray and pray meant to hold back the invader. Even though he was well-shielded from ground zero, the soldier slid a couple of yards farther down from the hornet's nest of bullets snapping through the doorway. Two million candlepower was set to light up the warehouse, turn the enemy into senseless petrified flesh. He squeezed his eyes shut just the same, looked away, slapped his hands over his ears. Riding out the crunching blast, the soldier made his move to crank it up, bowl them down.

Charging low through the doorway, he tallied up four badly mauled dancing hardmen in the immediate open vicinity ahead, guys teetering around in the smoke, growling oaths, hands grabbing at blinded eyes or bleeding ears. Amman was on the ground, blubbering something, somehow managed to clutch at his handler's leg, as if beseeching deliverance.

The Executioner marched ahead, took in the target area. It wasn't much as far as warehouses went. He spied a lot of empty ground, a few crates stacked here and there, some fifty-five-gallon drums, a scattering of workbenches, the catwalks free of potential combatants as far as he could tell.

Bolan directed a short burst of 5.56 mm lead toward the runner, stitching a ragged crimson line up his left leg. He left that guy to his howl of agony, began sweeping the three dancers to his left. In the span of two seconds it took Bolan to wax three more shooters, dropping them in a heap of tangled limbs, Amman's handler somehow managed to feel his way to the soldier's bait, slapping at the fingers that clutched, then fisting a handful of hair. Before Bolan could adjust his aim, a pistol was jammed into Amman's ear, the trigger squeezed, the bullet coring through Amman's brain and exiting the other side of his skull in a reddish-pink halo.

Bolan tapped the HK-33's trigger, biting down a curse of frustration, as he hit the handler in the shoulder with a three-round burst. No sooner had the man screamed his pain and toppled than Bolan was looming over him, kicking the PPK pistol away. The soldier sighted down the assault rifle at the mask of hate and agony.

"I counted eight," Bolan growled. "Anyone else around?"

The handler turned defiant. "What?"

His hearing was most likely damaged from the grenade blast, so Bolan placed the muzzle of the HK-33 between the handler's eyes to help clear the cobwebs. "I don't like having to repeat myself. Eight of you, including Amman?"

The man appeared to focus on reading lips, his face screwed up in pain. "Yes. Eight."

"Consider yourself warned. I don't give liars a second chance," the soldier said. He reached down and flipped the man over on his stomach, the guy yelping and cursing. Fastening his prisoner's hands behind his back with the cuffs, Bolan set off for the stairs, in pursuit of the injured Arab assigned the task to delete what he hoped was the mother lode. The guy had crawled out of sight behind a partition that shielded the stairs. Jacked up on fear and pain, the wounded man begin capping off shots from a pistol. Wood flew in Bolan's face as he reached the partition. No time to waste in some bogged down trading of shots, the soldier hugged the partition, hung the assault rifle low around the corner and held back on the trigger. He was rewarded by a sharp cry, made out the faint wet thud of steel-jacketed projectiles burrowing flesh.

Standing, Bolan moved to the bottom of the steps. Halfway up, he found the Arab a mass of red ruins, but the shooter was fumbling for the pistol even in his dying breath. A three-round burst spewed from the Executioner's HK-33 ended the Arab's play.

A quick search of the warehouse from where he held his ground, combat senses tuned to every inch of the place, and Bolan was satisfied he'd made Amman's killer a believer.

The Executioner began ascending the steps, setting his sights on an open doorway to what appeared an office. Topping the steps, he saw two computers beyond the doorway, a wall map of Boston, a fax machine and a shredder. At first glance it all struck him as some fly-by-night command center.

Or was the grand slam he'd gone swinging for just beyond the doorway?

Bolan swiftly moved in on what he hoped was the mother lode of intel, grimly intent on stealing whatever sinister knowledge they may be jealously guarding here.

Sudan

THE HORROR SHOW was starting earlier than usual. The sun hadn't even set over the barren plain beyond the People's Palace of Sudan, and already Nafud saw Sayid had tied on half a load, the bottle of cognac in his pudgy hand three-quarters empty. The lieutenant general wobbled his flabby girth toward a giant-screen TV roughly as large as two king-size beds, his belly jiggling as he chuckled and waved the remote around at his guests and soldiers. The grand master of this coming psycho ceremony, Nafud thought, was savoring his ghoul's spotlight.

"I am glad all of you could attend the showing of our noble fight against the SPLA savages who wish to destroy the government of Sudan," Sayid stated.

As if they had a choice, Nafud thought sourly, noting the tense looks, lowered gazes from the bankers. A few of the officers chuckled, looking proud and expectant as if ribbons were about to be pinned on their already over-medaled blouses.

Nafud thought he was going to be sick. Standing beyond the ring of soldiers, officers and the two CIA mercenaries, he sipped from his glass of merlot wine. He hoped enough wine would wash away the queasy churn in his belly, the Omani sure he was about to bear witness to the ghastly mother of all Sayid film productions.

Trying to shake the image of gaping crocodile jaws from his thoughts, Nafud took a moment to look around the sprawling living room. He wondered what sort of madness could spawn itself out of all these opulent surroundings. He wondered how such obscene wealth could get grabbed up by a few men—outrageous privilege and riches even by his own standards—who no more valued the lives of their countrymen than they would a cockroach's. Then he inwardly laughed at the sheer absurdity of even wondering such a thing.

This was Sudan, he reminded himself. Here the only thing that made sense in some irrational nightmare reality was, indeed, the madness of the men in power. Here death and suffering were the only constants counted on to rule the day. Here they starved to death daily by perhaps the thousands, the UN and Red Cross having long since seen and publicly admitted the naive stupidity of turning over cargo planes heaped with food and medical supplies to a bunch of patronizing soldiers on the tarmac, who promptly handed it all over to the likes of men like Sayid, who turned around and resold it all to cronies in Somalia or Ethiopia for hefty sums of cash.

Forget the sudden epidemic rise in HIV. In Sudan they died in droves from treatable diseases such as malaria, TB or syphilis. Oh, the horror alone that could be prevented by a simple vaccine, those antibiotics pilfered up by Sudan's ruling body for a few more dollars that eventually went toward marching along their campaign of genocide in the black south.

Nafud knew all too much about Sudan's plagues, in fact, as he shuddered at images of withered corpses strewed all over the country. He was well read about all the bacteria and disease carried by ticks, worms and mosquitoes. Truth was, he had made a point to educate himself with his research of the country over the past year, wanting to understand—if just to save his own skin—how he could avoid coming down with any one of a dozen illnesses that would prove fatal if left to run their course.

Wondering where such a fleeting soft spot for people he'd never met, much less really cared about came from, he shook the terrible thoughts and images of diseased or starving shriveled black mummies out of his head. He narrowed his roving gaze then, felt his eyes nearly hurt from all that glittered around him. Everything was trimmed in gold or silver, Nafud noted for maybe the twentieth time since his year-long exile. From the bar and adjoining whirlpool tub to the banks of wall mirrors, to the railings of the winding marble staircases hugging the north and south walls, it gleamed and yearned to sting the eyes. The hanging chandeliers, he figured, were perhaps half the size of some small cars, and they were made from cut diamonds, not the standard crystal. The floor was the most polished white marble he'd ever seen, seemed to shine a blinding white light against the twinkling blaze above.

Was that a vague shadow of his reflection on the floor? Did he look troubled? He looked up and toward the oversize couch, which was made from a bizarre mix of leopard and lion skin, teakwood base. Horseshoe in shape, fanning out around the center of Sayid's pride and joy, it was big enough to comfortably hold forty men, although only the upper-echelon officers and an assortment of bankers and other businessmen from Khartoum were deemed worthy enough to have front-row seating.

A dozen or so soldiers now worked their way around the couch or offered cocktails from silver trays to those lower-ranking officers left standing. A few of the soldiers looked a trifle surly at being relegated waiter duty, serving up the drinks and enough caviar, suckling pig and oysters it would have even shamed, he thought, his own father's lavish indulgences. Nafud was grateful there were never any women among the viewing audience. Sayid at least had enough common sense to not tweak the horror or outrage from the female populace that might dampen their enthusiasm to please a sudden urge. Turning his head, searching out something to fill his eyes other than the flabby drunken buffoon, he spotted the small contingent of imported beauties still out by the pool. He shot a longing gaze through the French double doors at the lounging nubile flesh out there trying to catch the dying sunshine, or making for one last swim before the onslaught of night and its bitter chill. Nafud sighed, seeing a few pairs of tender ripe lips lingering on crystal goblets, blond hair glowing his way in the fading light. The heat stirring in his loins, Nafud wished he could excuse himself to go in search of some more pleasant way to pass the time.

He couldn't, and not just because Sayid would notice and take offense.

The CIA war dog, Kragen, had moments ago whispered he needed a moment alone to discuss something. The grizzled, white-haired mercenary claimed it was urgent, and when Sayid started the show he'd make his way toward him. Nafud suspected it would turn out to be simply haggling over more money, but there was something else he'd read in the merc's tone that left him wondering. But what? Fear?

"The lights, turn them down!" Sayid called to a soldier, staggering away from the screen.

Nafud caught the dark looks exchanged among the bankers, smiled, grateful he wasn't alone in his disgust. The lights dimmed, casting little more than shadows around the living room.

Then a picture of death jumped out at the crowd with a jab of the remote in Sayid's hand. A row of skulls, either half-bleached to rotting by the sun, or the flesh picked clean by the vultures and the ravens, Nafud couldn't say, was lined up behind Sayid, who stood there on screen, grinning into the camera, an AK-74 canted across his medallioned uniform. He then looked set to retch, somehow kept the smile in place before he produced a thick bandana and wrapped it around his nose and mouth. During the pause, Nafud heard then looked at the thick rolling mats of hungry flies picking at whatever meat remained on gleaming skullbone.

"The smell of death," the celluloid Sayid began, "is all around me. Some of my soldiers succumb to losing their stomachs, vomiting from a stench I can only describe as something emitting from the very bowels of hell. I urge them, as their leader, to always stand tall, to take in the smell as a smell of triumph, of our destiny as holy victors over the savage hordes here in southern Sudan."

Cut to soldiers with machetes, lopping off the heads of dead rebels. Some of them didn't look any older than sixteen, eighteen tops to Nafud, two of them balking at driving their machetes through an exposed throat until an older soldier walked up and nudged them with his AK-74. But he'd overheard the rumors about youths during the drunken retelling of war stories by officers here in the palace, how they were kidnapped from their schools, sent to the front lines. Fight or die. It also occurred to Nafud the lieutenant general always showed himself to the viewing audience after the bodies were piled up and the blood had long since stopped running from shot-up, even dismembered SPLA guerrillas. The man never looked ruffled, or adrenalized in the eyes after his alleged close encounters with death. Not even the first bead of sweat on his face, not a stain anywhere from head to toe, the uniform so crisp and clean it might have just been pulled out of the closet. Sayid always

know the shipments in question fell into your hands and were rerouted to your sources in America."

Nafud felt his guts coil with anger and fear. "You have trouble, I have trouble, is that what you're implying?"

"The trouble is that one of these men made off with a satlink that can communicate with my American employers over a secured line. They might have passed the word on all's not what it seems in Sudan."

"Meaning fingers will point this way? Perhaps some commandos will come hunting for me?"

"That's certainly a possibility, especially if the weapons shipments are connected to their point of origin, my two running boys mentioning all the money we've been receiving from a certain Omani sheikh living here in exile. My employers can tend to play God. They have eyes and ears not even I can sometimes find."

Nafud started to bare his teeth toward the mercenary, then decided it was in his best interest to look conversational and relaxed, since Sayid did wander a curious eye their way before launching back into his patriotic diatribe. "I demand an honest reply from you at this time. Is this blackmail?"

"No, no. This is a business proposition, Sheikh. I'm going to be staying on, right here at the palace another two, three days until some details are hopefully ironed out between us."

"Such as more money?"

"It would certainly be incentive on my end to see you stay free, and breathing."

"What are the chances of you finding these two potential troublemakers?" Nafud asked.

"Slim to none. Unless, of course, I care to take a full battalion of men into the bush and root them out. That would be a suicide mission. The problem there, you see, is that a few of the higher-ups in the SPLA leadership are aware their CIA friends have duped them, gave them a serious shortage on weapons and promised funding."

"Both of which, especially this funding, went into your pocket."

Kragen softly chuckled. "Hey, we all have to look to the future. And mine certainly isn't dying in the biggest shit hole on the planet."

"And this business proposition?"

"I have a jet being sat on near here. I'm losing the transponder, working on installing an antiradar housing, mapping out a safe flight path through watching corridors, such as making sure I'm free of any AWACS, eyes in the sky, like that. Now I'm going to have a chat at some point with the lieutenant general, clear a few matters by him. Say he's sad to see you go, or feels some duplicity on this side. A hefty wire transfer to his account should take care of any hurt feelings."

"Or he might feed us to his pet crocodiles," Nafud said.

"Won't happen. I can be quite the salesman when I want to be."

"And just what are you trying to sell me?"

Kragen took a sip of bourbon, smiled. "Life." He held up his empty glass. "Why don't we, meaning you, me and Sayid, sit down in private later and discuss a plan that would make all of us happy."

"I'll think about it."

"You do that."

"I'll need and he'll need to know more details, what you think it is you know about some possible attack by U.S. commandos."

"I didn't say that was going to happen."

"But it could."

"During my tour here in this shit hole, I've come to understand two things about Sudan. One, life is cheap, and two, anything is possible if the price is right. Hey, you were the one who bailed from your country. You were the one hatched the jihad that is now underway overseas. You were the one marched out a known and wanted, uh, 'freedom fighter' to do your recruiting. I'm not looking to spook you any more than you might be, Sheikh, but I saw you standing here looking like you'd just swallowed a huge camel turd. I can tell when a guy's concerned about his tomorrow, scrambling in hopes of saving all that's near and dear to his heart. I'm saying the game here in Sudan is dead, played out. If none of us has to walk around and start pulling daggers out of our backs, we could all fly off into the sunset, free, rich and happy. I'm here to help, not hurt," he added, smiling.

Nafud wanted to tell the man he was already rich, but watched in silence as the CIA merc passed in front of him, then wandered toward the bar. The Omani didn't know what to believe, much less who he could trust. But if there was some trouble perhaps headed his way, and the merc was being truthful, then it might be in his best interest to secure some other safe haven. There may or may not be danger coming his way, but Nafud wanted to at least live long enough to see the jihad fully erupt in America. His mind wanted to sift through all the unanswered questions the mercenary had just put on the table. Then he became aware his gaze had somehow settled on the sight of a rebel getting chomped on by a massive crocodile. Nafud grimaced, looked away when the rebel was hauled beneath the churning waters, body and screams vanishing beneath the thrashing foam as he was devoured by the crocodile's death roll. He heard Sayid laugh. "Now, that is what I call food for thought."

CHAPTER SEVEN

Boston

Bolan's tear and search of their command center ate up nearly five critical minutes before he found the lockbox in a cubbyhole walled up by loose brick. Shooting off the lock with the Beretta, he'd turned up all of one floppy disk. Aware he had a wounded fanatic downstairs, eager to grill his prisoner, the soldier couldn't spare the time, booting up one of the computers, indulging a personal scour through what he believed was secreted knowledge about the terrorist organization. Whatever was on the disk was more than likely coded anyway. When he left this abattoir he'd find the nearest hotel, steal the time to turn over whatever was stored on the disk to the cyber wizards at the Farm. Aaron "The Bear" Kurtzman and company were the best at cracking encrypted intel.

HK-33 leading the soldier down the stairs, Bolan listened to the silence beyond the partition. Something felt wrong, too still and quiet out there on the floor, his instinct for trouble flaring to life. Hitting the bottom of the steps, he cautiously moved out into the open—only to find his prisoner was nowhere in sight.

The assault rifle fanning the warehouse in all directions, Bolan picked up his pace, heading for the open door when a rare and basic oversight on reading the situation nearly cost him his life.

The groan of metal above snared the soldier's attention at the last possible instant before he looked up and found his prisoner launching himself into a swan dive off the catwalk. The header meant to mash Bolan into a pile of broken bones became a solo act when the Executioner dashed ahead. Clear of the falling human missile, he looked over his shoulder just as the Arab slammed the vacated area, his skull cracking open with a wet thud, a shooting vat of blood and brains taking to the air, the length of his body seeming to fold in on itself as he bounced off the concrete, flipped on his back, legs twitching as the life was slammed out of his limbs. Bolan muttered a curse. So much for taking a live one.

The soldier had two quick calls to make. First Brognola to alert the Farm he had top priority work for the cyber sleuths coming their way. Then he'd contact Commander Jeffries. Since Agent Belasko was unofficially in charge of SCTU, the soldier wanted Grevey and Powers to come there and take a look at the mess he wanted them to personally clean up. It was a dangerous hand he was about to play, but if they were dirty, as he suspected, then they'd start sweating beads at the sight of the carnage. With any luck, they'd make a move, come gunning for him, perhaps create some ambush. In short, he was handing them an excuse to see he had an accident, as they chewed on their nerves, aware Special Agent Belasko was now something more than his Justice Department credentials claimed. A long shot, or was it? Bolan had to do something to flush them out, force open some window of opportunity that would produce a lead to see him hunting his faceless enemies. Beyond here, he suspected he would hit a wall, unless he rolled the dice.

The soldier was heading for the open door when he spotted two fifty-five-gallon drums in the murky depths of the far north corner. He couldn't quite make out the markings on the face of the drums, but as he began heading in that direction the universal sign for radiation leaped out at him. He angled away from the poison, recalling part of his talk with Brognola included the suicide bombers touching off their blast to Paradise laced with radioactive waste. A harder search, and he spotted a tarp covering a bulky heap behind the stairs. Reaching the hidden mass, he slid the tarp off the stack of unmarked wooden crates then unsheathed his commando dagger. Prying off the lid of two crates, he discovered the Arabs had been housing quite the armory. Plastic-wrapped bundles of gray-white bricks were packed in the top crates. Bolan figured he was looking at somewhere in the neighborhood of three hundred pounds of C-4. At least two dozen Italian Spectre submachine guns were loaded in the other opened crate. With all the hardware and explosives he suspected bulged the other crates, it left him wondering just how vast and entrenched was the terrorist cell in Boston.

The Executioner beat a swift exit from the warehouse, a sense of urgency propelling the soldier along. More now than ever he was grimly aware he was racing against some doomsday clock.

POWERS WAITED until Grevey slid his black unmarked Ford into his personal parking space of SCTU's underground garage. Searching the area, satisfied they would be alone, the colonel slid the Beretta 92-F from the shoulder rigging beneath his bomber jacket. Threading the sound suppressor to the muzzle, he held his ground, hidden behind the concrete post beside the basement door he knew Grevey would have to take to get to the bank of elevators. He heard Grevey open and close the car door, a resounding thud that echoed through the bowels of the garage. Powers heard the rap of hard-soled shoes on concrete coming closer, his heart pounding from the sudden anxiety of what he'd just learned from Jeffries.

Powers felt his grip tighten on the Beretta. A whiff of Grevey's aftershave passed him, and Powers whipped out from hiding. The colonel pounced on Grevey's backside like some enraged tiger. The shock forming Grevey's expression was instant, as the colonel slung the SAC against the concrete pillar, slamming the wind out of his lungs in a guttural belch, and jammed the Beretta's sound-suppressed muzzle under his chin, pinning him there like some bug beneath a microscope. Powers erupted in snarling rage.

"You want to tell me what the hell is going on, Grevey?"

Grevey's stare hardened with anger. "Maybe you'd like to tell me why you've got a gun shoved under my jaw."

"One word. Belasko."

"What about him?"

"Where have you been the past two hours?"

"Out. Driving around. Clearing up my head."

"Then I guess you don't know."

"Know what?" Grevey snarled.

"According to Luther, Belasko followed Amman to our boys near the river. Seems Luther wants us to head out with a special-issue HAZMAT team and eight body bags."

"You want to stop talking in riddles and spell it out?"

"Seems this Belasko waxed all eight of our terrorists there. By himself. Turned up two fifty-five-gallon drums of radioactive waste that may or may not get tracked back to us. I've gone to considerable trouble and expense, mister, to make sure my man out west safely delivered that little radioactive mix."

Was that look of surprise on Grevey's face sincere? Powers wondered.

"Wait a second. Belasko took out eight men?"

"Luther wants us to go there and personally clean the guy's mess up. But I'm thinking you know more about Special Agent Belasko than you're telling me."

Grevey's chuckle sounded bitter. "You actually think I'm going to cut my own throat at this stage? Hey, asshole, if this guy is something other than what he's pretending to be, maybe he came from your part of the country."

"I already checked the jackets of current and former Black Ops from Bragg, A to Z. He's not one of mine."

Grevey paused, turned grim but in a smug way. "So, what are you going to do? Blow my brains out now? Go ahead on your own? Go ahead, Colonel, pull the trigger, you think I brought Belasko onboard to ruin your life."

"Don't tempt me."

"Can you lose the gun? I'm not your problem."

Powers searched Grevey's eyes, looking for any sign of duplicity. He decided Grevey was playing it straight, slowly pulled the Beretta away, stepped back.

"Here it is, Grevey. Belasko has to go. I'm stepping up tonight's raid."

"I was thinking, I don't think my overseas man is going to appreciate us sacrificing any more of his recruits."

"I don't give a damn what he likes or doesn't like any more. I informed Luther about our strike. He gave it a thumbs-up. Strangely enough, given what's happened, our commander doesn't even want to be on-site when it's taken down."

"That's the last part of the cell here in Boston. We wipe them out..."

"There's others. Boston's finished for us. Listen up. I'm going to bail right before we strike. Give Belasko some song and dance I've got a lead on another cell."

"Take off on your little hunting expedition, you mean."

"Only Belasko will follow. He'll see the hunter in action, and during my jaunt, I'll make sure he catches a bullet."

Powers was tucking the Beretta away, his gaze falling off Grevey, when the blow to the jaw came out of nowhere. A blast of stars in his eyes, and he felt his brain threaten to become jelly, his legs nearly folding at the knees. Somehow, he held on, staggered back, considered reclaiming the Beretta when he saw

Grevey holding his ground, flexing out the fingers on the fist of the pile driver.

"Next time you pull a gun on me, Colonel, you'd better pull the trigger. Are we clear?"

Powers worked his sore jaw, massaging it with his hand. He held the SAC's angry look, then chuckled. "Crystal. I'll let that one slide, but the next time you so much as even lay a hand on my shoulder, I'll tear out your throat with my fingers and hold it up before your dying eyes. Are we clear?"

"Crystal."

WHEN BOLAN TOOK a room in a hotel near the Hynes Convention Center, he had quickly gone to work getting the satlink up, its specially installed computer hard-drive modem having relayed whatever was on the confiscated disk to the Farm. Some thirty minutes later there was good news and bad news coming out of Hal Brognola's office at the Justice Department. Bolan listened, indulging in a rare cigarette, as the big Fed spoke over the secured line on the mini-intercom of the satlink.

"What Bear's telling me, at first glance we may be looking at contacts, phone numbers, locations of other cells in various U.S. cities."

"And?"

"That's the good news. The bad news is it's all coded in Arabic."

"So, what's the problem? Bear has the translation software, doesn't he?"

"He does, but the problem is whatever the code, it's all written backward. Sentences, lettering, the works."

"How long before they break it?"

"It could be hours."

"Or days," the soldier finished when Brognola lapsed into a long pause.

"I've got something on my end that the Farm turned up, Striker. Unless they miss their guess, we've established proof of this link overseas to what's happening here."

Bolan smoked, listened as Brognola launched into a long revelation about the Omani sheikh in hiding. According to the big Fed, the sheikh was a known rabble-rouser, having spewed anti-West diatribe from his native soil to Sudan where he was under the care and protection of the thuggish rulers of the country's military infrastructure. It seemed the CIA, Brognola said, had a full platoon of military advisers from their Special Operations Division—translate mercenaries— who were taking Nafud's money for weapons and explosives that were supposed to go to the SPLA. These weapons, in a communiqué intercepted by the Farm to Langley, had somehow found their way back to the U.S. This was just learned because two of the mercenaries in Sudan were now on the run and hiding from their comrades, apparently having grown some sense of patriotic duty the past couple of days. Sudan was a known breeding and training ground for international terrorists, and it appeared a few fanatics had recently been shipped out of Sudan, straight to America. The rogue CIA element was believed to be shipping men and matériel via their new Air America.

"There's your source, Hal."

"Why do I get the feeling, while you may be sitting around, stalled in limbo up there, you want to go after the hydra yourself.''

Bolan had already brought the big Fed up to speed on his end, from the engagement with the Arab terrorists, the discovery of nuclear waste, down to the raid on some cell he'd learned from Commander Jeffries that his suspected rat bastards were staging for later that evening. The soldier had a decision to make. Stay on in Boston or pay Sudan a visit.

"How long would it take for Barbara," the soldier said, referring to Barbara Price, the Farm's mission controller, "to set the table for me to drop into this People's Palace where Nafud is having himself a good old time while he plans war against American civilians?''

"Well, we're talking about flight arrangements, getting logistics ironed out, nailing down a U.S. base in, say, Egypt, maybe the Sinai where I know we have a joint Special Forces, Israeli base established there, a launching point. Some calls, arm twisting, Grimaldi," he said, mentioning Stony Man's ace pilot, "over in Indonesia doing the flying honors for Phoenix, hell, a good six, seven hours to nail down the details.''

"Whatever it takes, have Barbara get me to Sudan ASAP. I'll need six blacksuits at my disposal. Whenever the next satellite passover of Sudan, I'll need a full and comprehensive layout of this palace. I'm going in, Hal. I cut the head off the hydra, my gut tells me it will unravel on this end.''

"And what about Powers and Grevey?''

"I'll go along with them on this raid tonight. I've

turned up the heat, I'm hoping they'll show themselves for the traitors I believe they are."

"You know what happened during their last two
so-called raids."

"I'm hoping three's the lucky charm. By then, Barbara should have worked out the details to get me to
Sudan."

"Striker," Brognola said, sounding grim as hell all
of a sudden, "Sudan is the number-one hellhole on
Earth, a Dante's Inferno of killers, terrorists, death,
starvation, plague—it's a witch's cauldron boiling
over with every ill of humankind not even the Four
Horsemen could drop on their heads. They're
staunchly anti-West. The legitimate world powers,
from our side to the world bankers, the UN and the
Red Cross have denounced the Khartoum government
as the most brutal and corrupt regime of cutthroats.
They make any criminal cartel out there now look like
choirboys coming into puberty."

Bolan knew the risks, the bottom line being he
might not make it out of Sudan. As far as he was
concerned, he was going in to trample through an
entrenched nest of vipers, utterly destroy and sever
the source of the jihad already underway in America.

"There's no other way. I'm going in just as soon
as Barbara makes it possible. The dragon is in Sudan.
I intend to hit this People's Palace," the Executioner
said, matching Brognola's dire tone, "and show them
a new horseman of the Apocalypse."

CHAPTER EIGHT

Some campaigns could find Bolan floating in the limbo of on-hold status. Riding it out was simply a question of how long the wait before new leads were dug up by the Farm or rooted out by the soldier himself, enemy faces on the next horizon confirmed, the finer details of getting in and out of the bad guy's backyard nailed down. Stony Man Farm was, he hoped, three hours, four tops, from hauling the Executioner out of waiting and getting him on his way to Sudan.

Not that Bolan didn't have something to do at that moment—far from it, in fact. The Executioner never waited for any problem to come to him. So while the day burned out he made arrangements through Commander Jeffries to fill him in on the night's proposed raid, ordered the commander to remain available at his office. The soldier wanted to see Grevey and Powers in action for himself.

After showering and ordering room service in his hotel, the soldier had grabbed a quick combat nap, aware once the Sudan phase was launched it could be days before he slept, even ate. The Farm would reach

Brognola and the big Fed would call him when he was set to fly.

So the sun had gone down, and all hands were now assembled in the parking garage of the SCTU command center. The soldier counted twelve commandos in full body armor, balaclava helmets, com links with throat mikes. Weapons and gear check, each commando toting an HK MP-5 subgun, and they began boarding three separate black vans.

Bolan had passed on the brief, gone straight to Grevey and Powers to get the particulars about the raid, the terrorists in question. Supposedly, three Iraqis had been linked to the dead men Bolan had left strewed near the river. What a coincidence, Bolan had thought. Powers claimed their intel gathering wizards had traced the phony paperwork found at the warehouse to two INS agents, one in Boston, the other working out of the Manhattan office. Conveniently, they weren't available for arrest, as Bolan recalled how Grevey informed him that both INS men—who might have proved invaluable sources of information—looked to have packed up and vanished. Hacking into the bank accounts of both INS men by the SCTU cyber team showed they had earlier that day made hefty withdrawals from mid-six-figure savings, sums that hardly jibed with the salaries of civil servants. None of this explained how Powers and Grevey always came up with locations on suspected terrorists, but Bolan wasn't in the mood to ask questions and hear the patented bullshit flung back. It also struck Bolan as mildly curious that neither Grevey nor Powers had offered any comment about his one-man strike and takedown of an eight-man terrorist cell, damn near right under their noses. Not so much as a job well done, even though Bolan was never one who needed congratulations and a slap on the back. And since Grevey and Powers always seemed to know right where to find the bad guys, how come they couldn't find the bunch Bolan had terminated? The stench of their rotting souls was growing stronger in Bolan's nose the more they blew smoke his way.

Bolan intended to do more than just go along for the ride. He intended to help lead the charge, take a prisoner. From his parked SUV, he took the war vest, filled with spare clips, a flash-bang, HE rounds for the M-203 grenade launcher. He shrugged on the vest, checked the loads on both the Beretta and the .44 Magnum Desert Eagle autoloader.

"I wasn't aware that kind of cannon was standard Justice Department issue."

Bolan found Grevey looking his way, the SAC locking and loading his own HK MP-5. It was the first tip-off to Bolan Grevey harbored suspicions Belasko wasn't any G-man.

"Personal favorite?" Grevey said, then forced a chuckle. "Or is that a throwaway piece in case you blast the wrong guy?"

Bolan dropped the mammoth gun into the holster riding his hip. "I've yet to shoot someone who didn't have it coming."

Grevey grunted. "That's comforting. Now, you want to saddle up, Belasko?"

The soldier wondered where Powers was, searched the garage. The colonel, he saw, was marching toward a black Ford, a cell phone pressed to his ear. "What's that about?" he asked Grevey, nodding at Powers, who looked back, seemed to hesitate then climbed into the Ford.

"The colonel won't be joining the party," Grevey said.

"And why's that?"

"He received a tip there may be another cell operating somewhere in Roxbury. He's going to check it. We get confirmation from his end this could be a doubleheader."

Bolan was catching a whiff of some hidden agenda ready to tear out of the garage.

"You coming or what, Belasko?"

The Executioner didn't answer, opened the door to his SUV. Whatever Powers's game, Bolan would play it out. Reading Grevey's act, the soldier guessed something was being staged for him, that he was meant to head out and follow the colonel. But why?

"Belasko! I'm talking to you."

"Three Iraqis against twelve heavily armed commandos. I don't see where the bad guys stand a chance."

"What the hell are you saying?"

"Looks like you've got everything under control. I'd just be in the way."

"Belasko…"

"Oh, and Grevey," Bolan said, shooting a grim smile at the SAC's bad acting. "Try not to blow the place up. There might be hard evidence there."

"Of what?"

Now Bolan heard fear in the man's tone. "When I find out, you'll be the first to know."

The Executioner settled behind the wheel, banged shut the door, the SUV's engine firing up with a throaty rumble as he keyed the ignition. The Executioner found Powers was already backing out, dropping his vehicle into Drive and rolling for the exit ramp.

POWERS FOUND HIM in the sideview mirror, four or so car lengths behind. Right where he wanted Belasko. The colonel kept a nice easy pace as he headed down Columbus, and the first grim telltale signs he was entering an urban combat zone began to show themselves. The creatures of the night, he thought, were out in force, as usual, same thing, different night. The dealers, the users, they were nothing more in his mind than sheer wastes of life, knew only how to take in some never-ending insatiable quest to keep their addictions fed. A few of the more paranoid, he noted, would scurry down alleys at the sight of what they feared was a lone cop car on the prowl. The more defiant ones held their lounging positions in stairwells or the steps of tenement buildings or the nooks and corners of the triple-deckered apartment buildings. One homeboy, Powers saw, decided to say hello, giving him the middle-finger salute.

Powers chuckled to himself. ''Welcome to the jungle.''

They were smoking crack even in full view and defiance of the law, he observed. Some tall black guy in white pants, white shoes and pink fedora was slapping around one of his girls. He heard the sound of a pistol capping off somewhere nearby, followed by a scream.

Animals, he thought. What was their contribution

anyway, he wondered, besides keeping the courts busy and the prison guards on their toes?

Another block or so and Powers slowly eased the Ford into a long alley. A few shadows stirred midway down, decided flight was called for when the unmarked Ford hit them with the lights. A quick look in his sideview glass, parking the car, dousing the lights, and Powers saw Belasko's SUV roll slowly past the mouth of the alley. Powers had the man's curiosity all flamed to hell.

Outstanding.

The colonel unzipped a small black nylon bag, hauled out the mini-Uzi. He threaded the sound suppressor to the compact SMG, then hung it beneath his jacket in the special shoulder rigging. He dropped four spare clips into his pockets, figured what the hell, and stowed away two fragmentation grenades. He never knew what or how many might turn up on a hunting expedition.

He climbed out, smiled into the enveloping darkness. It was time to go hunting. And, if Belasko caught up to him, well, Mr. Special Agent might just get caught in the cross fire. Life was tough like that sometimes, full of bad breaks.

THE EXECUTIONER found an empty weed-choked lot near the alley where he saw Powers park the Ford. He was glad he'd left the war bag behind in his hotel room, aware mere glass and metal wouldn't hold off any larcenous hands in this part of town. With only the necessities to see him through whatever was on SCTU's menu for the night, Bolan stepped out of the SUV, locked it up, slipped an arm through the

HK-33's strap, hanging it muzzle down before he did the best he could to conceal the bulk beneath the black leather trench coat he tugged on. He stepped through the gaping hole in the chain-link fence, hit the sidewalk, sights homed in on the alley where Powers ditched his Ford. He could feel the night people watching his swift progress, measuring him in paranoid silence, the thundering of rap bellowing from somewhere in the rows of tenements. Marching on, the soldier moved into the alley, gave the abandoned Ford a once-over, searched the far-reaching darkness ahead. He was stepping deeper into the alley when a shadow stumbled around the corner of a tenement building. Naked terror sought out Bolan as the shadow faltered, seemed ready to collapse in front of the soldier.

"You a cop, man?"

"Maybe."

"You gotta help, man, you a cop. This crazy white dude, he just started shootin' up my homeboys. All we done, ax for a smoke and he smiles, saying sure, then pulls out a piece and just starts blastin'."

Bolan looked past the terrified guy. A grim and sordid picture of what Powers's little solo act was really all about began to piece itself together in the soldier's mind.

"How did you manage to make it?" Bolan asked.

The guy took a moment to catch his breath. "I ran, that's how."

"I'll take it from here. And do me a favor."

"Yeah, anything, just nail that crazy bastard, he did my homies, man."

"Don't call the police."

"They wouldn't come anyway, man."

"Why's that?"

"You ain't never see a cop 'round here. Got more guns in this neighborhood, automatic weapons, no cop crazy enough to take a stroll here, 'less he pickin' up his cut from the crack man."

Bolan marched away, left the guy to his fear. When he rounded the corner, coming to a bisecting alley, the soldier spotted three bodies stretched out near a Dumpster garbage bin, the blood still running from their shattered skulls.

The Executioner unleathered the Beretta.

POWERS WAS a on roll. First the three homeboys— too bad one got away, but the guy moved like a rabbit. He'd popped off three quick ones, putting one 9 mm hole each between their eyes, but before he knew it he'd lost one.

What could he do? Shit happened.

Two shadows, he now found, were scrunched up in the framework of some broken-down door. The glass stems lowered away from their lips, the flames of their lighters dying at the sight of the lone armed man in black headed their way, smiling at them like some demon from the bowels of hell.

"Didn't your mothers ever tell you smoking that garbage is bad for your health?"

Powers saw their drug-addled brains were having difficulty understanding his little joke, so he decided to drive home the punch line. The Beretta was out and chugging, the 9 mm Parabellum rounds blasting through glass before drilling through their faces.

It was cherry pickings out here tonight, he thought,

rolling past them as they folded at the knees and flopped to the alley. He needed something more dramatic. Like a drug den, whorehouse, maybe a nightclub, a whole slew of zombies he could send to the big smoke out in hell. With any luck he'd find it, a real challenge to keep the juices flowing.

ALL BOLAN HAD to do was follow the trail of bodies. He found two more, heaped on another alley floor before a darkened doorway. Like the first three bodies, he found they were unarmed after a quick pat down. Powers was out here on some execution task, had proclaimed himself a one-man genocide campaign against what he saw as the wrong element of society, armed or not, criminal or otherwise. The soldier could well imagine the sort of bigoted hatred that fueled the colonel's killing march. He'd gone up against it before too many times to count. But why would Powers risk showing what he really was to a man he suspected of smelling him out as a rat bastard? This was murder, plain and simple....

Okay, Powers wanted him to see this, follow him deeper into this maze of alleys. This was staged, and even if the colonel had gone off before on what he saw as some kind of righteous vigilante hunt, Bolan's hunch was he was meant to get marched into an ambush.

The night was rent by the familiar thunderclap of a grenade. Powers was somewhere close, tallying up the body count, now winging around grenades. It took a few critical seconds, but Bolan holstered the Beretta, stripped off the topcoat and filled his hands with the HK-33. The Executioner set off, picking up the pace. He had Powers pegged as a stone-cold fanatic savage. If there was any doubt before this whether the colonel was capable of crossing over to the terrorist side of the tracks, it was gone now. The cold ball of anger lodged in his gut helped propel Bolan ahead in his hunt for the colonel.

POWERS BECAME light-headed with glee, fueled by a fresh burst of adrenaline when he hit major pay dirt. He'd found the steel door at the bottom of the stairwell, heard the racket of rap music thumping away, hardly muted by the thick barrier. Having armed the grenade, banging on the door, he'd taken cover back up the steps. A paranoid face framed in an Afro had cracked the door wide enough only to find himself obliterated by the shrapnel blast.

Powers had charged through the boiling smoke to shrill female screams, a few armed hulks barring his way, draped in enough gold and jewelry to clear the debt of most Third World countries, he figured, and started pouring out the lead storm with the mini-Uzi. A few wild rounds snapped past the colonel's head as he peeled off, taking in the large room with its oversize couches and chaos at a flying glance. The compact SMG stuttering in his fists, Powers nailed three would-be heroes with a facial 9 mm Parabellum stitching. A blur in the corner of his eye, and some guy was charging him like an enraged rhino. The haymaker craned for his skull, and Powers bent at the knees. The dealer's momentum carried him over the colonel's shoulders, Powers hitting the guy in the back of the skull with a three-round burst on his way down, cleaving off chunks of shaved head. Holding back on the trigger, he started spraying the room at random, catching semiclad females in the backside with long sweeping bursts, laughed next, experiencing gratitude, when one of the women was sent flying into the stereo. Her headfirst ram killed the noise that one second ago had been booming out of speakers the size of most people's beds.

He didn't want to waste more time here than necessary, instinct revved up, telling him Belasko wasn't far behind.

Arming his second frag grenade, the colonel saw them pouring out of the bedrooms in a narrow hallway, dead ahead. He pitched the steel egg into the human pack, bodies bowling into one another as they created a stampede, heading for what he assumed was some back way out.

His own exit stage left.

He took cover behind the wall, riding out the explosion, the shrieking of the wounded chewed up by countless pieces of lethal shrapnel the only kind of music he wanted to hear. Something was staggering near a massive fish tank. Powers burned up the SMG's clip as an angry black face, fists filled with a TEC-9, loomed behind the fluttering stuffing blown out of the couch by grenade blast one. A fresh magazine cracked home, leaving that guy to tumble, a bloody heap, through the fish tank, and Powers began raking long bursts down the hallway, clearing the path, his bullets chewing up naked flesh as hideous groans knifed the air and a few of his victims crawled ahead or tried to stand. He nearly caught a bullet as he flew past an open door. It was a glimpse, on the fly, but some guy was hunkered down inside, pulling the trigger on a semiautomatic pistol for all he was worth.

The shooter became less than zero in his mind as Powers growled, risked it and tapped off an SMG burst, catching the guy square in the chest with a figure-eight goring.

At the end of the hall, Powers saw a few runners heading for the door. He held back on the trigger, slamming them into the steel partition in a rain of shredded flesh and crimson. Checking his rear, satisfied it was a clean sweep, the colonel hit the door and burst out into the night.

THE SIGHT of such indiscriminate slaughter, whether these folks were engaged in illicit activity or not, coiled Bolan's gut with a rage that blew fire through his veins. HK-33 fanning the smoke and the feathery fall of stuffing, the soldier knew they were all dead. Was Powers leaving behind for him some message? Agent Belasko was next? Powers just wanted him to see he saw himself as the last line of defense between his vision of a better America and the poor and the desperate, the pathetic drug addict, all of them being, in his mind, on the same par as a common criminal? Whatever made Powers tick, Bolan needed only to stop this savage cold. Something in the colonel's way told the soldier this wasn't his first murderous outing.

Cautious but swift, Bolan advanced down the hallway, stepping over the sprawled mass of red ruins. The door was open. He could almost feel Powers, somewhere beyond the opening, laying in wait. The stink of blood and emptied bladders and bowels like an invisible hammer hitting him in the face, the Executioner stopped at the doorway, crouched. A gentle push of the door, and he saw he'd come to another narrow alley. Strangely enough, but just as the terrified runner had told him, he didn't even make out the first hint of a distant wailing siren. If he thought about it, the soldier would be disturbed that the residents of this neighborhood didn't even rate a visit by the cops when it was obvious to anyone with eyes and ears all hell had broken loose. There was no time for snap judgments, incriminating measuring on the politics between the haves and the have-nots.

Bolan spotted a shadow at two o'clock, the familiar marching gait betraying to the soldier he was mere seconds behind Powers. The Executioner made two abrupt decisions. The first choice was to turn the hunter into the hunted.

His second decision, if he pulled it off, would leave the colonel so stunned he wouldn't find himself capable to even eat, much less sleep anytime soon.

THE CONSTANT adrenaline rush seared his combat senses to new heights. Even as his blood boiled and he hungered to keep killing, Powers had held his ground in the alley, caught the door cracking open a hair, then set off into the mouth of an adjoining dark opening of yet another alley. He settled behind a garbage bin, knew Belasko was within striking distance. There was enough light still spilling from the doorway of the drug den. Belasko was a tall shadow stepping into view, wielding an assault rifle, a searching, confused expression on the man's face clearly framed in the soft glow. What the hell was Belasko doing? Standing there, looking all around, as if he'd lost the scent. Silently, Powers urged the guy to come his way, finger taking up the slack on the SMG's trigger. Another second of hesitation and Belasko moved away, setting off down the alley ahead.

Powers broke cover, reached the alley wall. Peering low around the corner, he found Belasko picking up the pace before he vanished into another alley, thirty-some yards away. Powers bit down the chuckle at the sight of the guy looking lost, as baffled as hell. And this was someone supposed to make him nervous? This was the big gunslinger waxed eight tangos? He could only figure the guy had gotten lucky somehow, dropped the hammer on those eight from pure shock factor, managed to nail them with the opening rounds, lucky shots all.

Powers set off in pursuit, hugging the redbrick facade. His mini-Uzi leading the hunt for Belasko, the colonel hit the mouth of the bisecting alley. He looked around the corner....

What the hell? There was no sign of Belasko, not even a sound of a dark silhouette traipsing ahead, kicking through the litter of discarded bottles and whatever else. It was hard to see down there, although the streetlights beyond the far end of the alley cast a murky white sheen. Enough light so he should have seen some sign of Belasko, even a shadow. The garbage bin. Belasko had taken cover. Powers rolled into the alley, sights set on the bin, mini-Uzi poised to start blasting as soon as the guy came into sight. The colonel was holding back the chuckle when he heard the voice from behind sound off like something that should have rolled up from the bottom of a tomb.

"Freeze. Lose the weapon."

THE CRACK in the brick wall had been wide enough to barely allow Bolan to squeeze through, wait in blackness that was choked with the stench of urine and vomit. It was a fluke, finding the dark slash in the side of the building, and he could only wonder how it got there.

It was enough, just the same, to see the Executioner boil out of hiding, issue the warning to the colonel's back and paralyze the man in his tracks.

Powers erased the surprise off his face as he twisted his head sideways and chuckled. "This where you read me rights?"

"The gun."

Powers released the mini-Uzi, sent it clattering to the broken concrete.

"Grab some air, Colonel. You so much as twitch for that side arm under your coat…"

"Yeah, yeah, you'll shoot me down like a dog."

"I'm considering doing just that."

Powers raised his arms. "But you won't."

"Not now."

"Am I under arrest?"

"No. This is your lucky night. You're free to go."

"What?"

Bolan wasn't about to show any more of his hand. "Only you and me need to know what happened out here tonight."

"Why am I having a hard time buying that?"

"That's your problem. See a shrink if you start having anxiety attacks."

Powers sounded a strange chuckle. "You don't even want to hear the speech why I did this?"

"Skip it. I've heard it before. It doesn't wash with me."

"So, if you're not arresting me, if you're not going to shoot me down, then what?"

"Face front. Turn your head again, and I'll put a few in your legs."

"I don't get you, Belasko. What I am beginning to think is you're no G-man. What are you? CIA? NSA?" Powers started to sound every bit as worried as Bolan had hoped before he'd made this snap change in plans. The colonel might figure it out in time, that Bolan was simply holding him out as bait, see him running scared, maybe bring whatever contacts he had in the shadows of the conspiracy to the light. There was Sudan for Bolan to consider next. Then there was Grevey, perhaps a whole slew of unknown targets out there, scattered around different U.S. cities, oiling their guns, priming the charges to high-explosives. While Bolan left Powers and Grevey to sweat it out, Brognola and the Farm should have no trouble keeping tabs on SCTU.

Sudan was the Hydra, and it sure as hell sounded to Bolan as if the place needed a personal visit from a fifth horseman.

"I'll be seeing you around, Colonel."

POWERS COULDN'T remember the last time he'd felt the first shred of fear. He found he was actually shaking inside, somehow mentally willed away the trembling. There was something in the guy's icy voice, all the mystery and riddle he'd hurled his way, leaving him to ponder and fear the future...something in the way he'd just turned up on his blindside, out of no-where…

Powers sensed he was alone. Slowly, hesitating be-fore he lowered his arms, he turned. Belasko was gone, vanished like some ghost in the night. Whoever the hell he was, he was good, and Powers had re-formed his opinion about the man.

The distant wail of the first sirens snapped the colo-nel out of grim thought. He snatched up the mini-Uzi and beat a fast exit out of the alley. The way Belasko had issued his last statement before departing left Powers believing the man was bailing from his watch-dog duty over SCTU, gone elsewhere to do whatever. But what? Leave him twisting in the wind? Make him sweat and worry when and where he'd show up next.

No matter. The guy had just blown his one and only chance to take down the hunter, Belasko betray-ing some kind of soft spot. Next time he even so much as glimpsed Belasko, Powers vowed to shoot the man on the spot.

CHAPTER NINE

Texas

Cody Caldwell was having serious doubts about the future. As he listened to McClintock briefing the thirty-plus members of God's Crusaders in the conference room, Caldwell had to wonder how his life had reached this critical mass where a former supervisory special FBI agent attached to the Organized Crime Task Force in New York was on the eve of aiding and abetting international terrorists who would massacre countless citizens in targeted cities across the U.S. He felt as if he were on another planet now, hearing McClintock's spiel with his angry "us" and "them" rhetoric.

How had it all come this far, gotten so crazy?

Sure, the money for him was nothing shy of fantastic, another fat eighty grand dumped into his offshore account in the Caymans yesterday, padding his golden years some more, putting him well into six figures since Grevey had talked him into joining up a little over a year ago. And at the finish line, beyond their helping to launch Holocaust USA, another hefty cash sum was promised each man.

But he'd been a lawman, dammit, and not all that long ago. Fidelity, bravery, integrity, the stuff of honor he used to hold near and dear. Where did he go wrong? he wondered. In the beginning he'd seen himself as something of a crusader against the shadowy monsters of organized crime, out there in the streets, working CIs, reeling in Mob turncoats for the Witness Protection Program, chalking up a few major busts along the way. Yes, making a difference, something to be proud of. The problem, as he recalled it, was his thirst for booze, then later on coke and crack, soon blaming his substance abuse problem on the endless raging war between himself and two ex-wives who never understood the job, much less a man's need to be somebody important.

Naturally, the end wasn't long in coming when his superiors received a tip he was huffing powder and sucking down Jack Daniel's whiskey on the job like there was no tomorrow from some bastard he'd always believed was his buddy. So the door on his FBI career had slammed shut in his face, pension and all, but another door—one that had led him down this road toward hell—had opened wide, some yawning chasm where he now teetered on the edge, staring down into the abyss at a new monster.

Only he saw himself once again.

But he'd been stone-cold sober, not even a cup of coffee or a cigarette for the better part of nine months. Funny, he thought, when the fog cleared how a man looked at the world, and himself, in a different light. Yes, he could see clearly now, no longer angry at everyone and everything, railing and pointing fingers of blame all around for his own personal failures and screwups. No longer did he feel a burning urge to break heads, put his fist through walls, take what he wanted and the next guy could go to hell. Somehow, he decided, the way he'd lived was wrong, plain and simple, and he had no one but himself to hold accountable for his fall.

And what he was now mixed up in was beyond criminal. Hell, as far as he was concerned, it was downright treasonous to the point of summary execution if caught.

He watched McClintock, standing tall and sure behind the podium, addressing his legion in the straight-back metal chairs, all of them armed with the computer printouts of their marching orders.

"This is it, gentlemen," McClintock said, appearing to want to finally wrap up the long-winded brief. "This is what we signed on for."

Speak for yourself, Caldwell thought, wishing to God he could just run out of that room, but knew that was impossible, unless, of course, he was willing to take a bullet in the back.

"Once you've boarded your assigned jets, you are to read, memorize, then torch what you each have in your hands. Now, I hope none of you is having second thoughts about this. We all understand what is about to happen. A lot of people will die within the next two days. Just make sure it's them and not us. Now, some little voice in your heads may want to whisper that we're traitors, but I'm here to tell you we're the ones who have been dumped on, abandoned. Just look at your lives. Lost jobs, disgraced, divorces, broken families, your women sleeping with other men, taking what little money you may have left. You came here, most of you, no money, no hope, no futures. Maybe all any of you ever wanted was a shot in life, but somehow shit happened. If it makes you feel any better, just look around at what this country has become, and don't look back when it's finished. We are already, gentlemen, living in a society that is on the verge of anarchy and self-annihilation. Even the powers-that-be know this. Why do you think so many politicians hunger for nothing more than reelection? Simple. They want to fatten their own bank accounts, grab up what they can while they can. Our government has turned corrupt, soft, evil, pandering to the whims of the unwashed and the immoral who anymore make up the majority of so-called American citizens. I know, I was a former Secret Service agent. I have no qualms about the road we are undertaking. Maybe by helping what are most assuredly enemies of the United States, it might send a wake-up call to Wonderland. Who knows? Martial law imposed on the masses might just be a good thing. It may weed out the weak from the strong. Once it's all crumbled, America might get rebuilt from the ashes up. Of course, when this is done—I've already informed a number of you—all of us are on our own. Bail the country. Live out your lives. Watch it all unravel from a safe distance and smile and tell whoever is near you 'I told you so.'"

It wasn't the most rousing call to arms he'd ever heard, but he saw the hypnotic effect dazzling a few of the others, guys on the edges of their seats, heads bobbing in tune to McClintock's "woe is us" spiel, eyes lit up with a strange fire to get out there and kick ass. But there was a note of rage and desperation

Caldwell had yet to see in McClintock's eyes. The man was telling all of them do what they were told, then jump ship because it was going to sink anyway. What did McClintock know that he didn't? Caldwell wondered. And why was half the force remaining behind?

He didn't like it, was already envisioning a knife in his back once he headed out.

"Any questions?"

Caldwell watched as McClintock held eye contact with him for a moment. He wondered if the man read the doubt and fear churning in his gut.

Forget McClintock, Caldwell had to find a way to save his own bacon.

When McClintock looked away, Caldwell made his decision. He still had a couple of friends in the Justice Department, guys who had helped him clean his act up awhile back, even though they didn't have a clue what he was set to get involved in.

"Dismissed."

Caldwell stood, linked up with the four members of his team. The first chance he got, he would put in a call to the Justice Department. He figured he owed it to himself, a shot at redemption, as much as he owed trying to reach out and somehow save the untold innocent lives poised to get slaughtered in the coming jihad.

THE GULFSTREAM C-20 had long since topped out at its maximum ceiling of forty-six thousand feet above the Mediterranean Sea. In less than one hour, according to Bolan's calculations, they would touch down at the joint U.S.-Israeli military base on the Sinai.

There, Bolan would launch into the final briefing for his blacksuit team. Following that, they would board a C-130 Hercules, rumble off for Sudan, escorted by eight F-15Es in the event the Sudanese military scrambled some MiGs in search of a dogfight with U.S. fighter pilots they were sure to lose.

The hydra behind the terrorist attacks in the U.S., Bolan knew now beyond a shadow of a doubt, after receiving the latest intel from Stony Man Farm before leaving American soil, was alive and seething in the People's Palace of Sudan.

Ahman Nafud.

The Executioner and company were going head-hunting, and if it came their way, armed and angry, it was fair game.

Sudan wasn't exactly a sovereign democratic country, the soldier knew, smiled on by the rest of the free world. The hard and ugly truth was the Khartoum government was ranked high up on the list by the UN, Red Cross, World Health Organization, World Bank and every law enforcement and intelligence agency in the West as brazen violators of human rights in every way, from blatantly starving their own countrymen to mass genocide. In fact, the military regime in Sudan was so brutal and corrupt they often made number one on that list for savaging their own, while in the same breath creating a breeding ground for international terrorists, the Khartoum powers nothing more than exporters of death and mayhem to points west. If at all possible, though, depending on how the action unfolded in Sudan, Bolan had given the order the Omani was to be snatched up as a prisoner, hauled back to the States.

The Sudan showdown was set for nightfall, North Africa time. And the President of the United States had given Bolan the green light, even when the Farm had jumped the gun earlier to engineer the Sudan foray before the word had come down from the Man to go.

Death was en route for the People's Palace of Sudan.

The soldier poured a cup of coffee amidships. The cabin windows were closed, blocking out the blazing sunlight beyond the sleek military jet cruising along at top speed. Bolan had wrapped up a long initial briefing for the team thirty minutes ago. He now found a few of the commandos attempting to catch a quick combat nap, two cigarettes going down the aisle, a couple of the troops working on coffee, reviewing intel jackets, complete with Farm photos and background on the key savages, with full detailed layout of the compound, down to Lieutenant General Yussef Sayid's crocodile pit on the eastern edge of the complex. According to Farm intelligence, Sayid was little more than a mass murderer of black rebels in the south, armed or otherwise. Sayid's track record screamed for blood retribution against the man, Bolan thought, the Sudanese butcher's so-called military career rife with accounts of mass torture of women and children, the man having no problem putting the torch to entire villages, while leaving the displaced masses terrified and starving as they marched for the borders and a grim uncertain future as refugees inside neighboring Ethiopia or Kenya. And Bolan suspected Sayid's crocodiles were penned up as more than just some bizarre showcase for visiting VIPs.

Before heading out from the Farm, armed with updated intel and sat imagery of the palace in question, the soldier had beefed the number of commandos up to nine, forced to alter the game plan with some late news. He wanted three teams going in, with himself the lone man out, advancing from the east. They would HALO to the compound, guided down and in by their GPS modules, which would see them land at their respective points of attack within six feet. According to the Farm, they would go in facing at least forty or more armed Sudanese soldiers. Throw in a smattering of officers and their cronies from Khartoum, so-called legit businessmen, and the soldier expected to find quite the contingent of players when they hit the ground running. The scuttlebutt from Langley, which Brognola had received from his own sources at the Company, warned of innocents held against their will at the palace.

Women.

It seemed the ranking Sudanese officers at the palace had quite the flesh-peddling operation. Translation—slavery and kidnapping of females ranging in age from fifteen to thirty, snapped up from various countries in Europe and as far away as the Philippines, and that came straight from a reliable CIA contract agent working deep cover in Khartoum. The soldier intended to give the women a choice when the time came—fly on from Sudan in the Herc, or stay behind in whatever they left standing of the palace. Already Barbara Price was working her usual logistical magic, inserting a team of CIA agents on the Sinai compound, ready to help see the women back home to their respective countries.

The main event, though, was still hours away.

Bolan decided a callback to Brognola was in order. During the hours in the air, he was hoping for some new developments Stateside. As he walked aft for his cubicle where the satlink was housed, he felt a haunting specter overlooking his shoulder, given what he'd witnessed in Roxbury. It galled a part of Bolan to know he'd let Powers walk after his slaughter jaunt. The soldier never second-guessed himself, and in this instance he was banking his sudden departure from SCTU's doorstep would have the rats scurrying to step up whatever agenda they had sold their souls to. Sure, it would have been easy to have eighty-sixed Powers in that alley, walked on with a clear mind, justice done. That would have left Grevey still at large, and, unless he missed his guess, the FBI SAC and the Delta colonel were in league with an unknown jihad devil. Hunches, right, but the soldier had come out the other side of a campaign often enough, relying on instinct, to know when to fold his hand at a critical juncture or simply blaze ahead. When Sudan was wrapped up, the soldier was going back for the colonel's head. By then, he hoped Powers or Grevey had chomped at the bit enough to make some glaring error in judgment, such as betraying whomever it was they fronted for.

The soldier took a seat in his cubicle, slipped on the radio headset, adjusted the throat mike, working up the satlink until he raised the big Fed.

"Anything new, Hal?"

"Was just thinking about you, Striker. I think we've caught a wave."

First Brognola stated the Farm was still trying to

crack the code on the disk he'd seized from Boston. They were hard at it, but vowed they were on the way to soon figuring out what was on the file. The Farm had also done its homework on Leland Property. The owner was Mike Leland, formerly of the FBI's Organized Crime Task Force in New York, retired two years ago. Leland had a sterling record as a Fed, on paper running a moving company with warehouse-office complexes in Atlanta, Oklahoma City and Richmond. Allegedly, Brognola said, the man snapped up the properties using an inheritance from his late father who was some sort of real-estate giant on the East Coast. The Boston property Bolan found harboring terrorists had been ostensibly sold back to the city, only a check by the Farm showed no one seemed interested in the property right then since Leland suddenly had it hung up in legal proceedings one week ago, something about the city reneging on its contract, owing him money for the land. Leland also owned small private airports in the three cities, plus one more airfield some hundred miles southeast of El Paso in the rugged scrub wilderness of Brewster County. The man had six Learjets, three twin-engine planes and two executive choppers at his disposal.

"That must have been some inheritance," Bolan commented.

"Yeah, well, I don't care if his old man was Howard Hughes, the numbers don't jibe on that guy's end. If I wanted to, I could nail the guy now, since Aaron tracked two accounts of Mr. Leland's to a dummy offshore company in the Caymans."

"White collar stuff, Hal. He'll putt eighteen holes

a day for three years and eat surf and turf for dinner
every night.''

"Right, he's connected to something, only what we
don't know yet. Let's tie some of this together,
Striker, if just for the sake of argument. Item—Leland
worked out of the same office as Grevey. I made a
call up there and found out the two were Frick and
Frack, best of buddies on and off the job. Item—
Leland began his coast-to-coast moving company
about a year ago, same thing with his airfields. The
man owns a home outside Atlanta, but he keeps a
sprawling ranch-style compound near the Texas-
Mexican border that is apparently rented out to one
Buck McClintock, formerly of the Secret Service. I
had to get that from the FBI office in El Paso after I
contacted the sheriff down there, got the feeling I was
being stonewalled when I asked him about the land.
El Paso did some low-profile snooping in a town near
the compound in question, and they told me a rather
strange little story about this place. Seems they've had
an eye on this compound for about six months. They
believe it's a little more than just a bunch of good old
boys, or in this case, former lawmen, running around
playing weekend warrior. Nothing the FBI can pin
down, El Paso just thinks it's weird to see a bunch
of ex-Feds and cops shooting up the hills down there.
Okay, you've got Grevey and Powers, and after my
conversation with the Man, it turns out it was Grevey
who recommended the Delta Force involvement in
SCTU, convinced the President personally to bring
Powers onboard. After you saw the colonel's vision
of urban renewal firsthand…''

"We're getting closer, Hal."

"But we're still in the dark. We don't have concrete proof of any involvement between terrorists and Grevey and Powers."

"They're dirty."

"No doubt on this end. These bastards sacrificed their own men, probably to show their jihad paymaster they were straight shooters. Problem is, SCTU took down three more terrorists last night while Powers is out shooting up Roxbury."

"The whole thing was staged."

"To nail Special Agent Belasko, whom Grevey and Powers thought had smelled them out for the traitors they are. I passed on your, uh, words of praise to Commander Jeffries, by the way. I kept the man in the dark, but if your angle works we just might get lucky and flush all the rats out of the dark. Question is, where do we go from here?"

"We're looking at a conspiracy, Hal. We have three different warehouses in three separate cities, situated in a near triangle."

"And you're talking big moving trucks, capable of transporting weapons, fifty-five-gallon drums of nuclear waste."

"Or entire platoons of fanatics."

"A roundup at these three separate Leland properties? Fly them out to different targeted cities across the country? Roll them out down the interstates in semis?"

"Can you get a few teams of your own people to stake out all Leland properties? And have someone keep an eye on SCTU's finest while you're at it."

"Until you return from Sudan?"

"Right. I want to lock and load as soon as I'm

airborne for the States. Powers and Grevey are going down.''

"It'll be a definite plus if you bring Nafud back here in one piece as a guest of Western penal culture.''

"That's his call. All I want is to shut down the monster on this side of the ocean,'' the Executioner said, and knew his grim-as-hell tone was loud and clear on the other end.

Texas

MCCLINTOCK WAS copying the disk in the computer room when the call came through on the secured line. He listened as the voice he knew all too well on the other end told him to fly out a jet for Mr. L's Atlanta facility, right away. Then Special Agent Grevey ordered McClintock to fly along four of his best guns to beef up his own security detail. Something was wrong on the FBI man's end, but before he could pose a few choice questions, Grevey hung up.

McClintock cursed, slammed the phone down, then relayed the order to Monroe.

"They're ready for it to go to hell, you know that, don't you, Buck?'' Jansen, the worrywart, growled.

"I only know we're getting paid to take orders and not ask questions. I only know we're waiting two more days tops for the final payment, then we're gone, gentlemen.'' He took the disks, slipped them inside a pouch of his briefcase.

"What?'' Monroe wanted to know when McClintock lapsed into a long silence.

"I'm not sure. Who's Caldwell riding with up front?"

Monroe checked his printout. "John Peterson. Why?"

"I don't know, it's just this feeling I can't shake. I pride myself on knowing men, anticipating their own motives, reading their fears and doubts."

"And you think Cody's getting a case of bad nerves?" Jansen asked.

"Raise Peterson after they land in OKC. Tell him to keep an eye on Caldwell. He smells a problem with Caldwell, he's to use his own judgment handling the matter."

"If somebody decides to start singing, Buck," Jansen said, "this whole place will be swarmed over. Shit, it'll make Waco and Ruby Ridge—"

"I know that, dammit!" McClintock rasped, pinning Jansen with an icy stare. "I want every man here armed with fully automatic weapons. I want four men patrolling the perimeter at all times."

"I noticed you didn't delete the file like our Arab friend wanted," Jansen said.

"It's called a trump card," McClintock replied. "Life in the Witness Protection Program is better than a lifetime at Leavenworth. Before you grow that constipated look, I'm going to make sure that doesn't happen."

"Meaning if we're hit?" Monroe posed.

"The ship is sinking, and I intend to go down with it. Any man not game for that kind of action can walk now."

Squaring their shoulders, Monroe and Jansen held their ground, and their leader's fanatic look.

Boston

POWERS LET Grevey walk into the basement elevator first. When the colonel was inside, Grevey threw his hand out, holding the door back.

"I'm telling you, Colonel, if Luther's calling us up top to his office, if he's going to sink you because Belasko saw you in action, you sink alone."

What could he say to that? Powers thought. If he was about to find himself arrested, well, the Beretta was coming out and he'd blast his way out of the building, even if it meant suicide by cop.

"Well, if that's the case, let's not keep Luther waiting."

Grevey released the door, hit the button for the top floor. Powers found it all strange, just the same, that the entire night had passed, Jeffries ordering the two of them to remain on-site with local cops after the three terrorists had been terminated, Luther saying stay there until he called for them.

Weird.

Powers didn't trust the moment as the numbers chimed above and he ascended closer to destiny, one way or the other.

When the car stopped, Powers told Grevey, "Good to know I've got a real stand-up partner covering my back."

"Kiss off, Colonel. I only damn near begged you not to do what you did."

"What can I say? Shit happens."

"You'll excuse me when I step away from you if the feces hits the fan."

"Not a problem. Deny everything, that your play?"

"Let's just see how this goes."

The door opened and they marched together down the short narrow hall for the double doors with the plaque reading Commander Luther Jeffries. When they were summoned here they never bothered to knock. Powers felt his heart racing as he grabbed the knob, twisted it and led the way into the spacious office. For a moment, Powers felt relief. No Belasko in sight, no squad of cops with cuffs ready. Jeffries, he saw, was hunched over some file on his desk. When Powers and Grevey stopped in front of the desk, Jeffries looked up and the colonel found himself pinned by a menacing look in the man's eyes. Powers was lifting his hand, a twitch in his fingers, heard something about Belasko calling. Seemed Belasko had seen enough, Jeffries said. Seemed Grevey and Powers appeared to have everything under control, they didn't need the Justice Department breathing down their necks. Powers was waiting for the punch line.

It never came.

He wasn't sure he heard Jeffries right next, the ringing in his ears, the pounding of his heart obscuring the man's words.

Powers felt his baffled expression freeze on Jeffries. "Sir?"

"Clean your ears out, Colonel!" Jeffries snapped. "I said Belasko said to pass on the job well done. Man said keep up the good work. Man said I couldn't have two better men working under me, that the SCTU program looks solid. Man said to tell you

hello, Colonel. Said he hoped to see you someday
soon.''

"That's it?"

"What the... What else would there be?"

Powers twisted his head. Grevey looked every bit
as puzzled as he felt. No, studying the FBI man's face
another second, and Powers spotted the fear behind
the mask.

"Now, I've read your report from intelligence, gentlemen,'' Jeffries said. "You state there's a clear and
present threat down in Atlanta. I suggest you pack up,
get to Logan ASAP. Your work's far from finished.
Dismissed.''

Somehow Powers moved his feet, followed Grevey
to the door. He couldn't believe it, wondered what
the hell kind of game Belasko was playing. Whatever
it was, he knew he'd see the bastard again. In fact,
he was counting on it.

Powers was saving a special hollowpoint bullet to
the brain for that guy.

CHAPTER TEN

Sudan

The last one to have jumped off the Herc's ramp, the Executioner was the final man to touch down. Landing roughly a dozen yards inside the east wall, Bolan had the chute pack off, bootstrap unfastened, war bag opened and HK-33 in hand, locked and loaded in several quick moves. Combat harness snug in place, webbing hung with a mixed bag of grenades, black cosmetics masking his features, the soldier padded into a tangled nest of tropical vegetation hugging the razor-topped wall. Hitting the vibrating button on his com link from the cover of darkness, the soldier got his bearings, waiting as three silent signals shimmied against the side of his head.

The blacksuits were hunkered down on the far west edge of the compound.

Show time.

Up close now, the People's Palace looked immense, but the soldier knew sat imagery—no matter how refined, high-tech and sophisticated—never did the sort of 3-D justice on some sprawling enemy compound that the human eye would observe from the ground.

Bolan surveyed the lit-up white granite structure. To penetrate and clear the place of enemy guns, secure his hostage and march the women to safety was going to prove quite the task. Two stories, running the length of over a football field on just his side alone. He wasn't even going to bother counting all the windows, most of which were curtained, or worry about how many rooms held how many guns or what sort of occupants. The word from Brognola's CIA mouthpiece was that the soldiers here pulled double duty as wait staff. That helped his play some, no servants to contend with or keep out of harm's way.

No guards were visible in his vicinity. He heard gentle splashing beyond the wall ringing the pool where someone was catching an evening dip. A slope, pocked with scrub, led to the wall. The soldier would stick to the game plan, go over that wall, advance through the back door when the fireworks erupted. Once the shooting started the women could pose a problem, perhaps scurrying all around, terrified and in danger of getting caught in the cross fire, perhaps even reeled in as human shields by the fainter of heart Sudanese.

Bolan would deal with each situation and individual as they showed his way. On the surface the plan was simple and straightforward enough. Then again, it always was—in concept at least. Bulldoze inside the palace, mow down the enemy, round up Nafud and the women. Team Three would penetrate from the south side, while One manned the front and Two secured a fire point from the west. If the officers and their corrupt lackeys chose to run outside to bolt for safety while Bolan brought the roof down, they would be greeted by a hail of lead. No mistake, Bolan and the blacksuits were declaring war on men who had willingly helped engineer some jihad against American citizens. Whether they toted a weapon or financed terrorism from behind the safety of some desk in a bank, they were all guilty.

And the Executioner had plenty of one-way tickets to hand out.

Getting inside on the business end of his HK-33, though, could prove the easiest chore before the night was over, Bolan knew.

Once the Omani and the palace's sex slaves were in tow, Bolan and the blacksuits would make their way on foot to a nearby airfield. En route, the soldier would raise the C-130. After the F-15E escort laid waste to the main control tower and rudely eliminated anything that might take to the skies after them, the C-130 would land for Bolan and company's extraction.

Or so went the soldier's battle scheme.

The Executioner searched the black waters inside the fenced-in pit. Even then he heard a rumble, spotted the scaly torpedo bodies slicing across the surface, dark bulky shapes sliding around in the far outer reaches of light thrown from the pool.

Hungry for blood, perhaps? he wondered.

Some structure, perhaps a guardhouse, he saw, was planted near the wall ahead and beyond his cover. Right then, Bolan didn't make out any Sudanese soldiers on patrol near the croc pen.

Scanning on, the soldier found the motor pool was

spread out in front of the massive colonnaded entrance to the palace. Twelve luxury vehicles, three
APCs with tripod-mounted machine guns, the sat pictures right on the money on that score. It was Blacksuit Team One's job to fix the C-4 to every vehicle.
Sat recon had shown two choppers grounded on the
roof. If they flew, Bolan had given the order to blast
them out of the sky.

Spotting no sign of armed guards out front, Team
One looked to have clear sailing to mine the motor
pool, as far as Bolan could tell. Another tap of the
vibrating signal to let Team One know he was free
of human traffic, and designated One-One patched
through. Checking his chronometer, the soldier told
One-One, "Move out. Two minutes and counting to
lay the gifts under the tree and fall back into position."

"Roger, Striker. Two minutes and counting."

The Executioner held his ground, cradling the assault rifle. In the distance, he made out the three shadows breaching the front grounds. Swiftly, their rear
covered by teams Two and Three, they began reliev-
ing the burden of their satchels, sticking blocks of
plastic explosive under the chassis of each vehicle, all
hell packs wired in to one radio frequency. These soldiers, like all hands who came to Stony Man Farm,
were handpicked from the U.S. military elite by Brognola, Price or Buck Greene. To a man they had been
sworn to an oath of secrecy about the Farm's existence and its covert operations. Army Special Forces
or Rangers, Delta, or SEALs, they were the best at
what they did.

Which was make war.

In short order, Bolan would give the word to light up this privileged oasis of the corrupt and the savage and get it started in earnest.

One last look at the enormous running facade of the palace, and Bolan took in the giant saucer jutting over the edge of the roof. The enemy's link to the airfield and any help beyond would have to go first. The warrior fed the breech of the M-203 attached to his assault rifle a 40 mm HE round.

Bolan held back for another eternal minute. He was breaking for open ground, preparing to haul himself up the side of the croc pen, when he heard the voices, and froze.

The matting of ferns and vines obscured the soldier's vision. A full two seconds later, easing to the side and surveying them through a gap in the vegetation, he counted two shadows, standing in the sheen of light spilling through the doorway of the guardhouse. They were looking toward the croc pen, seemed glued in place, the angry rumble of beasts suddenly agitated by the presence of humans so close rolling across the night. There was a distinct coppery taint of blood in the warm air, mixed with an odor of meat that warned Bolan these animals were well-fed, leaving him to wonder how much human flesh was part of their diet.

Bolan slipped the HK-33 around his shoulder, drew the Beretta 93-R, the muzzle already threaded with the sound suppressor. There was a chance that once he dropped them with a head shot and the blood started running down the muddy grade leading to the pen the crocodiles would start thrashing and growling loud enough to alert any more soldiers who might be standing guard inside the wall of the pool.

No choice but to risk a little reptile fury.

Bolan sighted down the Beretta, gauging the thirty-some-foot distance to the closest guard, who was in the act of firing up a cigarette when the Executioner caressed the trigger. A muffled chug, the subsonic 9 mm hollowpoint round shattering the smoker's skull, dropping the guy like a poleaxed steer, and Bolan tapped out another quiet message of death.

Two down, but were there any other soldiers in or near the guardhouse?

Bolan broke cover, his grim focus alternating between the wall and the palace proper to the guardhouse. Sure enough, the crocs caught the scent of blood, and a chorus of deep-throated rumbling hit the air, tails slashing the surface in great spumes.

Not good.

It turned worse for the soldier in the next heartbeat.

Hitting the front of the guardhouse, Beretta tracking the doorway, Bolan was about to burst inside when a shadow whipped around the corner less than two feet ahead. The warrior was bringing the Beretta to bear, but the AK-74 was already whipping around like a club in the shadow's fists. Before Bolan could fire off a fatal shot, the AK-74's muzzle swept across his gun hand, sent the Beretta flying. The Executioner was right on top of the guard, knew then he'd missed the guy from his point of concealment, the Sudanese soldier more than likely having gone beside the structure to relieve himself.

With the AK-74's muzzle flying back for Bolan's

face, the warrior ducked as the weapon chattered, blowing a hot three-round burst over his head.

NAFUD DIDN'T even want to think about the tens of millions he'd burned up over the course of the past year to see his dream of jihad come true. It was gone, never to be seen and spent again, and the dwindling money—even though he figured he still had forty or so million at his disposal—was now beginning to worry him. Cut off from Oman and his father's endless supply of petrodollars, he needed to find out exactly how much was left in the one Swiss account. At his age he still had fifty, sixty years or more to live, and he would need all the money he had left to assure him of a life of pleasure and, of course, safety. Unfortunately his own expenses, the payoffs to every bastard lately crawling out of the brush, were adding up at light speed. The CIA war dogs and Sayid were growing impatient for more money, and he'd stalled them all day, claiming a stomach virus, putting on the act, stating that he needed rest in order to haggle with his man in Switzerland.

The next day, he had promised them, he'd make the call and wire some more funds to the bank of Khartoum.

The fact was he wasn't feeling all that hot. Perhaps it was just his nerves, all this talk from Kragen about trouble on the way. Perhaps it was being cooped up in the palace for a year that was causing him doubt about his future. Could it be contaminated drinking water? Was he coming down with some virus? How much would that cost him if he had to pay for a vaccine? He shook his head in disgust, then felt his face

when a sudden burning flared up right behind his
eyes. Sure enough, the skin felt hot and clammy to
his touch. He was feverish. Why? Just his luck, coming down with dysentery, malaria or worse, and at his
hour of triumph, no less. Maybe Sudan was a big fat
mistake, he thought. If his recruiter could have so
easily created forged documents for the holy warriors
who had infiltrated America…

No. His face was too well-known. He was a sheikh,
worth something like two hundred million dollars, ten
times that much had he not slain his brother and remained in Oman.

Nafud let his gaze wander around his suite. The
two Swiss women were asleep beneath the black silk
sheets in the massive sunken bed. He allowed a smile,
recalling how he'd spent the afternoon wearing them
out. He went to the bar, poured a glass of red wine.
He decided some fresh air was in order, moved onto
the balcony. He was sipping his wine, hoping it would
calm the anger and queasiness in his belly, gazing at
the scrubland of the plain to the west when…

What was that?

It was a darting shadow, maybe two silhouettes,
somewhere in the dense vegetation near the wall. Silently, he cursed the lack of lighting on that side of
the palace. He peered into the vegetation, searching
for movement, but found only total blackness. And
where the hell were all the guards?

Of course, it was that time of the evening. They
were serving the drinks and the appetizers below for
another Yussef Sayid production.

Fools! Barbarians!

Nafud was lifting the glass to his lips, scouring the

darkness below, when he heard the tremendous peals of rolling thunder from some point out front where all the vehicles were parked. He was turning his head in that direction, some dark instinct warning him they were under attack, the glass slipping from his fingers, when he discovered night was turning into day and the crunching din of explosions kept on shattering the night.

Nearly collapsing from terror, it was all he could do to keep from throwing up.

THE HEAD BUTT might have knocked out Bolan if he hadn't felt the man recoil at the last possible instant. As soon as the bullets had torn past his scalp, the Executioner charged forward, wrapped his fists around the AK-74. The dark face on the other side of the assault rifle was growling, rearing back. The warrior twisted his head, took the blow off the side of his cheek to a blast of stars in his eyes and a hollow thud in his ears. Bolan held on to the weapon, nothing but iron will keeping him on his feet. The Sudanese soldier was good, lightning quick and pumped on adrenaline, aware he was locked into a fight to the death. He'd taken Bolan by near fatal surprise, and now the guy sounded the alarm again, holding back on the trigger, spraying the front of the guardhouse with slugs and racket enough to bring the reinforcements running unless the warrior finished it fast and final.

Bolan and his adversary danced, grunted, strained to wrench the rifle free. The Executioner was spinning the soldier, looking to hurl him toward the fence when his adversary lashed out with a leg whip. Bolan took the boot to the shin, white-hot pain shooting through every nerve ending. The warrior felt himself falling, but somehow held on to the AK-74, taking the soldier down into the sludge. The Sudanese hammering on top of him, Bolan felt himself skidding down the grade on his back. From some point just beyond the ringing in his ears he heard the roar-growl on the other side of the fence as his shoulders slammed into metal. Bolan wrestled the soldier off to the side, was yanking the guy to his feet when he slipped in the mud and his opponent seized an advantage. The Sudanese soldier hurled his weight into Bolan, pinning him against the fence, driving the AK-74 across his throat, wedging him there, straining to force the big American up and over the fence. The ominous roaring sounded nearly on top of Bolan, so close he could smell the stench of digested food like some noxious cloud washing over his face.

Feeling as if his spine were a mere heartbeat from snapping in two, Bolan speared his knee into his enemy's crotch. The guy woofed a sound between agony and surprise, and it was all the edge the Executioner needed. Bolan felt the soldier's grip loosen on the AK-74, the guy going slack long enough for the warrior to twist, shift his weight and sling his enemy over the fence. As the Sudanese soldier was going over the edge, a hand shot out, clamped on to Bolan's webbing. Bolan couldn't be sure, but glancing down he thought he saw the soldier's finger curled through the pin of a frag grenade, the guy's screams raking the air with all the wailing of the damned as the water behind him churned and yawned open like a giant wave breaking on the beach. The Executioner unleathered the .44 Magnum Desert Eagle, put the muzzle square between the Sudanese's eyes and all but blew his head off with one thunderous retort.

The problem next was that the frag grenade went with the body, only it plopped in the thick soup, resting against the base of the fence. The crocodiles came roaring up the bank, gaping jaws clamping over legs and arms, Bolan catching a glimpse of the raging behemoths ripping the body apart before he started scrambling away from the fence. He made it all of twenty feet, barely clearing ground zero, when he nose-dived, covered his head and rode out the blast.

In that one moment, as the fireball sent shredded chunks of the fence flying over Bolan's head, he knew the whole program was about to change, and for the worse.

CHAPTER ELEVEN

Max Kragen could appreciate greed. Money made his world go round, he thought, always had, and it didn't matter if he bartered gold, diamonds, teak or nubile female skin to grab up a fistful of cash, as long as he could go his merry marauding way in search of his next pot of riches at the end of the rainbow. Truth was, during his five-year stint in Sudan, he'd sold everything from drugs to diamonds to slaves, and right under the very noses of upper-echelon CIA operatives, in fact. Naturally, he'd greased a few wheels along the way, a few of the wiser spooks willing to look in the other direction with a wink and a grin as long as they got their cut of the action. As it stood, he had enough money already squirreled away in numbered accounts in the Far East to vanish, create a new identity, start over, live out his days swimming in booze and sex. Taking Nafud's blood money was simply an honor he figured he owed himself.

Greed was good, cowardice wasn't.

Which was why he'd just as soon pump a bullet through Sayid's face as look at him. The man was an obscene joke, Kragen thought, standing up there, hurling bald-face lies how he personally led kill hunts into the bush, kicking rebel ass by the scads, in-your-face, hand-to-hand encounters no less.

And the circle jerk of suits and uniforms looked as if they were buying it, nodding and grunting in rhythm to their Sudanese version of Patton.

As soon as the lights dimmed and the giant-screen TV flared up with yet more snuff stuff, Kragen had eased up to the bar to stand beside his fellow merc, Manson, a man's man and a soldier's soldier if there ever was, he knew. Kragen was working on bourbon number three, attempting to mute with enough alcohol the chortling voice of the fat baboon who was bull-shitting his soldiers and cronies from Khartoum once again about his heroic exploits in the black south. Kragen torched up a cigar, drew deep on the smoke, hoping to calm a sudden murderous impulse. The CIA mercenary knew both the real numbers and the truth about the killing fields in the black south, resisting then the urge to roll up before the crowd and let them have the mother of all tongue-lashings. There was a floating rumor that Sayid had wet his pants the first—and apparently the last—time he'd heard a shot fired in anger.

Sudan, he thought, was the devil's idea of a bad joke on the human race. Since their formally declared independence from the colonial vise of the British more than four decades ago, civil war, palace revolutions and state-sponsored mass genocide—according to the UN reports and Company numbers crunchers—had snuffed out more than a million folks in the south. Another two mil plus had starved to death, and five mil and change had been left wandering the countryside, hoping the Eritreans or Kenyans would take

them in—fat chance, since everybody with guns and
sense enough in those countries despised the Sudanese Muslim authorities for the bullies, thieves and
cowards they were. The reason for the ruling military
junta's barbarity toward the southern blacks, though,
went deeper than just ethnic or religious differences.
All Kragen had to do was take one peek at the arid
wasteland beyond the palace walls, then compare that
parched earth with the fertile paradise of the south.
The soil down there was richer than the banks of the
Nile, he'd seen, like some precious metal crying out
to be held in awe. There was enough tobacco, hardwood, cotton, gold, not to mention vast sweeping
crops of corn and rice, herds of goats and cattle...
Sudan, he knew, should be on the map as one of the
richest countries in all of Africa, instead of its citizens
wallowing in a poverty of $330 U.S. per-capita in-
come.

But, then again, the rainbow of differences made
Sudan pretty much what it was—a cauldron of corruption and hate, spewed out in the name of religion
for the most part. Seventy percent Muslim, twenty
percent Christian and animist, something like close to
160 languages and dialects spoken inside the borders... He knew Iranian terrorists and SAVAK spies
had proclaimed Port Sudan their home away from
home, throwing still more fuel onto the fires of religious and ethnic animosities.

Who cared? He decided it was time to fly. Five
years up the devil's ass here, and he'd long since
concluded there was little he could do except take the
money and run—and by the next day. If he had to,
he'd call in his troops from the airfield, raze the pal-

ace by storm. Shouldn't be much trouble, he decided, to seize the palace, if he acted with lightning brutality, showed these puppies what some real live ass-kicking was all about. Right, he'd seen Sudan's finest in action down south, and unless they had superior fire and manpower on their side they'd been known to turn tail and scurry off more than once, imploring God for deliverance from some righteous black rage.

Indeed, he'd heard the rumors of all the gold and diamonds and cash stashed away in vaults here. And the sheikh had gotten snippy earlier about the rest of his money, hell, Sayid even insisting he move his jet to his own airfield where his soldiers could watch his transportation out of there.

Sudan sucked.

"The longer we remain here," Manson said, running a nervous tongue over his black mustache, "the greater the risk we may never leave Sudan in one piece. I say they settle up within twenty-four hours or we give them a taste of what they're only dreaming about doing to U.S. citizens."

Kragen was about to agree with that, a mouthful of bourbon poised to go down his throat, when the whole damn palace shook and it felt as if the roof would come down on his head. He knew that sound of rolling thunder for what it was and nearly choked on the acid liquid in his throat. He was looking toward the foyer, felt the freeze of pure terror all around, when the bank of mahogany doors was blown off its hinges in a gust of smoke and fire. Something resembling a sheet of metal came winging down the foyer, scything through a couple of palm trees, bowling down a trio of stick figures in brown uniform, all but smashing them to broken sacks. A harder look, and he saw it was the hood of a Rolls-Royce, smoking and warped to hell from whatever launched it through the doors.

"Oh, shit," Kragen growled, and instinctively reached for his holstered .45 Colt.

The trouble he had feared the past two days had finally arrived.

THE EXECUTIONER scrambled to his feet, senses choked by cordite and the stink of blood, his bell rung to an agonizing chime by the concussive force of the grenade blast.

Searching the ground beside him, he found his Beretta, retrieved and holstered it, then adjusted the com link in place over his ears and throat. To hear his own voice he'd have to shout and tell them to bellow back when they copied. He was about to raise Team One, sound the order to blow the motor pool, when the blacksuit with the hell box took the initiative, obviously figuring out something had gone terribly wrong on his end, and lit up the night.

Fireballs, brilliant as the sun, intercoursed in a brain-splitting roar they could have heard maybe twenty-some miles away to the outer limits of Khartoum proper. Waves of fiery debris were slammed off the palace facing, ricocheted, then jackhammered back and forth on raging tongues of fire, bouncing up the pillars, screaming like a nail across a chalkboard as razor-edged wreckage scarred the granite facade, blew in windows, cleaved off whole hunks from the roof's edge.

For a dangerous moment, Bolan was outlined in the dazzling firelight, the soldier instantly becoming aware he was the sudden target of two types of predators. First, he saw the black waters ripple and heave with the surging mass of reptiles. Counting the number of crocs by sat imagery hadn't fallen on the intel scale during the formulation of his battle strategy. But a sweeping look of the countless reptile torpedoes slicing over the water's surface glowing beneath the halo of firelight, and the Executioner guessed a ballpark figure of eighty, maybe a hundred, judging from the size of the pen and the roaring chorus flaying his ears.

Time to go.

Steel-jacketed bullets stammered out of AK-74s. Bolan began a serious run for the hillside, beelining from the divots slapped up in his wake by tracking lead. Out of the corner of his eye, he caught the first of ten or so monsters shooting through the smoky maw, noses, no doubt, filled with the scent of blood, their pea-size primal brains charged up and consumed with one purpose only.

Devour.

HK-33 filling his hands, the shouting voices breaking through the ringing in his ears, the warrior set his sights on three armed soldiers on the wall, then found himself smack in the middle of a white light beamed his way. Angling out from the light, Bolan held back the HK-33's trigger, raking a long burst down the wall, mentally homed in on their positions. The light blew out in a shower of glass and sparks, the first three Sudanese soldiers flung from sight, screams trailing them over the edge to poolside.

Bolan hit the button to his com link that tied him to one frequency for all three teams. "Striker here!

Number Three, go in, take up position at the end of
the hallway on your end! I'll let you know before I
drop a flash-bang in that living room. I'm moving in
now for the pool. Your orders stand. If it runs your
way, drop it, unless it's one of the women.'' When
that was copied, Bolan added, ''We've got a problem
on this end, gentlemen. Keep your eyes peeled for
hungry crocs on the loose.''

The blacksuits copied, didn't bother asking a slew
of unnecessary questions. Seasoned pros, they knew
a soldier more often than not had to improvise on the
spot.

A look over his shoulder as he hit the bottom of
the incline, and Bolan found three of the larger beasts
had won the footrace to his first two victims. It was
a fearsome sight that not even a battle-hardened soldier such as Bolan could deny. Within a few eyeblinks, massive jaws had shredded the two bodies into
small red chunks, enormous heads snapping around,
swallowing other grisly slabs of human flesh whole
in one gulp.

Feeding time, the soldier suspected, had only just
begun. He wasn't any nature buff who claimed to
know what might turn a crocodile into a man-eater,
but he was bearing witness to bloodthirsty machines
that had—thanks largely to Sayid and his soldiers, no
doubt—grown an insatiable hunger for human flesh.

The soldier heard the loud voices before they materialized into AK-74-wielding figures on the wall.
Tapping the trigger on his M-203, Bolan blew them
off the top with an HE round that punched a hole
large enough in the wall to get him through to poolside. He made out the terrified cries of female voices

beyond the boiling smoke, men barking orders. Climbing higher, scanning the wall then the hole ahead, the Executioner filled the M-203 with another 40 mm HE round just as he saw three or four muzzles jutting on either side of the gaping yawn.

Hell bomb number two streaked on, impacted in a flashing light show and a peal of thunder, clearing the way.

Forging into the swirling cloud, the soldier crouched beside the jagged teeth, peering beyond, taking in the chaos as bikinis stampeded for the rows of French double doors at the other end. The soldier looked up, loading another HE round into the M-203. He sent the grenade chugging on, flying over the heads of a group of five uniforms who were swinging AK-74s his way. The satellite dish was lost inside a saffron fireball, sheared trash streaking back over the roof.

No cavalry called in for the enemy this night.

Bolan held back on the HK-33's trigger, hosed down a group charging past the cabana midway down the pool. As bodies sailed and splashed into the water, the Executioner decided to up the gory ante. Slipping an antipersonnel round into the M-203, Bolan wheeled around the corner and cut the bomb loose. A direct hit on the middle of five uniforms on the other side of the pool, and the Sudanese uniform all but disintegrated in a red cloudburst. Two more soldiers were shredded to the bone by flesh-eating steel piranhas, while their comrades were blinded and sent dancing and screaming for mercy.

The Executioner stepped through the hole, a dark, grim-faced wraith of death. Cracking home a fresh clip into his assault rifle, Bolan drilled the screamers with a quick burst, took them out of the play, boneless sprawls spewing out their guts over white-marble decking.

Bolan marched on. He could see them just beyond the fluttering drapery, hands flapping, uniforms bouncing around as they tried to get it together.

The Executioner filled the M-203 with a flash-bang grenade.

It was time to ratchet up the killing heat.

"THIS IS your doing!"

"Bullshit!"

Kragen didn't have time to dance around with Nafud, answer a bunch of crazy accusations simply because the Omani didn't have the stomach for the kind of action ripping apart the palace downstairs. With Manson at his rear, Kragen topped the stairs. Down the hall a few of the women were peering out the doors, clutching sheets to naked flesh while a couple of Sayid's higher-ranking officers were fumbling into trousers, snapping on gun belts.

"What is going on?" Kragen heard an officer bellowing down the hall.

Nafud was shaking a finger in Kragen's face as the CIA merc rolled up on him. "We're bailing, Sheikh!"

"I'm not going anywhere with you! You have betrayed me!"

Kragen cracked a backhand over the sheikh's mouth, a sound like a rifle shot, then reached out to wad up a handful of hair. He jammed the gun in Nafud's ear, locked an arm around his throat.

"Don't worry," Kragen rasped, nodding to Manson and indicating to his partner, also toting a .45 Colt, that he should lead the way down the stairs. "This is where me and my buddy here earn our keep. But you try and run, I'll shoot you in the back."

"You will pay for this."

"Wrong again. You're going to pay for this. As in a fat seven figures soon as I clear out. In cash."

Kragen started hauling Nafud down the stairs when the whole damn staircase seemed to erupt in a blinding white light, something, he imagined, that was like the sun imploding into a supernova. Even as his eyes were scalded, and it felt as if hot needles were piercing his eardrums, he knew some bastard had just dumped a flash-bang into the living room.

It just turned things down there, he knew, into a turkey shoot for the unknown enemy.

THE EXECUTIONER burned through one clip on his way through the smoking fangs of hanging doorjambs. Raking long concentrated bursts over the large group reeling and hollering around the horseshoe couch, he chopped up white uniforms into gouting scarlet sieves, sent them flopping to the marbled floor running red with their showering life's juices. One tall figure, festooned in enough medals to anchor a small boat, was stitched up by Bolan's 5.56 mm barrage, sent dancing backward on some bizarre-looking tiptoe jig before he crashed through the screen of a giant television.

Return fire was wild and way off the mark, since the Sudanese soldiers were blazing away blind and deaf. Even still, Bolan dropped to cover at the edge of the bar. He slapped home a fresh clip, swung the HK-33 around the corner and went back to grim work as a row of liquor bottles blew up and glass needles pinged off the bar top.

With the intel photos of Nafud and Sayid mentally filed away, Bolan had already done a quick but hard scouring of faces in the crowd. The Omani was nowhere among the panicked herd in the living room.

And the blubbery mass of Lieutenant General Sayid, waving a pistol and shouting at a trio of his soldiers, was waddling his way to cover behind a massive pillar across the room. Before Bolan could drop Nafud's host, Sayid made the pillar.

Putting the man out of mind, the Executioner let the HK-33 rip free in long stammering bursts. Uniforms were staggering around, begging for mercy, screaming at the top of their lungs, guys throwing up their hands, a voice here and there calling on God as if this were all some huge mistake. Bolan dropped them without blinking. Tracking on, he mowed down a dozen or so blind men holding back on the triggers of AK-74s, kicking them into the walls on great bloody splashes, or sending them flying into the Jacuzzi whirlpool to hurl red sprays toward the ceiling. A few officers somehow gathered themselves, went into a drunken-looking march down some chamber that led to the southern courtyard.

Fatal exit.

Bolan didn't see it happen, but he clearly heard their screams, the lingering rattle of autofire cutting through his own bursts as the doomed rabbit run charged into Blacksuit Team Three.

By now, the soldier found the women who'd raced

in from the pool bolting up the winding staircase, a few of them stumbling, crying out in terror from the other side of the living room. It was then he caught sight of Nafud and what looked like two men of Western roots. As Bolan surveyed the carnage, he stepped out from cover. The trio melted into the pack of women, vanished somewhere down the hallway.

Bolan raised his commandos. "Striker here. I'm going after our pigeon. My guess is he's heading for the choppers on the roof. Team Three, penetrate and begin a room-to-room sweep. Round up the women! I want this wrapped up in ten minutes and counting."

Three copied. Then Bolan saw the mass exodus of uniforms and whoever else going for the smoking hole at the end of the foyer. A moment later, he heard Team One greet them with a sustained burst of weapons fire.

Grimly aware of what he'd left behind, the soldier looked toward the pool. Beneath the still wavering band of firelight, he spotted the first monster sliding through the hole in the wall. Two more behemoths emerged, began helping their cousin out with quick savage chomps on the arms and legs of dead men. With any luck, the slaughter he was about to leave behind would keep them busy.

If not…

Bolan shoved that particular mental image out of his mind. The Executioner broke across the living room and hit the stairs running in pursuit of the quarry he'd crossed an ocean to bag.

CHAPTER TWELVE

To Yussef Sayid it sounded like a full battalion was out there, blasting away beyond the foyer. All the bodies he bore witness to getting gunned down as soon as they hit the steps running—a number of the dead his bankers, front men and weapons exporter cutouts for the CIA mercenaries helping the sheikh—nothing less than a hundred commandos, he believed, could have possibly stormed and taken down the People's Palace of Sudan. A mere hundred men? No, too puny a number, for sure, to wreak all this death and destruction in just a few furious minutes. It seemed more like a thousand commandos with guns, he thought, were circling the grounds, closing in and coming for his head.

Yet, as he looked over his shoulder and took in the strewed bodies, the smoking ruins of his prized giant TV where one of his officers was still impaled through the screen, his white uniform nothing but a shredded red mess, he was almost one hundred percent certain just one man—with eyes he could only describe as belonging to the devil himself—had created the slaughter he was so desperately trying to run from. Visions of that tall black-clad figure burning in his mind, his urgency to get the hell outside, and fast, grew with every long terrifying moment during which he heard the distant rattle of weapons fire. Gratefully, it sounded like the battle was now raging upstairs.

Questions such as who these commandos were exactly and what country they represented could wait until he was safely on his way back to Khartoum. Right then it was all Sayid could do to keep the floodgates to his sphincter under control. If he didn't somehow flee the grounds he knew he'd never hold in what was rumbling and threatening to soil his white trousers....

Images of himself, years ago, that first and last time he'd ever ventured with a gun into the bush and come under rebel fire, wanted to leap to mind. This was no time, he told himself, to feel shame. He needed to save himself, but how?

At least the devil in the skintight blacksuit wasn't chasing him with that massive assault rifle and grenade-launcher combo. Small comfort, since the way to freedom was still blocked off by some huge force of shooters, and the road to saving his skin would come paved by bullets.

Wishing he could squeeze himself into the pillar and just disappear, he saw the entire motor pool had been obliterated beyond the wall of smoke hanging like some dirty shroud where the doors used to be. So much for riding out in one of his three Rolls-Royces. And to make the roof for the choppers was out of the question. Suicide wasn't an option. The kind of firepower that was bringing down the palace walls would most certainly get dumped on those helicopters. Then he'd be stranded up there, nowhere to run or hide.

What to do? From his hiding point, he counted up seven of his soldiers who were looking his way, their eyes full of fear, wanting to know what they should do next.

Sayid knew there was only one play that would clear him of the compound. The problem was getting his soldiers to do it, offer themselves up as sacrificial lambs, human shields that would take the bullets for him once they bolted outside.

Sayid spotted a discarded AK-74 near a fallen corpse. He reached out a trembling hand, clutching and hauling back the assault rifle. At least he could make it look good, act the hero, inspire them, unwittingly, of course, to lay down their lives while he ran off in the opposite direction. He reasoned no army anywhere could ever survive unless its own generals could live to plan and carry out the next battle. Why should he be expected to give up his life?

"Listen to me," Sayid whispered. "On my count of three, we all go through the door at once. Shooting. Where does it sound like they're firing from, Sergeant Hassam?"

"The sound of their fire is coming from the west corner."

"You are positive?"

"Yes, sir."

Sayid nodded. "One..."

They stood, bracing their weapons.

"Two..."

To a soldier they drew a deep breath, steeling themselves.

"Three!"

Sayid hung back a full second but knew he couldn't wait any longer as his soldiers made the charge. The only thing that got him running and risking death was the mere thought of the devil being anywhere close enough to reach out and touch him.

Pure terror and adrenaline fueled his bulk, propelling his legs as he started hacking and gagging when he bulled into the smoke. He thought he was going to vomit next, or worse, as, sure enough, the unknown enemy opened fire and started dropping his soldiers ahead, then beside him as he ran on. Blood hit him full in the face, his nose pinched with the acrid bite of burning fuel and bodily waste. He heard the cry deep in his throat, the world on fire around him as he commanded his legs to carry him at an angle away from his dying soldiers. They were screaming and cursing but they were holding hard, he glimpsed over his shoulder, their AK-74s flaming even as their twitching frames absorbed lead and gouted open in red spurts. When he found he wasn't falling for the ground, discovered he had somehow reached the cover and safety behind the flaming shell of a Rolls-Royce, he could see the finish line. But now what? He only knew he needed to go as far in the opposite direction as possible from those hundred-plus gunmen at the west edge of the palace. He peered through the black smoke, his uniform drenched in sweat, his breath heaving in his ears between short bouts of coughing. He looked east, focused on the thick vegetation along the wall. If he could make the east wall, somehow keep moving, stay hidden, he had the code to open the front gate. Sure, it would be a long hike

to his airfield, but if he could get there he could radio
Khartoum, call in the reinforcements....

First he needed to make that wall.

Sayid heaved his bulk away from the scattering of
fiery hulls, scrunched himself low, hoping if they
spotted him they'd figure he was too small a target
or maybe not worth the trouble to go after. They were
here, he had to believe, for the Omani sheikh anyway,
which meant they had to be American commandos.
They could have the sheikh. Every man at that point
was on his own. By God, if there had even been some
other way, if the Americans had wanted Nafud so
badly, he could have negotiated a reasonable sum
with them to hand the Omani over in the first place.
They didn't need to come here like this, wrecking
his palace, killing his soldiers, upsetting his women.
Maybe later, he decided, once he made Khartoum,
and the dust settled and they had Nafud cuffed, he
could make the Americans see it was all some big
mistake, that he didn't know the first damn thing
about any jihad against U.S. citizens.

Later.

Sayid kept moving, glancing back, waiting for
those bullets to rip into him. They never came. Aside
from the crackling fire he was putting distance to, it
was strangely quiet back there. He was about to look
ahead when he thought he heard a noise, some deep-
throated rumble like a...

He tripped on something, his heart feeling like a
frozen weight in his chest as his mind wanted to reg-
ister that noise for what it was but at the same time
denied the horrifying possibility. He felt his face slam

into the ground. Looking back, he spotted the piece of fender that had sent him plunging.

He heard the roar, closer now, and smelled the stink of blood and guts in his face. He was rolling over, wondering why he couldn't find his legs, when he saw the dark mass boiling up in his direction. Sayid screamed as the jaws flashed open, the monster advancing into the outer reaches of the firelight. He bellowed, "No!" Then saw his entire arm swallowed up and ripped away before his eyes. His brain on fire with agony and his ears shattered by his own shrieking, the last thing Yussef Sayid saw before the blackness took him away was two more sets of jaws going for the legs.

SOME POOR SAP down below was in pure agony, terror or both. It was a scream that would have chilled even Kragen to the bone, but at the moment he had his hands full and problems enough of his own. Between jacking the sheikh along and barking out the orders for the Sudanese flyboys to get the choppers fired up, Kragen was also forced to look back and hope his six was clear. One bastard in black was bringing down the palace. If he hadn't seen it with his own eyes, he would have laughed it off.

One guy.

Before making the stairwell then hitting the roof, Kragen had barely outrun that bastard's lead storm. The nameless commando had topped the stairs to the second-floor landing, just started shooting up the second floor, kicking in doors or catching them on the fly, cutting down the officers and the gentlemen from Khartoum alike who moments earlier had been sa-

voring pleasures of the flesh. If they weren't armed,
that was their tough shit, it looked like. The nameless
bastard wasn't there to take prisoners, that much was
clear. Who the hell was that guy? Over the years,
Kragen had heard the unconfirmed whispered rumors
about a covert operation so secret no one knew the
first thing of its real existence, from the Pentagon on
down. Scuttlebutt about a secret group of commandos
who were the best of the best, only no one had the
first concrete detail. Could it be that was who he was
running from? Some ultra-classified unit of ghost
commandos?

The screaming stopped its knifing point beyond the
edge of the roof to the north. Kragen and Manson
kept up the pace across the roof, the way to the choppers lit by the climbing spirals of fire from the motor
pool. He was counting up twelve officers who had
survived the mayhem below and opted to fly on, then
started to look back when he saw the nameless bastard emerge from the dark shadows of the granite
housing of the stairwell leading to the roof. That assault rifle was swinging up, his way, no less, but it
was the grenade launcher that spoke chilling volumes.

"Hit the deck!" Kragen roared, slinging Nafud to
the pebbled roof. Kragen dared to look up even as he
nose-dived, glimpsed the missile streaking overhead,
flaming on before it pounded into the sleek executive
chopper. The fireball pulverized their ride out of
there, a crooked finger of a rotor slashing into the
cockpit of the other bird. Flames screamed over the
roof, lighting up three, no, four officers he saw, turning them into instant shrieking demons. A few of the

more brazen stood, began capping off rounds from semiautomatic pistols or AK-74s.

Where the hell was Nafud?

Turning his head, Kragen was swinging his .45 Colt around, discovered he wasn't a second too soon in searching out the Omani. Nafud had hauled up a discarded AK-74, was going for broke, cursing the CIA mercs as treacherous spawn of goats. Kragen gave the .45 Colt a double tap, blasting Nafud in the gut. Even before the Omani folded, pitched forward, Kragen knew he had to get off that roof.

Kragen liked living, especially when he had more money to burn than he knew what to do with.

As if the nameless enemy was hell-bent on driving home his own point of no prisoners, the second chopper was obliterated inside another fireball, whole chunks of the bird sheared away and sent sailing off into the night.

"Let's go!" Kragen told Manson, as wreckage dropped and pounded the roof behind them. "If I remember right, there's some thick brush and transplanted jungle trees off to the side. Looks like we jump!"

Kragen dashed for the western edge, smiled as still more flaming shards hammered behind in their wake, obscuring the shooter's target acquisition to his backside. There might be hope yet, he thought, that he would see the other side of this night of living hell, and live to spend his hard-earned loot.

HOLDING HIS GROUND, Bolan swept the HK-33 left to right. He kicked the shooters off their feet first, then unloaded into the flaming screamers and put them out of their misery. The soldier was cracking home a fresh clip, ready to lock on to the white-haired runner and his buddy, when they vaulted themselves over the edge of the roof, flying out for free fall, arms windmilling before they were lost to sight.

Bolan raised each team for a status report. The designated leader of Team Three patched back. "We're clear, sir. In the process of rounding up the women."

The soldier heard a shrill female scream, followed by a burst of autofire. "I thought you said you were clear, Three?"

"Of humans we are, sir."

The crocodiles were going to present quite a problem, Bolan knew. He wondered how much ammo they'd have to burn up to clear the way through the man-eating beasts, not to mention dealing with the hysterical but newly freed. "Three, use whatever discarded assault rifles are available if you have to take out some crocs. Save your bullets. We still have to take down the airfield."

"Roger, Striker."

Bolan raised Two. "Blow me a hole in the south wall. We're coming out through the courtyard."

That copied, Bolan had One confirm the sighting of the soldier's flying rabbits. Before the blacksuits could open fire, the two runners were up and over the west wall. Striding for the edge of the roof, Bolan spotted two shadows racing across open ground, heading, most likely, for the Sudanese military airfield, just beyond a chain of low hills in the distance. Bolan ordered Team One to assist with the evacuation, then patched through to Eagle Leader, ordered the F-15E squadron to fly in and drop the hammer on the airfield. That copied with an ETA for the bombs to start dropping, Bolan patched through to the C-130 pilot, ordered the crew to tag along with their fighter escort and make the airfield. Three called back, informing Bolan they had taken some general captive who claimed there was a wealth of intelligence about Sayid and Nafud's terrorist operation. The Sudanese officer in question stated he would gladly give it up if they spared his life. Sounded like a smart man to Bolan, and he ordered Three to have at it.

Signing off, Bolan was about to leave the roof when he saw movement, caught the moan near the flaming teeth of chopper cockpit. Nafud stirred, rolled on his back as the Executioner rolled out of the dark and stood over him.

"American?"

"Yeah," Bolan said.

Nafud laughed bitterly. "You…perhaps won here… will not stop…my jihad in…your country…"

"A man's gotta try," the Executioner said, and pumped a three-round burst into the savage's chest.

KRAGEN WAS wondering what could possibly go wrong next when he stopped cold in his tracks, turned back toward the sound of screaming thunder. The black shapes materialized into his worst fear, coming in low, blowing over his head. Kragen cursed savagely, already knew what they were about. They were so close to the airfield now, yet they might as well have been standing on the other side of Africa, as far as Kragen was concerned. He stood in the darkness of the sprawling plain, breathing hard after his thirty-minute run for freedom.

In this instance, he feared, freedom was just another word for death.

Those were F-15s, he knew, American fighter jets, or possibly Israeli. No matter. They were going in to eliminate any threat of pursuit. Laughing bitterly, he took in the control tower, with its banks of satellite dishes, sticking up high above the crisscrossing ribbons of runway, the whole picture a perfect target.

One Sidewinder shot away from its pylon and took out the tower, a perfect bulls-eye, the structure lost in a towering mountain of fire. The MiGs, twin-engine planes and choppers grounded near the hangars went next to a thundering tune of explosions. He lost count of how many Sparrows and Sidewinders were cut loose.

All things considered from his standpoint, it was more than enough.

His own jet, he'd been informed, was parked in one of the hangars at the far southern edge. He glimpsed a bunch of guys racing out of the hangars, wished he had his handheld radio. At least he could have warned his men to get their bird clear...

Now this.

He watched for another few heartbeats, maybe six 20 mm Vulcan Gatling guns hammering out the heavy metal, further eating up the hangars, shredding apart anything that could fly. He saw the shadows running from the line of explosions, racing for the deep cover of a teak forest to the west. That, he hoped, would be his men.

Thunder rumbled in the sky behind him.

Kragen looked back as the night was brilliantly on

fire once more, made out the massive bulk of the transport plane soaring in for a landing.

A C-130 Hercules. Come to round up the troops from the palace.

"Come on," he told Manson. "I've got an idea. We might just get out of Sudan yet."

CHAPTER THIRTEEN

Holding down the People's Palace before evacuation proved a far more difficult and worrisome task than even Bolan had anticipated. The reasons were varied for the time-consuming chore, and none of them were good.

His previous order for clearing out in ten minutes was a whopping long shot, but the soldier knew that already. Whatever the time frame, he wanted all hands hustling just the same, with a sense of dire urgency to wrap it up. Beyond the hell grounds here it was still a good hour's march as the buzzard flew to the airfield, with no telling who or what would turn up along the way. LandSat imagery had already warned Bolan the terrain leading to the airfield from the palace was too broken and craggy for the C-130 to attempt a landing. They would simply have to leg it all the way to their ride out, hope some Sudanese reinforcements didn't boil up on their rear along the journey.

At least one hundred rooms in the palace had to be swept, top to bottom, just for starters. Even then Bolan heard some autofire, stammering from somewhere in the building, as pockets of resistance blazed at

Blacksuits Two and Three of Team Two from behind closed doors. A quick check on those blacksuits, as they carried on a room-to-room sweep, their own HK-33s leading the way, and he heard, "Clear."

Bolan had dispatched Team One to the roof to stand watch for any APCs or curious Sudanese aircraft that might want to take a look at the hell grounds. Team Three was right then downstairs, the bulk of the women now dressed, calmed down some with assurances they would be safe, unmolested and were soon going back to their respective homes. Then there were language barriers, and the blacksuits were playing hell getting translations worked out down the line. Not only that, but it turned out Sayid had several wives on the premises, and they were proving themselves a major problem, squawking at Bolan's troops, issuing all kinds of threats, in general bent out of shape the party for them was over, the good life and all its trappings soon to be nothing but a memory.

Well, life was tough like that, as far as Bolan cared for them.

While Sayid's wives sported jewelry, diamonds, the finest of imported silk from the Far East, enough makeup to shame even a parade of prostitutes, most with pudgy faces that had obviously seen daily feasts fit for queens—bucking any and all Muslim tradition about women he'd ever seen—those women who had been brought here against their will were lean to the bone, disheveled from their ordeal, clearly terrified. A few of them even bore the marks of beatings from belts, or worse, on their backs and shoulders, a few black eyes and swollen lips turning up among their crowd. The older women questioned by the blacksuits about the numbers, some of the younger ones had to be searched for, even rooted out of hiding, gently co-erced when found into joining the others near the living room.

Then there was the crocodile problem.

Bolan had ordered all entrances locked up, with a member of Team Two standing watch in the courtyard for any lurking beasts. Luckily, it looked as if thick jungle vegetation out back, toward the east, would prevent any more hungry predators attempting to interrupt the coming evacuation. Where the doors had been blasted off by the pool and the foyer, Bolan ordered Team Three to build fires, using anything combustible they could lay their hands on. Initial croc sightings told Bolan the predators appeared content right then to feed on the dead out front and poolside. Even still, there were so many crocodiles roaming the grounds, and with not enough meat to go around to fill all bellies, it wouldn't be long before the fires died and...

Bolan would take it as it came their way, human or animal, and on that night, he knew, the enemy had shown themselves every bit as predatory as the reptiles.

The Executioner was making his way down an off-shooting chamber on the second floor when something began to nag him about the two runners. He'd only indulged a quick minute or so when grilling the general and two other officers who wisely opted to surrender, but the Executioner knew enough about what had really gone on here to keep his combat senses on full tilt. They were still a long way off from the home stretch, and he knew the worst thing to do now was to believe the tough part was over. Lightning brutality had so far carried the torch for Bolan and the blacksuits, but they had burned up ammo at a furious rate. Sure, the majority of Sudanese soldiers and their officers had cut and run when overwhelming force had dropped over them. Sure, Bolan and company had earned this staggering body count, but something warned the warrior the easiest phase was behind them. And whenever he had to bother counting up the clips and the grenades, Bolan could always feel the enemy hungry to put the squeeze on.

The Sudanese prisoners, he recalled, had confirmed a CIA involvement with Nafud's scheme to unleash jihad on America. Their names were Kragen and Manson, and they had been in south Sudan for several years, supposedly there to arm, train and equip the black rebels, only they'd worked both sides of the fence. A rogue element. It was clear to Bolan those two had gone for themselves. It also seemed Sayid had known about the Omani sheikh's hatred of all things west for some time, had been the man to reach out and bring Nafud to safe haven here at the palace, for a hefty price tag, of course. Bolan would learn more later, but right then he suspected Kragen and Manson wanted only to leave Sudan any way they could, get to whatever money they'd taken from Nafud's deep pockets, skip off and vanish somewhere on the planet. The soldier formed a grim mental picture of the CIA mercenaries and whoever else the Sudanese general claimed was waiting for them at the airfield, his enemies on the loose and going for broke once his C-130 was parked. Perhaps inviting the treacherous mercs to either commandeer a ride or blow it up.

Bolan raised the Hercules pilot as he advanced on the last closed door of the chamber. He had already been informed the airfield was under control of his borrowed flyboys. "Get that ship in the air until you hear from me again."

He patched through to Eagle One next and ordered the squadron's leader to take out any threat that moved on the airfield. Just as the pilot confirmed the order and Bolan signed off, the door ahead flew wide, an AK-74 tracking the soldier's way, spitting flame and lead.

KRAGEN FOUND his men at least had the good sense to bring along some M-16s, plus a few rocket launchers. With some luck and a little initiative he could shape things up in a hurry. He addressed their angry and questioning faces simply. "Problems at the People's Palace, gentlemen. Time for us to fly."

Enough said, and he was grateful no one bothered to push it. As he stepped toward the edge of the forest, he searched the skies. Like circling predatory birds, the fighter jets were patrolling the air above them, winging north to south, holding crisscrossing patterns as if something out there in all that raging inferno would rise up and pose a threat. It would be tricky, walking up to that giant transport, he knew, convincing the flight crew it was in their best interests to let them climb aboard. Kragen really didn't want to die in the cesspool of the world, but if he couldn't catch his taxi out of Sudan he intended to make life miserable for every living thing there.

"Just follow my lead," Kragen told his mercs. "We're taking that big bird out of here. If they don't want to let us onboard, shoot the tires out, hell, blast away at the cockpit, wings, whatever. If we don't leave here, no one does. Goetzman, feel free to unload with that LAW if those fly boys won't cooperate. Let's march."

He was moving out when he suddenly saw the C-130 rumbling down the runway, rolling north. Cursing, he was breaking into a sprint as the crew put some thrust to the turboprops when he looked up and found one of the F-15Es swooping down, leveling out and boring in for a strafe. Someone had anticipated his play, and he had a good notion who it was.

The unknown one-man army. It was as if that damn guy could read minds, and from a distance.

"Fall back!" Kragen roared, as he heard the thunder of 20 mm Vulcans erupting dead ahead. Beside him, Kragen saw Manson burst apart from a direct hit, spewing gore, disintegrating before his eyes as flaming projectiles started scything apart the forest like some steel wall of blood and fire from hell. Kragen found the edge leading down into a gully, went airborne as his whole world once again went straight to hell and he heard guys dying in great pain all around.

BULLETS SNAPPED over Bolan's head, gouging furrows in the wall, whining off down the chamber. The Executioner caught sight of an enraged face, a guy naked from the waist up, then hit the trigger of his HK-33. Zipping him crotch to sternum, painting a red line of doom up the hardman, the soldier bounced him back into the door frame. As he slumped on his haunches, bleeding and twitching out, Bolan made the door.

"No shoot! Please!"

Peering inside, the Executioner found a Filipino girl, no older than fourteen, clutching a sheet to her chest. He scanned the large bedroom.

"You alone?"

She nodded.

"Get dressed. Hurry up."

She went to the closet, Bolan watching her, listening for any sound, any movement that would betray a gunman in hiding or creeping down the hall. She found some pants and a shirt, several sizes too large, then made her way with tentative steps toward the big black-garbed invader. She stopped at the door, and despite her tender years, Bolan read the feral hatred in her eyes toward her abuser. She spit on the dead man.

"These...they like animals. You not believe what they do to us."

"I can only imagine."

And Bolan damn well could.

"You here...take me home to parents?"

"Yes," the soldier told her, and gently took her by the arm, leading her out of that chamber of horrors.

WHEN THE F-15E screamed on, Kragen discovered he was down to eight men, soon to be seven. Goetzman was minus his left arm, blown clean off at the shoulder, the glazed stare in the man's eyes telling Kragen he was quickly lapsing into shock from blood loss. Kragen took care of the wounded in short order. The

.45 was out and thundering, one round through Goetzman's brain.

"Anybody else can't make it?"

They were struggling to their feet, dazed, but the survivors looked in one piece. Kragen needed to get it together in a hurry. He pondered the situation all of five seconds when the answer came to him. The simplicity, the beauty of it made him chuckle. Why hadn't he thought of it before? There was no way, given all the crags and generally broken up ground between the palace and here...the nameless bastard would have to come to them. Not only that but, unless he was dead wrong, the guy wouldn't leave the women behind. If he was some Western commando he'd probably be bound to some sense of chivalry, honor, crap like that.

An old-fashioned kind of guy, Kragen thought. If he played true to form, as Kragen believed, the commando's sense of being one of the good guys would get him killed—or see Kragen commandeer that C-130.

"Listen up, gentlemen, this is what we're going to do."

"THE MILITARY authorities are sure to be on the way. You American barbarians will pay for what you have done to the sovereign and democratic nation of Sudan. You will be captured, tried for crimes against our country and publicly executed, I assure you."

Bolan was about to enter the command and control room on the first floor when a woman hurled those words at his back. Turning, he dropped a level gaze on another of what he assumed was one of Sayid's bejeweled and well-fed wives. Autofire sounded then from somewhere around the corner. Bolan patched through to Team Three, holding the woman's angry look. He was informed one of the bigger crocodiles, at least a fifteen-footer, the blacksuit claimed, was getting impatient for fresh meat, the monster having batter-rammed through a French door before it was shot up.

"Get the rest of the women out in the courtyard. Two minutes and we're gone," the soldier told the blacksuit. "What was the final head count?" Bolan heard the number, signed off, then looked at the woman, who launched into a long diatribe in Arabic. "If you feel that way about us, I can always leave you here."

She spit at Bolan's feet, muttered something in Arabic, then the soldier nodded for the blacksuit to take her away.

"Striker, you won't believe what I heard, from the good general here, was on this."

Marching into the room, the walls lined with control and radio and radar consoles, a bank of computers running through the center of the place, Bolan found the blacksuit holding up a videocassette. The Sudanese general and his officers watched Bolan with mixed curiosity and fear, their hands fastened behind their backs with plastic cuffs.

"I'm hearing Sayid made snuff films of prisoners he tortured, executed, even threw to the crocodiles."

Bolan wasn't surprised. According to Team One, Sayid had met an end that would have been quite the encore for one of his flicks. Somehow a cosmic justice, Bolan figured, couldn't have been dished out more fitting.

"How many women did you count?" the soldier asked.

The blacksuit shut down the monitor, punched out the hard drive. Earlier Bolan had been searching for a way to expedite the evac, make sure all women were present and accounted for. One of the prisoners volunteered some aid in that direction. Sayid kept records of all the women he brought here as sex slaves. The place of origin, how much they cost him and how much money he might make if he decided to resell them was all logged on disk, along with a diary about Nafud and the terrorist operation on Sudan's end.

"Sixty-eight," the blacksuit said. "The general here says we also have all of Sayid's wives who were on the premises, sir."

The number worked. "Any way to find out if they were able to call out an SOS?"

The blacksuit indicated the radio console. "According to our prisoners, they didn't have time. The only frequency was a military one. Everything that hooked them to the airfield, the nearest outpost and even Khartoum down to their cell phones was linked to the dish you took out."

"You take us hostage now? You come here and murder Sudanese citizens, declare war on a sovereign country. Now we are prisoners?" the short, beefy general said. Even though there was fear in his dark eyes, Bolan heard the undercurrent of defiance and resentment. There had never been any doubt there was a real and viable threat to America's national security here. But the more Bolan learned about the

People's Palace and its military occupants and esteemed guests from Khartoum, the more he felt he
couldn't have gotten here a minute too soon.

"Let's move them out," Bolan told the blacksuit,
who took up his own HK-33, slipped a satchel chock-
full of any pertinent intelligence he believed was in
that room and waved the officers to the doorway.

The Executioner fell in behind two blacksuits ush-
ering the last of the women down the corridor that
led to the courtyard. A shattering of glass and a roar
from deep across the living room, and Bolan saw the
first of two beasts bulling their way into the palace.
If he had the time to think about it, he knew there
was some comparison between the dead savages here
and the animals that were about to consume their
flesh.

Putting the palace of death behind, Bolan gathered
speed, hit the courtyard and quietly urged the women
to pick up the pace.

CHAPTER FOURTEEN

Oklahoma City

The last time Cody Caldwell had been in Oklahoma City he was so strung out on Jack Daniel's whiskey and dope it was all he could have done back then to just remember what month it was. How things had changed, he thought, since those days when he'd been some runaway human freight train, fueled by chemicals, propelled by some senseless rage inside he couldn't put a finger on even if the blinding light had hit him square between the eyes. With all cylinders pure and clean now for some time, sobriety had certainly helped him to memorize the entire "war sheet," as it had been called, with almost no effort involved.

Caldwell was ready to redeem his sins.

Marching orders for the jihad mentally filed away, they came complete with names, phone numbers and addresses of safehouses for terrorists in the Oklahoma City area, the route and final destinations for depositing the fanatics even part and parcel of those orders. He had burned the paper on the jet, as ordered, along with the other God's Crusaders of the OKC unit, but committed every detail so iron-clad to memory he couldn't help but feel momentarily pleased with this newfound ability for recollection. The problem now was both his unfamiliarity with the city and being able to get through to his friend at the Justice Department.

He was grateful when he spotted the pay phone in front of a deli, knew he had only traveled three blocks from Leland Moving. With any luck no one would miss him at the warehouse. All day, he recalled, they had pretty much just sat around after riding in from yet one more private airfield owned by Leland, waiting on God only knew what. He didn't understand the delay, but overheard something about caution, last-minute details that needed shoring up, whatever those were.

He picked up the phone, slipped the calling card out of his wallet. The street was choked with traffic that time of day, when folks were heading home from the various downtown businesses to their suburban enclaves. Searching the human traffic sweeping by in both directions, he felt his paranoia flare up, suddenly believing somebody would notice he was gone, decide to come hunting out the reason for his AWOL status. He told himself he was just nervous about what would be perceived as betrayal if he was caught in the act. Do it, get it over with, he'd feel better about himself. If innocent blood was shed because he stood by and did nothing, he knew he wouldn't be able to live with himself, feared a guilt driving him to one final binge that would take him over the edge, plunging straight down into the abyss. Fingers flying with urgency, he punched in the one-eight-hundred, his PIN then the direct number to his buddy's office.

Four rings, his nerves taut as piano wire. "Come on, Jack, you've got to be there."

The familiar voice finally came on the line. Skipping past any catch-up between old friends, Caldwell got right to it, hardly had to work up injecting any urgency in his voice. He gave his friend everything he knew about the operation, wrapped it up by telling him about McClintock, the compound, how transport and hit teams were flown out likewise to Richmond, Atlanta. He wasn't sure when they'd move their human cargo along with weapons and explosives down the interstates, but it could happen anytime.

"Jack, you need to get this to someone high up the chain of command."

"How can I reach you?"

"You can't. I'll have to call back," he said, was looking at the crowd when his heart lurched at the sight of John Peterson rolling his way, the big man in the black leather bomber jacket grim as the devil. "Yeah, that's right, honey, I shouldn't be more than another two, three days," he said, pasting a smile he hoped was longing on his face. "I love you, too, baby," he said, as Peterson stepped up in his face, looming over him, suspicion frozen like chips of ice in his eyes. "Listen, gotta go, baby. Yeah, I miss you, too. See you soon."

Hanging up, Caldwell showed Peterson an apologetic smile, shrugged. "Women."

"You couldn't make that call from the warehouse?"

"Hey, you know how it is."

"No, I don't. Why don't you tell me how it is."

"Macho posturing, women wanting you to tell them you love them in front of your buddies, that kind of thing."

"I wasn't aware you had a woman."

"New love, six weeks we've been seeing each other. Since I got sober I've tended to lead a quiet, simple life. Not the man I used to be."

"Meaning?"

Caldwell shrugged, flinched inside as a car horn blasted out on the street. "I'm not some swaggering braggart anymore when it comes to the women in my life."

Peterson didn't move, peering, gaze narrowing, the dark look boring into Caldwell, who was certain the man was set to call him a liar.

"Okay," Peterson said. "But we've got serious things to do. Forget your woman, you'll see her soon enough. No more phone calls. Understand?"

Caldwell nodded, smiling, held down the sigh somehow, even as trapped air swelled his chest with tension. "Sure, I gotcha. No problem," he added, and heard the note of fear in his voice where he wished he'd sounded confident and truthful.

Washington, D.C.

HAL BROGNOLA WAS jolted by the phone ringing just as he drifted off for some desperately needed sleep. Jerking awake on the couch in his office, he checked the time, lifted himself up, grumbling. Too much coffee and antacid tablets, not to mention too much stress, made sleep these days a rare luxury, coming only from sheer bone-numbing exhaustion. He saw the light flashing on the phone bank for the interoffice line. Who the hell would be calling him from downstairs? It had to be urgent, maybe a lower-ranking agent under his command calling to tell him there'd been another terrorist strike.

Just what he needed, more trouble.

He threw his legs over the edge of the couch, rubbing his tired face, wondering why he hadn't heard from Striker. But he always feared for the safety of his friend whenever Bolan was out of touch, especially now, when the big guy and a team of blacksuits had launched a covert war against the Democratic Republic of Sudan.

Democratic republic, right, Brognola scoffed to himself. Briefly he recalled how the President had given the thumbs-up to Bolan and company to blow down the People's Palace when intelligence confirmed all manner of traitors and savages hunkered down in Sudan, using the country as some command and control springboard to murder U.S. citizens.

Brognola hoped to God he heard from Bolan soon. The Man was sitting on the edge of his own seat over at the Oval Office, waiting word, probably wondering how much flak would get blown his way once the dust settled, the bullets stopped flying and an Omani sheikh was en route for the States to get reamed out, grilled then dumped in a federal pen for a dozen life sentences. Talk about a strain on U.S. relations overseas with one tiny oil-rich country and another nation that represented a clear and present terrorist threat to the free world. Thankfully, that wasn't Bolan or Brognola's headache.

Brognola made his way to his desk, grabbed up the phone, hit the interoffice button. "Brognola here."

"Sir, this is Special Agent Jack Turner. I know this is highly unusual for me to call you like this…"

"Skip the explanation, Turner. What is it?"

"Sir, I just received a very strange phone call from a friend of mine. The man was an FBI agent. In light of, uh, recent events, sir, regarding the three terrorist attacks, he told me a disturbing story regarding his situation out west…."

Brognola listened, couldn't believe what he began hearing, but the big Fed found himself hoping they'd just caught the wave that might take them into shore.

Sudan

KRAGEN STIFLED the nervous laughter, but felt the mean grin carving his face. Some other situation, where his ass wasn't in the fire, and he would have enjoyed a good belly rip at what he saw heading their way. It was almost looking too easy, too good to be true, for damn sure. The nameless bastard, he thought, had to have seen himself as some kind of Moses, heading up his own version of a twenty-first-century Exodus. In this case the wandering tribe was a flock of women.

Kragen and his men were concealed—or so he hoped—near the edge of the hardwood forest, looking down a rise that led to the northern edges of the airfield. He had taken one of the two M-16/M-203 combos for himself, full clip in place, a 5.56 mm round chambered, with a 40 mm grenade up the snout of the attached launcher. Strung out beside him, in a staggered formation, the rest of the troops were hunkered dark shadows, eyes wild with the adrenaline rush, to a man knowing it wouldn't be much longer until their fate was decided one way or another.

The damn fighter jets, he noted, were still roaring across the skies above the airfield, the noise and the constant threat of another decimating strafe tweaking his own frayed nerves some more, even raising the hackles on the back of his neck. After what he'd seen those war birds do, and given the kind of carnage he'd left behind at the palace, he knew it wouldn't take much provocation on his part to find himself blown off the map. He had no choice any more but to risk it. Some edge, maybe some deception on his part, was all he needed. Perhaps make it look as if he'd been one of the good guys all along, simply playing Sayid and Nafud, gathering intel for the Company.

He watched the parade of shadows advancing. Without infrared binos, he couldn't hope to accurately count up the armed opposition, the number of women, but there were plenty enough targets down there to choose from if he had to cut loose.

All he had to do was announce his intentions.

They trudged over the broken ground, a few of the damsels from the palace, he heard, crying out as they stumbled, nearly fell until some gentleman in a combat blacksuit held out a hand. What a bunch of swell guys, he thought.

One hundred yards and closing, he began to see his targets take on shape as they moved into the outer limits of the firestorms still roaring from the flaming kindling of everything those F-15s had shot up. One last look at the troops, and he found them holding tight to their weapons. Two LAW rockets were ready to either dump their loads into the exodus or send destruction flying into the C-130, and at that point Kragen didn't much care.

He was ready to give it all up, he decided, if only to see Mr. Ass Kicker eat it here in Sudan. For some reason, he was starting to take it all personal where that guy was concerned.

It galled him to think he'd turned tail and fled the palace when a part of him knew if he'd held his ground and brazened it out, he might not even be here, sweating out his own immediate future.

Or dreading his potential extinction.

"Come on, puppy dogs, just a little closer," he quietly urged. "That's right, come to Daddy."

He heard the distant rumble of the C-130, made out the dark mass as the behemoth bird came their way. Ass kicker, he thought, had called the bird back, feeling he was clear and homefree.

Or was it something else? Why did he feel so uneasy?

Kragen stood, moved out and held his ground at the edge of the rise, hollered down, "Freeze it up now! Or I'll start shooting the women!"

"EAGLE ONE to Striker, come in."

The Executioner had anticipated trouble once they made the airfield. A mile or so out, he had passed on the orders for the blacksuits to keep moving after raising Eagle One. The pilot had turned up eight live ones on his heat-seeking screens, no movement in the forest's edge at the point Bolan and his party would come walking in. Stationary positions for the enemy spelled ambush to Bolan.

The Executioner, crouched and surging up a long rise, swiftly shadowing in on their blindside from some hundred yards out, made the edge of the teak forest, froze and got his bearings.

"Striker here," Bolan whispered.

"I've got movement somewhere just beyond the bonfire. Don't ask me how we missed it, but it looks like a full squad of Sudanese hostiles are ready to bail the premises in an APC."

Bolan mentally gauged the distance he'd need to cut to the enemy before he opened up with his recent acquisition of hardware. The soldier was toting a squat, stainless-steel rocket launcher. Ten chambers filled with 40 mm grenades, it was called Little Bulldozer, the weapon created and dubbed its nickname by John "Cowboy" Kissinger, Stony Man's resident weapons genius.

"Two minutes and counting, then take that problem out."

The order was copied, and Bolan, hoping some more fireworks would distract his enemies, moved on at a cautious pace. Opting not to use NVD goggles, Bolan was counting on the firelight striking the forest edge where they were laying in wait to guide him closer in.

It did.

Moments later, he pinpointed the white-haired merc standing on the lip of the rise, bellowing out his situation.

Smoke screen. The soldier had seen enough greed, bloodlust and savages caring only about number one in his War Everlasting to be able to see through Kragen as if he were nothing more than a pane of glass.

"We don't want to have to kill you, hell, I'm thinking you're Americans, we're on the same side, right? What happened at the People's Palace, I can explain, you give me a chance. Sometimes, a man has to make the bad guys like that fat piece of cheese, Sayid, think he's on their side. I was gathering intelligence about a major terrorist operation about to be launched against the United States. Here it is, folks, I want to fly on with you, me and my men. Take care of me and mine, I've got what you need to root out the mother of all jihads back home."

Padding ahead in absolute silence was impossible. But with the thundering scream of the F-15s overhead and Kragen shouting, the little bit of noise Bolan made—boots cracking over a twig or crunching leaves—was covered.

Bolan closed, lifting Little Bulldozer, ready to drop the first couple of rounds into the middle of the pack, the assault rifle slung around his shoulder bouncing gently off his backside. Backup piece only, if, by chance, he needed it.

Only Bolan was looking to blow them off the ridge in so many pieces there wouldn't be enough left for croc bait.

Eagle One, he next heard, was driving some thrust to his turbofans, and Bolan saw the F-15E streaking low over the airfield, bearing down from the north, fast and hard, a dark bird of steel blurring past his position. The roar of the fighter jet drowned out Kragen's shouting, then the soldier heard the Vulcans thundering away in the distance, a far-off pitifully small scream raking the air for a heartbeat before it was muted altogether by a thunderclap. The distant glowing wash of the fireball flared like some oversize illuminated screen off to the side of the Executioner's enemies. Bolan dropped to one knee.

They were lined up, savages all in a row. No better time than the present to nail it down.

"I hope that's not your answer!" Kragen yelled. "I've got eight guns aimed your way, ladies and gentlemen! Maybe you're thinking you can call down your flyboys, tough guys, maybe blow us clear into Kenya, but before that happens I can mow down plenty of those women! You hear me, damn you! Say something!"

Little Bulldozer told them everything they needed to know.

The Executioner tapped the trigger. A chug, a tail of fire and smoke and the 40 mm round streaked on through a gap in the forest. The first explosion tore into the heart of the mercenaries, as planned, hurling ripped scarecrow figures toward the head merc. Bolan squeezed the trigger repeatedly, raking the launcher down the line of hardmen, pumping out the noise, death and fire, the jaws of annihilation yawning wide on their blindside, clamping down, eating them up, so much human refuse to be decimated and cast about. Downrange, a few guys were scrambling for their lives, trying to outrun the crunching fireballs, as if a quick sprint would save them. Somehow, Kragen was lost to Bolan's sight as blazing sheets of flames ate up the forest's edge, muting screams and curses, the warrior loosing two more bombs, further spreading a blanket of pure raging noise from the forest

clear up to the thundering F-15E din. One of Kragen's
buddies was somehow clearing the line of fireballs
when Bolan managed to nail him dead center in the
back with one hell bomb. The runner was vaporized
by the blossoming fire cloud, a pair of boots flying
from the flames all that was left to mark the guy had
ever existed on earth.

Rising, Bolan shouldered Little Bulldozer, slipped
his arm through the strap. He took the HK-33 in hand
and rolled ahead into the floating grit and wafting
smoke, his nose stung by the ripe stench of blood and
pooling guts, guys pouring out dammed-up loads in
the final eyeblink, soiling whatever was left. One of
the mercenaries squirmed up in Bolan's tunneled
death vision, a bloody and mauled figure, writhing out
of the smoke like some giant worm, one arm bent at
an impossible angle, gleaming bone shard jutting for
the fires.

Evil men, Bolan knew, never wanted to gurgle out
their last foul breath when there was still other life
left to be consumed. They always seemed to die hard
and angry, unless they were simply cowards by nature. The evil brave always clutched and clung to life,
somehow instinctively aware they had gone for broke
on this plane and lost, that it might get real ugly for
them on the other side, furiously determined to the
end to go out with a roar and not a whimper for their
lives to be spared. To this savage's credit, Bolan
found no beggar.

If nothing else, it made it that much cleaner.

The guy looked back, all hate and snarling, doing
his damnedest to haul in an M-16, when the Execu-

tioner ended it with a quick burst of autofire up the spine.

Where was Kragen?

"Oh, you lousy..."

Bolan parted the smoke, rolled out onto edge of the rise, homed in on Kragen's vicious cursing. There was so much blood covering Kragen, head to toe, Bolan couldn't judge the extent of the man's injuries. Kragen rolled on his side, craning his neck, staring at the warrior. The way Kragen held his arm out, slowly bringing it back, Bolan knew the guy was holding a weapon and not his guts.

Kragen wanted to go out with a bang. Fair enough, the Executioner thought. The wounded lion never crawled off into the brush to die quiet, anyway.

Raising the C-130, Bolan gave the order to land, told the blacksuits, next. "We're finished here."

"You know...it could have been different... whoever the hell you are...still can..."

"I don't see how."

"You dumb...I have money...stashed...get me help...I don't want to die...like this...in this shit hole of the world..."

"It was your choice from the start."

"Hey...give me a chance..."

"I already did, and before I ever even saw your face. You drew the losing hand when you took Nafud's money."

"You rotten...you're telling me...no...to a quick two, three million...think about it here...hold on a second...it's easy...this ain't no game show...I'm not America's favorite game show stooge here...I'm a man...I fought for America... Hey, come on...you gotta think about your answer..."

Kragen made his move, rolling over, somehow finding that last reserve of strength the damned always found, the .45 Colt coming up, swinging across his mangled body.

The Executioner lifted the HK-33 and gave Kragen his final answer.

BOLAN WAS on the satlink, updating Brognola, as soon as they were airborne and all radar screens showed they were free of approaching air traffic, hostile Sudanese MiGs looking for some dogfight over the Nubian Desert. Soon they'd hit Red Sea airspace, where an Israeli backup squadron of F-15s was already scrambled, just in case.

Sudan was almost a wrap.

Standing aft in the huge belly of the Hercules, Bolan watched for a few moments as the blacksuits handed out blankets and water to the women.

The soldier was feeling the grind himself, tired, hungry and aching. Despite that, he indulged a moment of compassion and hope for the women they'd rescued. They were going home, back to husbands, boyfriends, children, a return to sanity and something normal that had been temporarily stolen from them. There would be scars both physical and emotional, no doubt, but time, the soldier knew from his own hard experience, always healed the wounds inflicted on the human heart and soul. Sayid's wives, in turn, would see themselves quietly shipped back to Sudan, if that's what they wanted. The Sudanese power structure, Bolan thought, might bawl their eyes out on the diplomatic front, cry foul for the rest of the fanatical Muslim world to hear, railing about some future call to arms against the so-called Great Satan.

So be it. Bolan was a soldier, and in his world diplomacy was only achieved against the savages at the business end of a gun. There would always be another Nafud or Sayid. It was the only promise tomorrow held for the warrior.

Somewhere up amidships, the soldier found the young Filipina looking his way. The look in her eyes said it all. No voiced thanks were necessary.

But the campaign was far from over as he heard the news from the big Fed's end.

"Here it is, Striker. What we now know, what my own people are watching as we speak, and the fact that the Farm has what you need to move ahead, Bear and company having broken the code down, well, the Man says since you've come this far, it's your show the rest of the way. Call it, Striker, tell me what you need."

And Bolan did. According to Brognola, a Stealth B-2 had been scrambled from the American air base in Saudi Arabia, would be parked and waiting to whisk Bolan back across the Atlantic. With a max cruising speed at just under Mach 1, a high-altitude range of seventy-six hundred miles, it was the fastest available ride to see the soldier back in the States and moving to hunt down enemies still on the prowl.

The good news on Brognola's end was that Powers and Grevey appeared content to remain, for the time being, in Atlanta, prepared, no doubt, to do whatever it was they were going to do. And, so far, there had been no more terrorist attacks on U.S. turf.

If Bolan's hunch was right, that was about to change, and sooner than he wanted, if his enemies on the other side of the ocean tried to contact their Sudan sponsors. The hours ahead could prove an eternity, but there was little else the warrior could do except hold on to grim hope the savages were only geared up, sharpening their blades, biding time for whatever reason.

And wait for their own date with the Executioner.

CHAPTER FIFTEEN

Atlanta

"I've been trying to reach you for almost twenty-four hours now. What the hell is going on?"

"Do you realize at what hour you are calling me?"

Grevey checked his watch, scowling, thinking only about the entire day he'd lost, wasting precious hours trying to find out about his money—with no luck—so he could finish tying up the loose ends and fly on for his tropical slice of heaven. He felt his expression harden even more as the front door opened and he saw Powers striding in, two giant bags in hand, a foot-long stogie jammed in his yap, the guy just letting a couple inches worth of ashes drop from the glowing tip to the carpet. Since Boston the colonel had been acting very strange, and for a solid twelve hours and change now Powers had been AWOL. The pissing contest was getting old.

It had been a long, nervous day already, mounting a snow job at SCTU's small command central in downtown Atlanta, putting bogus strikes against phantom terrorists on the drawing board, ducking calls from Jeffries. Then riding out to Leland's airport in his rental, paid for under one of his half dozen assumed identities, to double-check and make sure McClintock came through with the jet and extra gun-power. For hours, despite the fact he'd been unable to reach their cutout to the man overseas, Grevey had been grateful for the solitude, having grown weary to the point of some massive eruption of rage with the colonel's sullen and bizarre demeanor, believing the earlier disappearing act was staged as some sort of warning. Now what? he wondered. Then Grevey watched as Powers dumped the bags on the couch in the living room of the apartment in suburban Atlanta they used as their private retreat. The colonel zipped open the black nylon bag. It was a big one, the kind they used for diplomatic pouches, large enough to squeeze the corpse of a full-grown man inside with room to spare.

"I didn't think you'd be able to sleep, not with what's in the wings," Grevey said, trying to ease into the real matter he wanted to discuss.

And felt his hand twitching toward the holstered Glock 17 beneath his windbreaker. As if he wasn't even standing there, holding what might be the most important conversation of their lives, Grevey felt his heart start to race as something dangerous crept into the colonel's eyes, Powers acting oblivious to every-thing but the bags. A cautious step forward, and Grevey saw enough hardware in that dip pouch to field a full squad of commandos. Like some kid checking out his Christmas gifts, making sure he got what he'd asked for, Powers hauled out one, then two

HK MP-5 subguns, cracked home clips, ran an ap-
preciative eye over the SMGs. Some kind of slotted
belt came out next, stuffed to the gills with hand grenades. That got dumped on the couch, too.

"I believe I know why you are calling me."
Grevey heard the silky smooth voice of the Arab on
the other end of the telephone line, the FBI man
watching his counterpart closely. "There has been a
most unfortunate development, if I am to believe a
source of mine over there. Actually, I have been
forced to deal with another troublesome situation,
also. Improvising the operation due to unforeseen circumstances has created delays for my launch."

"How come I don't like the sound of all this?"

Grevey sidled away from the couch. Semi and automatic handguns were getting the loving once-over
from Powers. There was the bull-pup-configured Aus-
trian AUG in 9 mm, an Uzi subgun with a smaller
version of the famed Israeli piece getting deposited on
the couch. Powers took out a sheath, slid out a commando dagger, its razor-honed edge winking in the
lamplight thrown from beside the couch. The colonel
lifted a leg, snapped the sheath with tucked-in blade to
his ankle. There was a pair of brass knuckles, displayed
for a moment, then disappearing into the pocket of his
black leather bomber jacket. A closer look inside the
bag, and Grevey found a SPAS-12 automatic shotgun,
more clips and bandoliers of shells. A stun gun, five
or so mini handheld radios, the high-tech variety, he
knew, that could be scrambled once the Keynote microchip was installed. Powers put everything back except for one HK MP-5, zipped the bag up, slipped

an arm through the SMG's strap, hanging it around his shoulder.

"Beer?"

"In the fridge," Grevey said, and wasn't sure what he saw in the colonel's eyes, but he suddenly felt he couldn't trust the man any further than he could spit.

"Cold, I trust?"

Grevey nodded and trailed Powers a few feet as the man marched into the kitchen and helped himself to a Heineken.

"Are you there?"

"Yeah, yeah. I'm still waiting to hear about the rest of the money."

"As I was attempting to tell you, there will be no more payments. Not for you nor your friends in Texas."

Grevey heard the roar rushing into his ears. "What did you just say?"

"You heard me correctly, I believe. Before you start hurling around abusive language, listen to me. You have not been able to reach me because I have done little else today except covering my tracks and making that call overseas. Information just reached me that our source, our sponsor as you call him, is believed dead. Reliable sources tell me they were hit by an unknown group of commandos. I am told the body count is so staggering, it is believed a small army must have stormed the place. I have even heard the term 'of epic Koranic proportions,' in reference to this slaughter of soldiers and officers and men who were mere business partners in this venture."

"You're telling me that Na—"

"No names! Yes, I am telling you he is dead. Likewise, I understand, the pipeline has been effectively closed."

"Who? Americans?"

"They believe so."

"Okay, so, what's the problem? Just proceed with what you've got. Plenty enough, according to my last estimate of all available hands."

The Arab chuckled. "Oh, my American friend, it was not supposed to be this way, but as I sometimes say, hope for the best, but prepare for the worst."

"That's just the way I'm starting to feel, and then some. All this doesn't exactly make me want to crack open the champagne."

"Nor I. I was forced to track down and eliminate a situation that didn't work out. Shortly, I must take care of another similar unpleasant situation on this end. I am beginning to see trouble flying around, armed ghosts in the night, perhaps heading my way, and from out of nowhere. Is there anything I should know?"

"Like what?"

"You tell me."

"How come I'm standing here, friend, feeling something going way up my sphincter?"

"There is no duplicity on my end. I'll take your reply as a no. It doesn't matter anyway. As you suggested to me, take what you already have and be grateful."

Grevey bared his teeth. "I'm out another three mil, if I'm hearing you right, and I'm supposed to feel happy? Listen to me, friend, if it weren't for me and my contact you and our alleged late sponsor would have never gotten your own gig this far.''

''It was a mutual effort. We extended our hands to each other at a timely, critical juncture. You, for the money. Me, for principle.''

Grevey watched Powers come back, sucking on his beer, blowing up a cloud of smoke. ''That may be true enough, but if this is the end of our arrangement, if I'm not going to see another dime from you, let me be clear on something. Should I even see a shadow following me where I'm going, I can still reach out and find you.''

No reply, Grevey thinking the Arab had hung up, then the voice said, ''That will not happen.''

''And I'm just supposed to take your word about that? It's all sweetness and light?''

''Yes, something like that. You see, what you don't understand, could never possibly fathom…well, within twenty-four hours, I will be dead.''

''What?'' Grevey asked, thinking the whole damn world was suddenly insane.

''You heard me. Dead. I did not come all the way here, risk my life, invite and convince many others to sacrifice their own lives just so I could live to reap the glory of their sacrifice.''

''So…you're…''

''Yes. I will lead them all to Paradise, although I will be the last martyr to follow them to heaven.''

Whether or not the man was bent on suicide—and this crazy Muslim nonsense about jihad and martyrdom was working on his last nerve—Grevey didn't much care, but he wasn't about to just drop the money issue. "Listen—"

"No, you listen," the voice said, snarling it out, nearly shouting, the Arab getting intensely jacked up with all his talk and visions of jihad, no doubt. "This will be our last conversation. We each go our separate ways. What is done is done. You have most of what you want, and I am about to get, or, rather, give what I so richly deserve to give. As soon as I hang up, this line will be disconnected permanently. Goodbye and good luck."

"Wait a second! Hold on—"

Grevey cursed the phone as the dial tone buzzed in his ear, then some electronic whine pierced his brain, forcing him to shut it off as the Arab delivered on his promise, severing the line instantly with a special microchip he had tied into the scrambler.

"Problems?"

Grevey shot Powers an angry look.

"No more money?"

"You don't sound too upset we're out three million dollars, which, for your information, was to be our last payment!"

Powers shrugged, worked on his beer. "Man has to plan accordingly."

"What the hell's that mean, Colonel?"

"Means a week ago I liquidated all my assets, cashed in on some stocks, cleared out three accounts, some IRAs, a few other investments I made over the years. Plus what I've received for my—our—part of the operation."

"Well, I'm tickled you're feeling so peachy about your own nest egg."

"My money's sitting down in the Bahamas already. I could live comfortably off the interest alone. Who knows? If I get bored sitting on the beach, copping a rum buzz and getting mean hummers from island girls, I might go farther south. Understand the cartels are always looking for a few good men. Understand Brazil still has a few death squads. Maybe they could learn something from a man of my experience, if, of course, the price was right."

"You know, something isn't right here, between us."

"Really?" Powers said, and chuckled.

"I think we need to talk. First, you mind losing the piece?"

"What, Grevey?" he said, shaking his head, looking exasperated. "After all you've put me through, all the blackmail and sweating out our SCTU project, all the bullshit we've flung around and all the smoke screens we've put up, sacrificing young men to advance our own dream of an island paradise, you think at this point I'm interested in us going for it, shooting each other up?"

"You tell me."

Powers drained his beer, set it on the coffee table, then unslung his subgun and laid it beside the dip pouch. "So, I'm assuming we're ready to catch our plane out of the country?"

"You assume wrong."

A dangerous shine lit up the colonel's eyes. "Do not fuck with me, mister."

The fire was back now, and that was the colonel Grevey knew and didn't like. "I'm not. You knew the particulars, you knew the timetable."

"Refresh my memory, mister."

"A little matter of our friends down in the islands. That Panamanian freighter they arranged."

"The shrimp boat? The decoy vessel, the one the Coast Guard will be informed is stuffed with fifteen or so tons of coke?"

"That's the one. There's the little matter of all available Coast Guard and Customs folks moving out at the appointed hour tomorrow night to board that vessel and search it stem to stern. Our window then, to see us clear through U.S. airspace beyond Florida."

"I've been thinking about that," Powers rasped, then swiftly headed into the kitchen, popped open another beer. "I've got some problems with your scheme."

"Like what? And it's no scheme."

"Us crashing our jet into the Atlantic."

"We're parachuting to a drop site where our island contact will pick us up by boat."

"Maybe he decides he already has enough pocket money. Maybe he decides to leave us for the sharks."

"Maybe I'll swim all the way to the island, hop into one of the two cigarette boats I already know are docked there and hunt his ass down and cut him up into a thousand pieces with a rusty machete and use it for some deep-sea swordfishing. You know the arrangement, Colonel. He's contacted once our airspace is clear of any traffic, we make a visual of his boat first, then bail. Say he's not there, made that call to

ditch us, we simply fly on. Hell, no, I'm not about to
see us get swallowed up by the ocean.''

"I forgot, you have all the answers."

"What's the matter? You telling me you're losing
your nerve?"

Powers chuckled, then downed the beer, rolling
into the living room where he tossed the empty on
the floor. "What the hell, huh. We've gotten it this
far. I figure I owe myself a few days just sitting on
the beach, doing nothing anyway. All work and no
play tends to make the colonel a mean mother. So,
you're telling me we have to sit around another
twelve, fifteen hours, thumbs in our sphincters, Luther
maybe ringing the phone off the hook, wondering
what we're doing. Maybe Belasko shows up in Atlanta…''

"I get it now."

"Get what? Belasko? You're thinking I'm worried
the guy will piss on the parade."

"You certainly came here prepared for that event."

"Damn straight, I did. You haven't even seen
what's in the other bag yet."

"Our Sudanese sponsorship was burned down by
an unidentified group of commandos. Nafud is history. No Nafud, no more money. Maybe they got to
him before he croaked, and he talked. Maybe the CIA
goons I used to bring him onboard through my man
in Oman at the time the sheikh's daddy was screaming for his head talked, also."

"And maybe they didn't. All the more reason to
shake a leg and get the hell out of the country."

"I'm sticking to the timetable."

"All right. But I'll tell you this," Powers said, and his eyes seemed to harden into two pieces of stone. "No one, not Belasko, not you, not Luther is going to keep me from leaving the country and starting over. I want what I want and I'll have it. If the Arab doesn't get his jihad, that's not my problem, either. My only problem is maybe how many bastards I have to drop on my way out, how much blood I need to dirty my hands with before I'm looking toward that paradise to the south."

Grevey knew not to push it, the colonel growing that frenzied laughing glow in his eyes, telling the world he was a little tougher, smarter, better than everybody else, and he could prove it. The FBI had special experts profiling guys like he was now facing off, Grevey knew. Serial killers, sociopaths, pyschopaths, however they chose to categorize a man who killed for pleasure, who felt nothing for anyone but himself. There was always something weird in the eyes that the profilers never failed to comment on. Guys like Powers, he thought, went about their daily business, laughing at the world, telling folks they were just shit on a stick, something to be stepped on and scraped off the shoe if they couldn't be used as human pawns on their own personal chessboard. Wasn't he like Powers in some ways? Grevey wondered. He didn't want to quite believe that, but they were alike in some ways. Twice divorced, married more to careers or personal agendas than they could have ever been to a woman. Wanting something larger than life, a bigger slice to call their own.

Power? Control? Shaping their own destinies?

Holding themselves up as icons to all the little folks they stepped on? Rugged individuals who took no crap, did what they wanted and damn the odds or the consequences?

Grevey decided not to think about it.

"You know something," Powers said, "if it's all right by me our relationship with Sudan has been severed it shouldn't bother you, either, more money or not."

"And why's that?"

"That's just one less asshole can point the finger our way."

AHMED JABAL COULDN'T bring himself to look at his wife right then, not without his soul burning up from overwhelming guilt and shame.

The time had come, and they were here.

Without knocking they slowly came into the apartment, the one called the Messenger, he found, escorted by two big men. One glance at the bulges beneath their expensive suit jackets, his heart skipping a beat, the world seeming to revolve like some whirling dervish in his eyes, set to hurl him off its axis into oblivion, and he knew they had come there with one purpose in mind. One of the Messenger's two men closed the curtains to the parking lot beyond, shutting out the light of a new day, casting shadows across the living room while the Messenger settled onto the couch. This was the end, he knew. His bodyguards, warriors or whatever they were, he saw, took up standing positions on either end of the couch, folding their hands in front their crotches, drilling their contempt at him from across the room. Why wouldn't the Messenger, though, look him in the eye? Jabal wondered, but feared he already knew the answer. The bottom line here was very simple. The Messenger was disappointed that one of his chosen warriors had seen his own calling from God and chosen to defy him.

"You have not returned my calls. You have forced another delay. Time is running out, for both you and me."

Jabal felt the lump stick in his throat. It felt as if he'd swallowed some live raging bird of prey whole, and its claws were now tearing away to set itself free. Against his better judgment, he looked at his wife when he was jolted by some sobbing noise she made, the fear so strong in Mahjida's eyes he thought she would be erupt into some hysterical tantrum, shrieking and begging the three men to leave.

To spare their lives.

As if that were even possible.

It was something—this moment of truth—he had discussed with her just last night, the two of them quickly becoming embroiled in a bitter argument as to how to handle their dire predicament. Did he or didn't he do their bidding? In the face of her anger and despair, he had considered his options, which were next to none. Finally, after much weeping and gnashing of teeth, she said he shouldn't, that she would rather have the blood of their own.

Jabal felt cold as he looked at the Messenger, imagined everyone could hear the beating of his pounding heart, silently laughing at him for being such a coward. Running, hiding in some other city beyond Richmond, he recalled telling his wife, was out of the question, since everything they owned—the apartment, the deli with its assorted Lebanese and American cuisine, the passports and visas, the bank account, the cash in the cut-away-floorboard vault— belonged to the Messenger, anyway. He would find them no matter where they went. It would be far better, so they finally decided, if they went to God together, their souls clean, free and pure of the kind of sin he was being asked to commit.

Still Jabal couldn't believe it was all happening, that he was, in fact, being called upon to make the ultimate decision. This dark mysterious man who had taken them out of poverty in Syria, blessed them with a life of material promise, a better tomorrow for their children in America...

But a price tag was attached to Jabal transplanting his wife and three sons to America, a marker he never believed would get called in from the very moment he'd heard what was expected of him. He had reasoned during that moment, a little over one year ago, that the plan had been so insane the Messenger would have never pulled it off, no matter how much money he tossed around, bribing those who would cover his tracks, shadow men who had helped to lay out the foundation for his jihad. Surely the Messenger and whatever warriors prepared to sacrifice their lives on American soil would get arrested. So he had thought he could come to America, build a new life at the expense of this man who would simply eventually vanish to rot away in the prison system here, forgotten at worst, killed at best, in the act of his madness.

It hadn't worked out that way.

"Would you mind, Ahmed? Kindly ask your wife to take your children to the bedroom, close the door so we may have a few minutes alone."

Somehow, Jabal found his legs but felt as if he were watching himself moving like some wooden figure in a bad dream. He took his wife by the shoulders, his children sitting at the dining-room table, spoons frozen above the cereal bowls, staring at their father, confused and frightened.

"Please, do as he asks."

She shook her head, tears welling up in the corners of her dark eyes, the first sign her terror was about to turn to grief and perhaps mindless rage that would devour any dignity from this moment.

Jabal swallowed, his mouth raw and dry. He was so ashamed right then he couldn't look his children in the eye. "Please. Go, and pray." She dropped her head, shot a look of pure hatred toward the Messenger. "Be strong, my wife. I love you, our children. Forever."

It felt like the longest few moments of his short life of thirty years, time freezing in his eyes, as he watched his wife gently take each of his sons by the shoulders. They stood—Hasim, Farouk and three-year-old Fawzi—and he fought off the urge to run to them, grab them up, embrace their small bodies, make assurances he knew he could never deliver. The bitter taste of an acid sob squeezed off the air in his throat as they slowly walked off, melting all too quickly into the shadows down the hall. His three sons turned to look back, but his wife gently ushered them on through the doorway.

Go with God, he thought, and silently asked Him to forgive him this weakness of selfishness. He had sacrificed their lives, and for what? A dream for his sons they could better themselves here in America, armed with an education, fortified with a self-esteem he'd never known, to go out there and secure a life of dignity and self-respect? Become something more than he had been in the world, more than a petty thief or a sometime opium dealer in the Bekaa Valley of neighboring Lebanon, a man who had always agonized whether he had the guts and the willingness to sometimes work the land of his fathers? A simple farmer and shepherd? Fighting and chasing the dream to hand down to his own blood something real and honorable, to not have to struggle and rage through poverty, all the desperation, the despair and anger that came with having to worry simply about how a man would even find shelter and food?

He had no answers, but something deep inside told him there would be an answer, and he wasn't worthy enough to know the truth.

Let it be.

They disappeared, one by one, into the bedroom, looking so small, so innocent, so lost. Could they possibly ever understand? Perhaps it was best this way. They would leave here with their innocence, never having been tainted by the evil in the world. Surely there would be a place for them. His wife looked back, a fire lighting her eyes, and in that instant he was sure she'd break, rush into the living room, screaming, threatening to call the police. She malingered, the shadow of a ghost down there, beckoning him perhaps, her look seeming to want to tell him something, but what he didn't know. Then she vanished into the bedroom and shut the door.

Gone. The last time, he knew, he'd ever see her or their children again. At least in this world.

"I see the way you look at your wife. I am moved. I can spare you, and them. I tell you, before God, it does not have to be this way, Ahmed."

He silently implored God to grace him with courage, strike him in the eyes with some blinding light, place the right words in his mouth. He wouldn't beg for his life.

"What you have asked me," he told the Messenger, drew a deep breath, screwed his eyes shut, squared his shoulders and found he could look at the mysterious man who had never told him his name or his origin of birth, right in the eye. It was the most beautiful sensation he'd ever known, something erupting from deep inside, calling, urging him on. He was suddenly strong of heart, a newborn lion cub among jackals, as he felt some strange warmth settle over his body, a feeling that left him light on his feet, some power outside his own body, it seemed, that wanted to send him floating for the sky. "It is…an abomination. I have three sons. They are in school, an American public school. We are talking about children, the innocent who have done nothing wrong. It occurs to me right now, as I look at you and know what you ask, that when children are murdered, you murder those also they would give birth to, and so on. You want me and others to just walk into American schools, shoot children, set off bombs. I have given this much thought, I have prayed about it. I cannot.''

"I am disappointed in you, Ahmed.'' The Messenger looked up, his eyes flashing with some fanatical burning. "I chose you because you were once a freedom fighter.''

"That was many years ago, when I was young and foolish and rebellious and didn't understand the world. And they were men, soldiers.''

"You have deceived me.''

"I am offering you my life in exchange for my family.''

The Messenger chuckled. "We are at war with the infidels. It does not matter if we slay adult males in uniform or the spawn of their evil. It is all the same. All you need to do is come with me and carry out your holy duty. I understand your grief, your hesitation in this matter. Yes, your family will live on without a father or husband. You knew this when I took you out of Syria. That was our arrangement. What, has your soul become so stained, your thinking become so warped by their decadent ways that you would rather die a coward than go to God in glory?''

"It is not like that.''

"Then explain to me what it is like.''

"I have come to see that what you wish to do is wrong—no, it is evil.''

"How dare you, a mere peasant, speak to me in

such a way. I gave your family hope. I gave them this life, which you so blithely take now for granted!''

"And it is yours to take away. If I were to carry out your wishes, should I go with you to murder children...the blood of the innocent would blacken my soul. God does not want that."

"You foolish and wicked man. You dare to assume to know what God wants?"

"There is no assuming. There is only what is right and what is wrong. There is only one God."

"You would sacrifice the lives of your family then?"

"You have my answer."

The Messenger nodded, heaved a breath and stood.

"May I have a few moments to pray?"

"You have twenty seconds to make peace with God," the Messenger said, reaching inside his jacket.

He turned his back as the Messenger's men walked past him, squeezed his eyes shut when he saw them fastening sound suppressors to their pistols. Ahmed Jabal would normally hit his knees when praying, but, as he asked God for forgiveness, to take his family to heaven, he smiled and let the glow envelop him— some living fire that before now he sensed had always been there but he'd kept dormant because he'd been busy with the chores of the world and the selfishness of his own wants and endeavors—from the very depths of his soul.

Let it be.

If nothing else, he would die on his feet. If God, in fact, despised the coward, then certainly he would consider Ahmed's courage in this final moment, some atonement for what might be seen as a selfish act of sacrificing his own family.

Strangely enough, he found himself wrapped, even spiraling down in the warm cocoon of utter peace and calm as he felt the Messenger moving up from behind. It was as if he could see everything suddenly, the entire world beyond, with some diamond-sparkling clarity right then, even with his eyes shut and the voice in his mind crying out for his family's salvation. The faces of his children and his wife, holding each other in the bedroom—there they were! Calm. Assured. Willing to let it go. Some brilliant light coming down from above, blinding him, calling him home, where he and his family belonged from the beginning.

He felt the Messenger stop, even saw the man considering something in the tunnel of light. There was doubt, and great fear, in the man's eyes.

''Do it,'' Jabal said.

CHAPTER SIXTEEN

New Mexico

No one was coming.

Cody Caldwell became convinced, many miles and hours ago, his SOS was in vain. He was in a world of hurt if that was the case. No saviors from the Justice Department, no preemptive strike against the terrorist operation he was now an unwilling accomplice to, no shot at redemption, a clean slate.

He was on his own, twisting in the wind.

Dammit!

If it went down the way he believed it was going to, he'd either be dead or in jail within two days. If arrested, he would find himself the object of national fury, vengeful headlines and lynch mobs screaming for a speedy trial and the death penalty to be sure. What was planned, he thought, would exceed the Oklahoma City bombing in body bags alone, ten, maybe twenty, thirty or more times the dead once the bombs stopping going off, the bullets stopped flying and the Arab terrorists had committed suicide by cop.

What could he do, he wondered, to not only save himself, but to stop this madness from happening?

It would take at least twenty more hours just to get to Los Angeles, he believed. Their first stop, he knew, was Phoenix, so it could end up being as much as a full day, maybe more. There, twelve terrorists would be unloaded from the cargo hold. Four groups of three, weighted down with wraparound bundles of dynamite and plastic explosive, marching off into that city, suicide soldiers for the jihad. Between the two trucks, that left another seventy-four fanatics, according to his math, to be dumped off, dispersed around Southern California, a group of twenty-four shipped up to San Francisco. It coiled his guts with horror and revulsion to know at least six of the planned strikes were against private and public schools, both elementary and high schools. How many children would die unless he did something? And just what were the four fifty-five-gallon drums—two labeled toxic waste, the other two stamped with the universal radiation sign— for? How were they going to get used? The problem was he wasn't armed, and Peterson was, a big .357 Magnum Colt Python shoulder holstered beneath his jacket. The big buzz-cut man's silence ever since he'd found him at the phone back in Oklahoma City didn't inspire Caldwell with confidence he would be rescued, much less live to proclaim his own innocence.

The brown lunar landscape of New Mexico only served to deepen his despair. For as far as he could see beyond the interstate there was nothing out there but scrub brush, broken ground and cactus, a smattered jumble of mesas or sawtooth hills breaking up the monotonous terrain every few miles or so. Despite the air-conditioning, on full blast, Caldwell felt the shirt pasted to his back from sweat. The way the sun beat down on the hood of their eighteen-wheeler, he figured it was a hundred-plus out there, and he wondered how far he could make it on foot without water. A day? Two tops? That was provided, of course, he could find a way to slip off, use the desert to hide in until he could reach some form of civilization, make another call. He adjusted his shades, glanced at Peterson, who was a stone fixture at the wheel, staring ahead at the arrow-straight black ribbon.

According to his watch and the last posted sign, they were still an hour or so out of Albuquerque, if Peterson maintained his sixty-five miles per hour. Oddly enough there was next to no traffic, just a couple of SUVs, a travel trailer up ahead. But this was desert country, he figured, and several county roads had what looked like brand-new signs up warning travelers to venture on but ride with drinking water. In the jutting sideview glass he saw the second Leland truck in the rear.

Caldwell wondered what his chances were if he flung the door open and bailed. If he spotted a suitable and deep enough gully, something with brush in it, he figured he could survive the fall. And what would Peterson do? Stop the bus, send out a hunting party and risk throwing away the whole operation over one man?

Caldwell found just what he was looking for, the

rig thundering toward a deep swale off the roadside. He was reaching for the door handle when he felt the iron jammed into his ribs.

"Where do you think you're going, Cody?"

Peterson's voice sounded alien, faraway to Caldwell as icy fear clutched his chest. He turned slowly, saw the big man grinning behind his dark shades.

Peterson knew.

"Something's been bothering me, little buddy. I checked back with Buck in Oklahoma City while we were waiting around last night. Funny how things happen. Man knows everything about you, everything you've been up to the last year. Buck, he puts in a call to a buddy of yours, you know, Jimmy from AA, from downstairs in your apartment building. Turns out old Jimbo says you don't have any girlfriend, part of the first year of getting sober, something like that, no relationships with the opposite sex."

"Doesn't it bother you, Peterson, you used to be a lawman? Those...fanatics or terrorists or whatever you want to call them back there," he said, nodding at the panel separating the cab from the cargo hold, "are being sent out to murder children, for God's sake."

"God doesn't have anything to do with it. And, no, it don't bother me. I'm getting paid well, more than I ever made with the FBI. All I've gotta do is drop them off at the scheduled stops, where their vans will be ready to take them to whatever they think their own glory's gonna be. It's all about the money." He smiled, laughed. "A man with enough drive and ambition can always make it in this great country of ours, I always said. America is about to be very, very good to me."

"Kids, Peterson, they're going to be shooting up grade-school kids."

"You need to talk to somebody who gives a damn about this country, or rather what it used to be. Before we let the great unwashed have a voice raging all over the TV talk shows about their tawdry lives and how they're proud they're sleeping around with their best friend's girl or his wife or we're supposed to applaud and accept every sickness and perversion known to man. Before the criminals took over and armed themselves with more firepower than three big-city police departments or the frigging U.S. Army put together, or we allowed the courts and the politicians full, Big-Brother access to every area of our lives. This society's finished. I'm getting out while I can before it all really goes to hell. Me—about those kids? They can go straight to hell, too. I was tossed out of the FBI for roughing up a few of those kids you want to coddle so much. Kind with do-rags, a bag of dope, a gun and a lot of attitude. I sure hope our Arab friends do some urban face-lifting before they're checked out. But I guess you never understood the philosophy of God's Crusaders, little buddy. It's us and them. I guess since you sobered up, you've seen the light. You're better than the rest of us, that it?"

"I called the Justice Department, Peterson." Caldwell saw the fear and anger harden the man's features. "They know. And, no, I don't share your points of view. Probably never did. What is it they say about evil? It flourishes if a few good men stand by and do nothing, something like that.''

Caldwell was sure Peterson was going to pull the trigger, the man baring his teeth, when the handheld crackled on the seat.

''Peterson, pick up.''

''Pick it up and hold it for me,'' Peterson said. ''Real slow, real easy.''

Caldwell did, heard the other driver, Mulroy, say, ''Something's going on, Peterson. I've been wondering why there's no traffic out here. I was watching three smokies on my six, tailed me about four miles, just dropped back and formed some kind of barricade to the east. No westbound cars, tells me the same thing is maybe set up down the road. Not only that, I just spotted a chopper, flew in over the hills, headed your way. It's a military chopper. What do you want to do?''

''Pull ahead of me, I want to take a look. Keep going. Under no circumstances do we stop. Order your human cargo to arm themselves and be ready for anything. Got that?''

''Roger.''

''Put it down, you bastard,'' Peterson snarled. ''Maybe you think the cavalry's arrived. Maybe you think you can just hand yourself over, tell them it was all some big mistake, start squealing. You're a gutless sack, you know that, Caldwell?''

Caldwell inched his hand closer to the door handle, saw the trailing semi loom up beyond Peterson, gather speed and thunder on, finally swinging back into the right lane. Peterson pounded on the sliding window of the partition. It opened, a bearded, swarthy face edging up to the screen.

"We may be looking at trouble," Peterson growled. "Arm yourselves, get ready to bail and go for broke if we're stopped by cops."

Without a word the angry face disappeared as the slat was slammed back.

Then Caldwell spotted the black chopper in the sideview. Nose down, it was hugging the desert, blowing up dark funnels of grit, racing up the side. It blew past, right on top of the truck, the rig shuddering, Peterson cursing, fighting to control the wheel with one hand.

"That's a Black Hawk!" Peterson said.

Caldwell's cavalry. The former FBI agent thrust the door open, was leaving his seat when he heard the gun blast. He was so pumped on adrenaline, propelled out the door by pure fear and airborne in the next instant, Caldwell wasn't even aware at first his guts had been blown out the other side of his ribs.

TIRELESS DEDICATION, red-line phone calls authorized and backed by a presidential directive, and a stroke of good fortune found the Executioner one minute and counting from hitting the interstate and unleashing the next phase of the campaign against the enemy.

They were surging past the lead eighteen-wheeler, Bolan staring past his two-man blacksuit crew, when the soldier gave the order. "Set me down a good two miles beyond this point, then clear out and stay in the air.''

The interstate, he knew, was blocked off in both directions by New Mexico Highway Patrol, free now of noncombatants.

As good as it would get.

The soldier still counted his good fortune in several areas as he moved into the fuselage, took up arms. The long hours in the air during his transatlantic flight hadn't been wasted. In near constant contact with Brognola and the Farm, Bolan laid it out. The fickle gods of war had seen fit to smile on his mission, pave the road to his next hell zone.

Item. A former FBI agent named Cody Caldwell had put in the call to a friend of his at the Justice Department detailing the direct route, the enemy numbers and targets for their terrorist cargo, now housed in the backs of both rigs, clearly marked Leland Moving, all of it finding its way to Brognola's office.

Item. For reasons unknown the enemy at all three identified Leland operations, targeted and watched by Justice Department units sent by Brognola, had stayed put the entire night, the Oklahoma unit the only one moving out sometime in the morning. But, according to what the Farm had decoded, there was a method to their madness. The Oklahoma unit was designated first to move out, since they had the longest trek, California their final destination. If the enemy stuck to their timetable, Richmond was moving out at twenty hundred hours, Atlanta leaving five hours later. The brains behind the opposition, it appeared, had calculated the distances to some sixty-plus targets, road time then dispersal by van of the individual suicide teams down to within perhaps an hour when the holocaust would blow in savage and horrible earnest from coast to coast. The army of terror and murder, according to the Farm's discovery, was going after schools, museums, government institutions, including INS and IRS buildings. Post offices, police precincts, shopping malls, movie theaters, trains, buses, car bombs on crowded city streets or walking human time bombs setting themselves off in restaurants and hotels...

The horror of such wholesale mayhem and slaughter, if they succeeded in as little as five or six sites, wanted to boggle even Bolan, stoke him with a burning anger. Instead he was juiced on full combat alert, laser-focused, grim and coldly hell-bent to start a clean sweep of mopping up the enemy.

Beginning now.

Of course he couldn't be in three places at once. Just to get it to this point had seen Brognola and Price come through with logistical brilliance. His Stealth ride had ferried him to Kirkland Air Force Base in Albuquerque, where the Farm's handpicked crew was on standby with the Black Hawk SOF MH-60. State police had been brought onboard to tail the targets, ordered by Brognola—who could use his presidential directive if forced—to do nothing other than seal off a ten-mile corridor on I-40. With the interstate free of innocent travelers it was the soldier's task to bring down the trucks, declare all-out war, take no prisoners. A special Justice Department HAZMAT team was already in the sky, circling beyond the distant hills, prepared to clean up any toxic or radioactive spills.

The Executioner was fully intending to make a big mess. From there, he had a date to keep with someone named Buck McClintock, the leader of a right-wing group that was now shuttling and driving around their army of fanatics.

First round one needed to get nailed down.

If the Richmond and Atlanta teams moved out, Brognola was prepared to have units of heavily armed agents monitor their movements. The President of the United States was more than willing to let this be Bolan's show, start to finish, unless the enemy panicked and rearranged their doomsday schedule.

The Executioner wasn't about to the disappoint the Man. Much less let the enemy snuff out so much as one more innocent life, not without letting the HK-33/M-203 combo in hand and Little Bulldozer hanging from his shoulder speak loud and angry volumes on his behalf.

Bolan felt the Black Hawk stop, hover, then touch down. Dropping a 40 mm round into the M-203, the soldier hit the door, dropped to the highway. As the chopper lifted off and the rotor wash died, he walked across the right lane, felt the first few beads of sweat mottle up his forehead.

It was hotter than hell out there, as quiet as death. He looked down the empty highway, peering into the distant shimmering haze, listening.

He didn't have to wait long.

The shimmering bulk of the lead rig materialized in the mist.

The Executioner held his ground, the road beneath his boots vibrating as the monster rig with its savage cargo grew, closing.

He waited, then lifted the HK-33, sighted at the engine housing and squeezed the M-203's trigger. A muffled pop, and the hell bomb streaked on, Bolan thinking he glimpsed the driver jumping up in his seat, eyes popping out of his head as doomsday flew for his face. There was a squeal of rubber as the driver crushed on the brakes, as if slowing the truck would save him and his load of savages.

The 40 mm grenade impacted, detonated, hurling up sheared debris, the fireball and wreckage blowing in the cab's window, the face of shock and horror lost to sight.

The Executioner had officially declared war.

CHAPTER SEVENTEEN

Hot air gusted through the cab, flinging specks of Caldwell's blood in Peterson's face, spattering his lips with a bitter reminder of the guy's treachery. Peterson caught the flashing specter of the guy tumbling off the road in the sideview, all arms and legs, a mirrored wink of windmilling sunlit doom, then the desert swallowed him up.

Good riddance.

Only Peterson wished to God he'd had an hour or two to work on the traitor. Briefly it called to mind the old days when he'd worked the FBI's Special Gang Task Force and he found himself alone in an alley with some punk gangbanger. Pipe, sparking electrical wire, glowing cigarette tip, anything to hear Caldwell scream and blubber for mercy while bleating out just what he'd told whoever was now coming to crash the party.

It couldn't be that bad, he told himself, eyes ahead on Mulroy's rig. One chopper was all he'd seen, and there was nothing else on the road. Even still, why were all lanes, east and westbound, empty? And why weren't those smokies, if they suspected something, flying up, lights flashing? What was with the barricade? A gauntlet? A trap? Whatever, it all felt wrong somehow. He was sure any minute he'd find an army of Feds waiting down the road. If that was the case, he'd bulldoze his rig right through the heart of any barricade, pedal to the metal.

"Peterson!"

He winced. There was some note in Mulroy's voice, like urgency—no, terror, he decided—a tone he'd expect reserved for maybe the pilot of a 747 calling ground control, shouting their plane was going down, scramble the firefighters, the ambulances.

Peterson cursed himself for letting his imagination run wild.

He was snapping up the handheld radio, Mulroy wailing on how some guy was standing in the middle of the road, lifting up a big assault rifle, looked like he was aiming a grenade launcher their way.

"Run the bastard over!"

"He's firing! I'm putting on the brakes! Back off, Peterson, I'm trying—"

Peterson heard the frantic cries, raging so loud and clear over the radio, he could have been right inside Mulroy's cab. And the guy was laying on the brakes! Screwing not only themselves, as the rig's end sluiced away, whipping out across the highway, momentum sure to send the whole thing jackknifing....

Peterson heard about dying folks who claimed to have seen their entire lives flashing before their eyes. But at his own frozen moment, where he found himself rushing toward doom, Peterson didn't find himself locked in that rumored cosmic experience.

Peterson saw the future, instead, and all the money he'd never spend if he didn't bail the cab, flying away before his eyes. He still had a good hundred yards before impact, knew there was nothing short of jack-knifing the rig now if he tried to slam on the brakes.

Screw the load, the job. Everybody was about to find themselves on their own, and he offered up a silent good luck to the others.

He tapped the brakes just the same, cutting the speed by maybe ten mph, enough he hoped where he wouldn't hit the pavement and get pulped to a sack of broken bones and spewing innards. He bulled into the door and jumped.

THE TERRORIST CARGO was in a state of frenzy, angry looks shooting his way, dark faces framed in the soft glow of the overhead light, eyes full of suspicion and accusation. Jim Barker and his three pals sent to ride in the back and keep an eye on their human death machines—the whole load of killers worth another forty large in his own pocket—were getting nervous. Barker was looking in the face of mutiny unless the guys got it under control.

"What is going on? What is this talk I am hearing about police?"

Barker was digging out the Italian submachine guns, handing them out, while the dark face kept on bellowing in his ear. He would have sworn he heard a gunshot from up front but with the Arab in his face he could barely hear his own thoughts.

"If this is..."

The guy went on in his blind rage. Barker wasn't listening, tossing out weapons, but heard Petey Garner roar for everybody to shut up. Thank you, Petey, he thought. He looked around, saw they were somehow pulling it together, men now and not mice, tough guys all, and no one there to dance. They were all bunched up near the crates, but way too close to those fifty-five-gallon drums of poison for Barker's margin of comfort. Hell, they made him nervous just to look at the markings—roped together, yes, but if Peterson bounced them through a pothole he could just envision them tipping over, seals broken....

Images of himself burning alive, smothered by a cocoon of toxic goop, the flesh melting off his bones...

"Hey! Listen up!" Barker snarled at the Arabs. "This truck stops, that door opens to a bunch of cops, I suggest you start blasting away."

End of discussion. Now they got it. They were all going to sink or swim together.

A heartbeat later, and Barker knew they were sinking fast.

Barker was feeding a clip to his Uzi submachine gun when he found himself flying, Peterson hitting the brakes without warning for some godawful reason. Airborne, Barker was vaguely aware of shadows pitching all around, blurring ahead right beside him, human missiles, then angry weight bounced off his back and shoulders, slamming into the sides of the wall, guys grunting and hollering in two sets of languages. He was tasting the cold steel of the partition that separated them from the cab when he felt the entire back end of the cargo hold swerving, first one way then the other.

Barker fought to stand, guys cursing and shouting out their fear. He grabbed the steel handle to the partition slat, slid it back to a blast of wind. He was ready to bellow at Peterson when he found the cab empty of their driver.

What in the—

It was only a blur, something looming up right beyond their unmanned rig, and he knew what was happening even before he looked through the windshield. Barker didn't have time to wonder what had happened. The cargo hold shot up like some ghastly billboard advertising his own death, rearing up, holding fast in his bulging eyes, inviting them to crash right through it, steel, flesh, the whole works of both trucks one heartbeat away from the mother of all collisions. Barker barely lasted long enough to stand there and start to scream in horror and rage before the truck's nose plowed into the housing.

ROAD RAGE.

Did he say that out loud, or was it just a thought, attempting to form a picture, or make sense out of the carnage he saw, his own voice talking back to him from somewhere in the strange laughter of his mind? He knew he was dying, wouldn't make it but maybe another minute or so, that much he knew. Whatever had happened down there to cause it all, Cody Caldwell was witness to the worst open highway wreck he'd ever heard about. It looked like the earth had opened up and the sky was falling at the same time, nothing but fire, smoke and thunder.

Somehow, some way he had staggered out of the ditch, his landing cushioned by dense brush, like the hand of God or something wanting him to live long enough to watch the trucks mesh on impact, the walls of both rigs blowing up, stick figures hurled skyward, across the highway, flying out for the desert.

Holding in his guts, he teetered on the edge of the low rise he'd climbed, heard something like the buzzing of a great insect through the ringing in his ears. One second he was hot, his whole body on fire, the next moment a wall of freezing cold dropped over him, head to toe. He couldn't be sure of what he heard as the din shattered his senses, the desert trembled and the sky flashed.

Road rage.

Everything down there was still hurtling in all directions, but wreckage and things that appeared human seemed to hang in his sight, a series of slow-motion picture frames pumping out the images of raging death. Weird, but beautiful, he thought. Was this what dying was like? Was this the sweet taste of redemption, found somehow in the final breath of his life? For damn sure, vengeance belonged to somebody, but who was dropping the wrath and the hammer?

The firestorm blew on from that direction, gas tanks no doubt, topped out back at Tucumcari, ignited from the impact, or maybe the high explosives were touched off.

The sky was burning, either way.

He was vaguely aware of the dust storm, the cold falling over him once again, taking out his legs. The ground rushed up to meet him. The world spun, he sucked wind, but had to give it all one last look. He thought he was laughing, shadowy images of some army of lawmen down there blowing things up, sealing the doom even as broken bodies looked to still be flying around, smoking black mummies launched away on serpentine tongues of fire. Giving it all back and then some, in their faces, to monsters who would have done the same thing to countless innocent people.

Cody Caldwell rolled onto his back, stared up at the sky on fire. This wasn't exactly how he ever saw himself dying, not even in his worst drunken nightmare. Alone, bleeding like a carved-up steer, sucking in his guts, somehow having been on the verge of getting his act together, the promise of a new and sober life where he could make amends, find whatever part of himself, his soul, he'd lost along the way. Now no one would even be aware it had been his call that had saved hundreds, maybe thousands of lives.

Children spared. Parents who would never grieve.

Maybe that knowledge alone, he decided, was tribute and honor enough. Maybe his slate was wiped clean. It was simply time that his marker got called in.

Fair enough. God, he thought, maybe did work in mysterious ways.

It was all starting to fade away, then he felt the grit slapping him in the face, reviving him, cutting away some of the haze. He heard the loud bleating, his mind putting it together then.

The chopper had landed.

He found a shadow, some guy in black standing over him.

"Hey...I'm...Caldwell...you get them..."

"It's in the works."

"I guess...had I been on...truck...my tough luck..."

Was that compassion on the face of the man in black?

"You did right, Caldwell."

"Good...enough...thanks...I needed that..."

The shadow disappeared, Caldwell suddenly feeling no pain, no cold, nothing at all. The sky faded to black.

THE EXECUTIONER WAS digging hard, sprinting for the desert when the lead truck's cargo hold started to topple for the highway, some heaving metallic behemoth only one that was a heartbeat from getting gored and spread all over the road by its homed-in and rampaging cousin.

This strike, Bolan knew, could have been dropped on the enemy here by air, but the soldier wanted to do this up-close and personal, even though he was grimly aware he risked exposure to perhaps radioactive waste, sure to get blown around the highway now.

But this was his show, and he was determined to nail it down and move on.

God's Crusaders, or whatever they called themselves, he thought, were next on the shopping list.

The soldier hoped he cleared ground zero when it happened.

A few more yards, bounding over a boulder and landing inside a ring of rocks, and he looked back. The trailing eighteen-wheeler blasted into the cargo housing, shredding the length of both walls as if they were nothing more than flimsy tin.

Explosions marched down the highway, bodies spinning out of the shooting debris, sailing on, most of the occupants lost to Bolan's view, bodies slamming off the road, skidding off to be devoured by flames when fuel sparked almost right away from ruptured tanks to create a roaring wall of hanging fire.

As he rode out the thunder and the fire, Bolan looked back down the highway, clear accept for some rag-doll figure flopping off the shoulder of the road.

The Executioner was forced to hold his cover for a full minute, wreckage and balls of fire containing UFOs of whatever—human or something else—floating to earth, an arm or a leg, maybe torched up by the inferno out there, plunking off the asphalt. Above the climbing black smoke, Bolan made out the distinct shapes of two fifty-five-gallon drums, suspended above the field of banging debris and smoldering bodies, then dropping, hammering the road, spewing their contents.

The Executioner stood, made a mental note to steer clear of the poison he saw bathing a few unlucky survivors. Some guy started screaming his lungs out, slapping at his face, reeling about, demanding mercy from God somewhere in all that shrieking and cursing.

There were other survivors, somehow thrown clear, bodies trying their damnedest to stagger to their feet. They wobbled, choked on all the fumes, a few of the wounded looking around, dazed, but searching for weapons, a battered hard force looking to find the source of this conflagration and personal misery.

Bolan decided it was time to announce his presence, deliver up the final judgment.

Little Bulldozer paving his march, the warrior strode ahead, pumping out three quick rounds. He caught them in tight packs of six or seven, maybe more. With all the smoke obscuring them, dousing them as not much more than dancing shadows, it was hard to tally up the coming body count when he started the encore of slaughter.

Not that the numbers even really mattered.

The Executioner wasn't in the mood to spare any of these savages who had plotted wholesale slaughter of innocents. The cylinders of the squat rocket launcher kept chugging out 40 mm doom.

HE CRAWLED out of the ditch to the sound of rolling thunder. Peterson dragged himself along on his elbows, wondered why he couldn't feel his legs. Tasting the blood in his mouth, he stared through the fog in his eyes. Craning his head back and around, he saw his legs were still attached to his body, but what had happened during his fall?

No, he heard his mind cry, a pain unlike any he could ever imagine shooting up his spine, bringing tears to his eyes. His back was broken—or worse. Did it mean he was paralyzed from the waist down?

If he was in agony, somebody down the road was in pure hell, he next heard. With the invisible knife digging into his back, he fumbled through the shredded holes of his jacket. Incredibly, he found the .357 Magnum still hanging in its holster. Some sound he couldn't identify left his mouth, and he couldn't tell if he was laughing or crying. The mist started to clear as the pain reached some fiery point between his shoulder blades, digging up the back of his skull, cleaving his brain. What was he doing? He was actually crabbing along, some human snake, delirious from pain or shock, or both. Some big guy was down there, something like a spherical rocket launcher in his hands. The man in black was adding yet another firestorm to that inferno, driving one series of explosions after another into whatever was left over from the crash.

Impossible, he thought. One guy?

He was lifting the .357 Magnum, thumbing back the hammer, when the sky fell, something heavy that sent fresh bursts of fiery agony slamming off his lower back, pinning him there like some bug on a petri dish. He thought he'd pass out from the pain alone, but somehow the picture of one guy down there laying waste to one-third of the operation and pissing all to hell his golden years of sun and fun away carved a bitter anger through him, fueling him to crawl on and give it one last shot.

STEPPING BACK UP the highway, Bolan squeezed Little Bulldozer's trigger, dumped one last explosion into the inferno. The soldier had determined a nice little hot breeze blowing from the east, figured with the gale force of fireballs he was hurling in that direction, whatever toxic fumes or threat of contamination by radioactive waste was getting driven the opposite way.

The soldier had already seen the figure crawling down the highway, trying to raise a big handgun, but the hardman was groaning in mindless agony, his senses shattered and tweaked into fiery pinpoints to every nerve ending, the gun shaking, clearly unable to draw a clear line of fire.

Bolan listened to the firestorm, wondering if anything human could have possibly survived, when he spotted a couple of guys who weren't finished going to the mat. He drew the .44 Magnum Desert Eagle, Cowboy Kissinger's spent labor of love hanging low by his side. Two armed shadows were weaving around somewhere inside the tendrils of smoke. The Executioner dropped them both with two quick taps of the hand cannon's trigger.

The soldier turned toward the crawler. He saw the Black Hawk hovering at some distant point to the east, watching, waiting for the pickup.

Bolan eased away from the cloying stink, the wind gathering some newfound strength, hurling the stench of what he suspected was toxic waste the other way. It was quite the mess he would leave behind, but he was far from wrapping it up.

If Bolan had anything to say about it, the worst was yet to come for any survivors of this conspiracy. He was already thinking ahead, hoping the enemy wouldn't get the word by way of the media about the beginning of the end for them here on an isolated, lonely stretch of desert highway.

Of death and destruction coming for them.

He needed to touch base with Brognola as soon as he was in the air. Somehow, he needed the big Fed to make sure this slaughter show was kept quiet from the public as long as possible.

"What the—"

The crawler looked like some great crimson slug to Bolan, his bomber jacket and jeans tattered from his dive to the highway. Bolan stopped a few feet beyond as the guy sounded off with a fit of croaking laughter.

"I was so close…I can't believe it…"

"Believe it. You're finished."

"Yeah…a broken back's the least of my problems…that it?"

Bolan heard the fire, raging stronger during the silence as the doomed guy looked set to burst into tears.

"Where are the rest of them?"

"Rest of who?" Bolan said.

"The others...where's...the rest of you guys... stole my retirement?"

The Executioner lifted the Desert Eagle. "You're looking at it."

CHAPTER EIGHTEEN

The leader of God's Crusaders could feel the imaginary bull's-eye stuck to his back.

Buck McClintock felt the trouble coming even before it showed up on the monitors. A few belts of bourbon didn't stop the images of gunmen from boiling up, ready to storm the premises, raze the walls. The end was out there, moving in.

No matter how much booze he tried to calm himself with, the images still hung there in his mind's eye, living demons, things of doom, preparing to hunt all of them down one by one. They were burning, determined, inhuman things of fire and death. As he pictured armed but faceless shooters who were prepared to give him the bottom line, that the strong did not inherit the earth, after all.

He wasn't about to go out with a whimper.

Was he just paranoid? Too jacked up on fear, worried the gravy train was rolling out of the depot, his sponsors waving bye-bye? Duping him? Was he just a pawn? Maybe there was an answer. Maybe someone had simply stumbled onto the grounds by mistake. It was dark out there, with the exception of a few lights fixed to the hangars, and they probably hadn't seen the posted No Trespassing signs.

Rage and paranoia aside, his gut told him the end was on the way, just the same, and he didn't need Monroe, Jansen or any other wannabe revolutionaries to tell him that.

So he sat there in his office—barren except for his big teak desk, the mini wet bar, the hanging gun rack with its assortment of rifles, shotguns and pistols—even as he heard Monroe sound the alarm.

Another whine ball, in his face, pointing fingers, scared.

Stress, he thought, was really an unseen killer. Some guys folded under the pressure, others stood tall, made their mark, found their way.

His people didn't understand what he saw, never could in a million years, no matter how much money they were armed with, but that didn't mean he was about to cut them any slack. They hailed from the big cities—no small-town hillbillies need apply—but they still thought it was all some huge good-old-boy joke, whiskey, Johnny Cash, the Rebel flag.

The middle finger to the masses at large. For some reason he suddenly despised all of them.

Okay, he'd misread their hearts, told them what they thought they wanted to hear, playing the role of some scaled-down version of a Hitler or Napoleon preying on their fears, getting them to do what he wanted, as long as he had a pocket full of money. Good God, how the world had really passed them by, he decided. He was a dinosaur, after all, just like the rest of them, shoved out to pasture maybe, wheezing his last breath, still trying to tell them all he'd been to hell and back, listen up or the America the Founding Fathers created would be eaten up by others.

McClintock tipped back the glass, half-empty now. It was like some last request, he thought, sucking down the booze, big tough guy getting marched down the row, look out, dead man walking. What was he thinking? This was the sort of crisis where he was expected to lead.

After he built another drink, he finally looked at Monroe. "You said what?"

Monroe squared his shoulders, standing there, macho posturing, telling him the infrared beams had been broached, heat-seeking scanners on swivel mounts around the perimeter picking up an invader.

One guy? That was it? Lit up on the screen like some alien visitor from a distant galaxy, glowing red on green, somebody out there who didn't give a damn if they went hunting to hang his head next to the bighorn sheep in the game room.

Like they didn't even exist, guy coming in, scythe and all, looking to separate the wheat from the chaff?

It was too much to stomach.

McClintock felt the rage stoke a new fire to kick ass when he heard them out there, pool balls clacking, guys chuckling, glued to the sports channel, something about this year's latest home run race between the two national league sluggers filtering through the thick mahogany double doors.

McClintock killed the drink, slammed the glass

down, maybe it was his desktop, even the floor, who cared. Some uncontrollable rage took over, jolting him, warning him once again his own D day had arrived. It had been what? A day or more since he'd gotten a call from cutouts and sponsors? Standing around, wondering when it would hit the fan? Where was the rest of their money?

No mystery Arab.

No Grevey.

Not so much as a kiss-off, everyone's on their own.

As if he needed to be told that, anyway.

McClintock found himself staring at the wall, wondering where the hell it had gone, and why. He turned and told Monroe, "Go take care of our mystery guest."

"I'M LOOKING at one guy out there. He just made the east corner of Hangar Number One."

Jansen watched the darkness, crouched on the edge of the rise, waiting to hear the order from McClintock. Their fearless leader, he thought, didn't sound so confident when his voice crackled over the radio.

"Proceed, Jansen. Muller and Jenkins are with you, right?"

"They're on the way. What about that chopper I saw?"

"What about it?"

"That was a military bird I saw."

"Monroe's coming out there. If possible, I want you take the intruder alive."

Jansen took the infrared binos. He couldn't believe

just one armed invader was looking to tackle more than twelve men. There had to be more gunmen, maybe moving in from the hills.

"Jansen, you hear me?"

"I heard you."

He jumped, grabbing up his M-16 as the shadows of Muller and Jansen, making more noise than a Macy's parade, stumbled up behind him, their assault rifles poised, fanning this way and that. Both of them reeked of whiskey. Wonderful. They were being hit, and while these two were supposed to be guarding the fort they were busy copping a buzz. Morons. This God's Crusaders thing, he thought, had seen better days. This gig was dead, and maybe he was long overdue to find a life.

"How many guys down there?" Muller wanted to know.

"Just one."

"One?"

Jansen scowled at Jenkins. "Come on, Muller. Jenkins, you wait here for Monroe."

M-16 in hand, Jansen set off down the incline. He gave the desert to the north one last search, but the big chopper that had dropped their mystery guest off was gone. Jansen listened to the silence down there. He didn't like it. Their guy was heading right their way, he was certain, a big assault rifle in his hands, tripping their electronic security devices, several of which were out in the open. It was as if this unknown gunman didn't care whether he sounded the alarm.

Spooky, but Jansen wasn't about to let one shooter put the fear of God into him.

BOLAN DIDN'T CARE that his presence was announced by the motion sensors mounted on the hangars. The soldier wanted to bring the troops running straight into his gunsights. He needed a quick wrap here. Aerial recon earlier in the day had provided him with detailed blowups of the compound. He had the lay of the land, his sights set on the ranch house in the distance. There were still Richmond and Atlanta to consider, Grevey and Powers on the other end.

First he intended to sever one more tentacle of the hydra here before he called in his jet fighter ride.

He was making his way up the back of the hangar, heard then smelled them as they edged up to the corner. Lowering the HK-33 to the ground, the squat rocket launcher loaded up and hung down his back, the warrior palmed the Beretta, the sound suppressor already snug in place on the muzzle.

The few lights that hung along the hangar weren't much to steer him, but they were enough for Bolan to nail the two drinking buddies.

They rolled around the corner and the Executioner caressed the trigger, delivered a subsonic 9 mm message of instant doom. The first hardman was toppling into his comrade when the soldier chugged out another round, coring the guy right between the eyes.

Two down.

The Executioner peered around the corner. At the top of the rise he made out the shadow watching the hangar. The range mentally marked off, the soldier tapped the Beretta's trigger. A heartbeat later he was rewarded by the sharp grunt, the M-16 flying from lifeless fingers, the shadow stretching out in a boneless sprawl.

There would be others. And even if he was going in blind, no fix on numbers, Little Bulldozer would even the odds.

Before moving up behind the hangars Bolan had counted three aircraft parked on the tarmac. A twin-engine Cessna, a Bell JetRanger and a Learjet. He was considering backtracking, unloading some of the C-4 he'd brought to the party before making his final move on the main house. Or maybe he would just blow back into the hangars with Little Bulldozer. The latter made more sense at that point.

The soldier was heading up the side of the hangar to do just that when he heard a voice issue a quiet curse at the sight of the dead man somewhere just beyond the edge of the rise.

MONROE DIDN'T KNOW whether to report to McClintock that Jenkins was dead, grab the infrared binos or proceed down the hill.

He couldn't possibly know another decision altogether was about to made for him.

He looked down at the death mask, framed just barely in the moonlight, but it was a good enough view to spot the dark line of blood trickling from the hole in the side of Jenkins's head. He looked at the ranch house, spotted a few more heads near the SUVs.

They were armed, but they were just standing there. What the hell were they waiting for?

He was about to report to McClintock when he saw the big shadow rise no more than ten feet away, some black wraith that seemed to just grow right out of the ground. The last thing he heard was a chug, then the lights went out.

THE EXECUTIONER crouched beside his third victim, looked toward the main house. He counted maybe ten shadows, most of them grouped near the motor pool.

The soldier decided it was time to announce his presence to the standing guard. He saw a big man filling the doorway, barking out orders. Half the group began to fall back inside the house when Bolan let a 40 mm grenade fly from the M-203. He was filling the breech, tracking on for the motor pool, when the first explosion shaved a few more numbers.

McCLINTOCK ORDERED half his force back into the house. He couldn't raise Jansen or Monroe all of a sudden. The silence out there was fueling his paranoia.

Then the night blew up damn near in his face. Bodies were sailing across the porch, a scream shooting out from somewhere in the smoky thunderclap. The shock waves knocked McClintock down in the foyer, where he skidded on his haunches. Somehow he managed to keep his hold on the M-16. He was standing, survivors scrambling inside for the safety of the house, when the second explosion tore into the heart of the motor pool. The floor shook, and it felt as if the walls would come crashing down. Another fireball blossomed out front. McClintock hauled himself into the sprawling game room.

He was just in time to see a giant sheet of wreckage come hammering through the bay window.

THE EXECUTIONER saw the runners retreating into the main house. They would take up defensive positions, wait for him to come to them.

Fine.

The soldier had more than enough firepower to bring down the house. Just in case a runner or two should make the airfield, he wasn't about to leave anything to chance.

He heard them shouting, wondering out loud what the hell was going on, as he forged down the runway. Little Bulldozer in hand, he closed rapidly on the trio of birds.

The rocket launcher pumped out three quick rounds, and any escape, other than on foot, was shut down.

The night was lit up as the trio of fireballs took to the sky. As it rained fire and trash behind him, the Executioner marched for the scrubland that would take him to their back door.

It was far from a wrap, he knew, but the end here was in sight. Turn up the killing heat a few more degrees, and the soldier could quit this place for another rendezvous with the forces of murder and terror.

CHAPTER NINETEEN

This was crazy, he told himself. This shouldn't be happening, but it was. All he wanted was to get the money, clear the premises, start a new life. Now his whole world was crashing down, going up in flames, everything going straight to hell without rhyme or reason that he could see.

It just wasn't right. So much sweat and toil, so much worry spent to get himself this far, so close to the goal line.

McClintock was searching the area beyond the wavering band of firelight, somebody out there groaning for help, two of his people beside him crouched beneath the windowsill baffled as to how one guy could do all this damage, wondering how much worse it could get—

When it did.

It was all McClintock could do not to shriek his outrage at the sight of the balls of fire climbing for the skies in the distance. He didn't need to see it to know his aircraft had just been blown off the face of the earth.

"Those aren't any cops doing that kind of damage, Buck!"

He looked at Winters's snarling visage, fought down the temptation to just blow the guy away. But he knew he'd need every last man now standing if he was to defeat the force...

Force? He silently laughed to himself. A force of one was about to blow down his door, kick even more ass, and the guy wasn't there to have a chat with any of them in cuffs. This was some kind of military strike, some commando out there winging around grenades, dropping trained so-called professional former lawmen like they were nothing.

"Bentley," he called down the line, "you and Winters move out and watch the back entrance. You see anything, call me."

They left him and the others still alive to watch the burning night, the fires of destruction out there, roaring on like some beacon from hell.

"Who the hell is that out there crying like that?" McClintock rasped.

"It's Richards."

"Well, drag him in here and shut him up somehow."

Someone moved out of the foyer, a little too slow and unsure for McClintock's liking. He cursed, gripped in a near paralyzing fear right then, aware all of them were being hunted like animals.

And that they were marked for extinction.

ENOUGH TIME WAS spent knocking out the aircraft, and enough of the edge of surprise was now lost that

Bolan knew he had to turn up the heat all the way past scorching.

It was time to drop the fires of hell on earth over the enemy.

During the jaunt to circle in and claim this next point of strike at their back door, Bolan knew they were getting it together by now, scared enough to throw everything they had back at the man who'd come here to rock their world into oblivion.

Brognola and the Farm had already run a background check on his enemies here. They were former FBI, ATF, an ex-Secret Service agent from the previous administration heading up this pack of cannibals. As a general rule, the Executioner didn't gun down lawmen, present or former, on the take, dirty as a sewer. He knew there were cops out there grabbing up a bag or two of dope before it went into the evidence locker, or greased with an envelope on a regular basis to look the other way, even help the criminal maintain his ongoing enterprise. Sometimes, though, even iron-clad principles needed fine tuning. This was a judgment call, no more, no less. Whatever these men had been, they had now become traitors, the worst of savages who were all too willing to sell out innocent life, and for pretty much just a buck, if he read between the lines on the intel for this bunch right. They had long since spit on their sworn duty, retired or not, bounced out of their jobs or leaving under other circumstances. Whatever, they had outright sold their souls to America's enemies, forfeited their right for any consideration by Bolan simply because they once had the law on their side. They were bloodthirsty animals, no mistake, out-of-control, going for themselves, armed with some extreme view, no doubt, that America was no longer the land of the free and the home of the brave, where good men and women of honor and integrity could pursue life, liberty and happiness.

No hope, no redemption for any of them here on this night. It wouldn't be the first time Bolan had bucked up against this warped perspective of modern American life, and against men who used to wield the law on their side. Sure, he'd heard the question posed before. Did a doped up, gun-toting, lawless society appearing on the verge of anarchy make the cop, or did the cop make that society? If you couldn't beat them, did you join them? Sure, the soldier knew there were serious problems out there in his country, and some days it all looked lost. But as long as there were good people still in the game and worth fighting for, as long as there were still folks willing to step up to the plate in the face of long odds, when maybe their families and friends and co-workers and certainly the criminals next door were doing their own thing while laughing in everybody's face, he wasn't about to say it might as well just all go to hell, why bother, what's the use.

Not tonight, not tomorrow.

Not ever.

The Executioner walked the talk.

Two extremists materialized in a doorway that

looked as if it led to a kitchen. Crouched beneath a bay window, the soldier armed and let fly a frag bomb. He slipped into a narrow crevice beside the bay window when the metal egg blew.

HK-33 leading his charge, ears ringing some, the soldier burst through the swirling cloud, flying over the sprawled bodies, the assault rifle sweeping, searching for fresh targets. Light, natural or man-made, led the Executioner's run down the hallway. Senses primed to full tilt, he dropped an antipersonnel 40 mm buckshot round into the M-203. They were jacked up on fear. Autofire was unleashed from some point in the living room, spraying the corner.

Bolan took a knee, pulling up a few feet from the corner as angry voices lashed the air.

"Hold your fire!"

"Up yours, Buck! He came in from the kitchen!"

"Move it out, then."

The Executioner pinned down the direction of the voices, knew he'd get only one shot before all hell broke loose again. He hit the floor, crabbed ahead, turned on his side as he made the edge. He had less than a second to take in the numbers, made a group of four on a beeline for cover behind the first pool table. The soldier sent the buckshot charge zipping their way, then threw himself back as autofire opened up.

The weapons fire died in the next eyeblink.

A thunderclap, then two, maybe three sets of lungs were shrieking out their pain and horror.

Arming two more frag grenades, Bolan whipped

his arm around the corner, lobbed the first steel baseball toward the foyer at two runners, then chucked the
second bomb toward the pool tables in the direction
of the screamers.

The twin peals of thunder shuddered the floor beneath Bolan's rubber-soled boots.

Time to nail it down.

The Executioner rolled out, the HK-33 fanning the
smoke and the flying debris. A bloody figure staggered, choking, out of the boiling cloud. Minus an
arm, the hardman still tried to draw a bead on Bolan,
the M-16 snapping a few rounds across the living
room, then the soldier cut loose, stitching a figure
eight over the shooter's chest.

The Executioner gave his flanks and rear a search.
Clear.

"You...who the..."

Bolan stepped into the smoke. A big man, shredded
to scarlet ribbons by buckshot and shrapnel, was
stretched out on the last pool table. All the blood and
chewed-up flesh he saw, the features nearly savaged
to the bone around the jaw and cheeks, Bolan couldn't
be sure who he was looking at, even though he'd
mentally filed away Brognola's faxed jacket with
photo on the leader of God's Crusaders.

"You McClintock?"

"Yeah...you...why...I just wanted the money...I
was set to retire from this bull..."

"Money, huh? I'm hearing that a lot these days.
Must be a sign of the times."

The guy was delirious, going fast, lost in the ashes

of his dead dream. "Sheriff...lot of good he did me..."

The red mass heaved a final breath, convulsing, then rolled off the table. The soldier gave the carnage a look, heard nothing but the firestorm raging beyond the charnel house.

A ROOM-TO-ROOM SWEEP, covering all points of the compound, and Bolan found he was alone with the dead. After calling in his ride, the soldier entered McClintock's office. An aluminum briefcase on the desk caught his eye. He opened it, found rubber-banded stacks of cash, a few computer disks in leather pouches. ETA was five minutes before the jet touched down, so Bolan booted up the computer. He figured McClintock would have whatever was on file coded, but the soldier discovered he wasn't wasting his time. Just like that, he was on-line and reading about the operation here. For some reason, McClintock named names in the organization he coined God's Crusaders—background, duties and so on. Other data. Scrolling on, he read a running diary, complete with routes the terrorist cargo would take—scratch the Oklahoma crew—from Richmond and Atlanta. Looked like the bulk of McClintock's followers were drivers or watchdogs.

And the name Grevey popped up on the file. Blackmail on SCTU's field general, in case it hit the fan? Some more blood money going into McClintock's pocket? Bolan wasn't surprised. It was simply the way of greed.

Bolan was in the act of dropping the disk in his pocket when he heard movement in the living room, two voices echoing horror and disbelief his way.

"Holy...I want to see the army that done this!"

The soldier stepped through the doorway, spotted the two uniforms and said, "That would be me."

They wheeled, started to swing their revolvers at the soldier when they froze at the sight of the assault rifle already trained on them.

"Lose the guns."

They hesitated, thinking about it, but knew they were SOL, then dropped their revolvers. One big fat guy in a Stetson, a short, skinny version of the law to his side.

The county's Abbott and Costello.

Cautious, Bolan stepped across the living room, the HK-33 aimed at a point between the two lawmen. "You alone?"

No reply. A quick burst of autofire over their heads, twitching them into reality check, and the younger lawman blurted, "Yes."

"Shut up, Biff!"

"You must be this sheriff McClintock was talking about."

"You did this? You killed all these men?" the kid said, looking as if he might faint the closer Bolan came.

"Cuff the sheriff."

"Why, you son of—"

Bolan was forced to trigger a three-round burst to

get Biff moving. When the sheriff was cuffed, Bolan told the kid to get on the floor.

"Now, I suppose you're going to kill us, too?" the sheriff growled.

"No." Bolan snapped the cuffs on Biff. "But I'm going to make a suggestion you'll want to give serious consideration to. Tomorrow both of you will retire."

"You're crazy."

"I just might be. Crazy enough to come back here to your county. Maybe pay you a quiet visit some midnight hour when you're tucked in bed and counting McClintock's money instead of sheep. Thing is, if I come back here and find either of you still wearing a badge, I'll be very unhappy."

"And we don't want to see you unhappy, is that it?" the sheriff rasped, but the fear in his eyes, despite the defiance, told Bolan he'd made the guy a believer.

"Sounds like we understand each other."

The Executioner left them to ponder their next career moves. Outside he found their cruiser. Just in case they freed themselves somehow, Bolan held back on the assault rifle's trigger, hosing down the interior, reducing the radio to sparking ruins, then shot out the tires.

The lone warrior found his ride touching down in the distance as he moved off for the low hill that would take him to the airfield.

Richmond was next on the Executioner's menu of death.

Atlanta

"YOU WHAT?"

Grevey listened as Powers handed off the lame explanation. All day they'd holed up in the apartment, putting in the obligatory call to SCTU command in Atlanta. Jeffries, apparently, was flying down, armed with a list of angry questions about the sudden AWOL status of his top field commanders.

"Agents Riley and Burton should be here any minute," Powers said, checking his chronometer. "Makes you feel any better, I ordered one of my own people, Stanton, to come along for the ride. I figure I owe them a talk, try to clear up a few matters. Deflection, that's all."

"You actually gave them the location of this place?"

"I'm assuming we're leaving shortly?"

"We would have been gone already. Now this!"

"Hey, understand, we can't have a few nervous guys, suspicious as hell, maybe tailing us out to the airport."

"So, what are you intending to do?" Grevey asked, as if he had to. The colonel's bags were heaped on the table in the dining room, just on the other side of the wall, the nylon dip pouch opened. "Never mind."

"Just get them to talking. Find out what they know, or think they know. By the way, something's bugging me about our drop to the ocean."

"What?"

Powers didn't speak right away, instead went to the

kitchen and helped himself to a beer. "How in the world are we going out the door of that jet without getting sliced and diced in the engines?"

It was all Grevey could do anymore to keep from bolting for the door, run from this maniac and not look back. "It's already taken care of."

"How?"

"Leland and myself had a section of the floorboard in the cabins of all his jets redesigned, cut out, from the beginning."

"A hole in the floor?"

"A chute. A small ramp we'll jump down, slide off. We'll clear, no problem."

Powers smiled around his beer. "Like I've been saying, you've got all the answers."

"Anything else?"

Grevey jumped at the knock on the door.

"There they are."

Powers faded away into the dining room, rounding the corner. Grevey sucked in a deep breath, heart racing, sure he would find himself staring down assault rifles when he opened the door, that it was over, Jeffries knew about the colonel's ideas on urban renewal, thanks to Belasko...

The knocking turned up a notch, nearly an insistent pounding. Grevey considered pulling the Glock, ready to blast his way outside, make the car, tear ass for the Leland airfield. He looked through the peephole instead. He calmed down some, the pounding in his chest subsiding to a sick flutter at the sight of the three SCTU men standing there, no weapons in hand.

Grevey opened the door, held it back. "Come on in, gentlemen." Was that suspicion on their faces? He tried not to look at them, aware why Powers had called them here. He knew they weren't much older than thirty, wives and kids all three of them. He wanted to be sick, but he'd come too far now to let a few kids stand in his way. "Guys want something to drink?" he asked, closing the door.

"No, sir," Riley said.

"Have a seat," Grevey said, holding an arm toward the couch.

"If you don't mind, sir, we'll stand," Burton replied, sounding tough.

"You want to tell me what this is all about?"

"Commander Jeffries, after the colonel informed us you were here…" Stanton stopped, looking around the living room toward the kitchen. "Where is the colonel, sir?"

"In the can. He'll be out in a minute."

Something was seriously out of kilter here, Grevey knew, then saw Riley stepping toward the kitchen. "Riley, you want to get to it."

Riley stopped, turned and said, "I don't know how to tell you this, sir."

"So, just say it!"

"The word is that Commander Jeffries is en route as we speak."

"En route to where? Here? The command center?"

"He's just left Logan, sir," Stanton chimed in. "We don't know all the particulars, but word is he had a long talk with the Justice Department."

More silence, the three of them trying to say something without saying it. They were on the verge of dropping some bomb.

"Rumor, sir, it's just rumor," Riley continued. "Commander Jeffries hinted at some suspicions about the three previous operations. He did some investigating. He wanted to know why Colonel Powers wasn't on hand for the last raid. Uh, sir, there was... how do I say...a mass murder in Roxbury."

The room wanted to spin in Grevey's eyes as he heard how an eyewitness to the colonel's butcher run had given Powers's description, a sketch artist doing a spitting-image composite of the rampaging killer from Roxbury in question. The colonel, who had worked some with Boston police, he knew, was well-known to the cops. Boston cops laid out their suspicions to Commander Jeffries not more than a few hours ago. Jeffries was finding gaping holes in the latest proposed strike by SCTU ordered by Grevey and Powers. The snow job had melted, Grevey knew.

"So, what's the bottom line?"

"Sir, I'm afraid—"

Riley never finished the ultimatum Grevey knew was coming. It died on his lips as Powers marched around the corner. Grevey dived out of the line of fire, hitting the carpet as the HK MP-5 opened up. Despite the extended sound-suppressor on the SMG, the constant burping, as Powers hosed them down, kicking them all over the living room, sounded like some great trumpet blast in Grevey's ears, a death knell that would have the neighbors dialing nine-one-one.

Stanton nearly cleared the Beretta from inside his coat. He died wheeling toward Powers, a look of confusion on his face as the man he'd followed, from the military and beyond, cut him down where he stood.

Grevey looked up at Powers, as cold as ice, the colonel inspecting the slaughter, something close to admiration in his eyes.

"Believe it or not," Powers said, "I really hated to do that. Stanton was a fine soldier."

Grevey picked himself up, watched as Powers toed the dead, confirming his kills, then the colonel said, "Now, can we leave?"

CHAPTER TWENTY

"We're looking at a runaway train. These guys, I keep hearing 'show me the money,' and it's making me real angry, Hal."

"I hear you, Striker," the soldier's friend told him over his headphones of the satlink with its secured line to Brognola's office. And went on to tell the Executioner the media, along with a few highway patrolmen in New Mexico, were trying their damnedest to pin down the source of all that anger. No sense in crying over spilled toxic and radioactive waste, Brognola had the New Mexico problem covered, stating one worst-case scenario would be for the Richmond or Atlanta crews to turn on CNN and find their plan was quickly getting shot to hell.

Bolan listened to the update, taking in the starlit black heavens beyond the two-man cockpit of the bat-shaped B-2 Stealth.

Good news. The big Fed's teams were monitoring the Leland properties in Richmond and Atlanta, HAZ-MAT units on standby, Virginia and Georgia State Police and the FBI alerted to both situations, but only on Brognola's need-to-know orders. All buildings in a six-square-block radius had been quietly evacuated beyond the targeted warehouses, roads sealed off. Both McClintock's driver-handlers and their terrorist cargo had yet to bail either location. Thanks to McClintock, Bolan had already passed on the routes, final destinations where the murder crews would be off-loaded.

If they pulled out before the soldier could carry out the presidential blessing of "terminate them all," Brognola would act with all available resources at hand. Washington, D.C., Baltimore, Philadelphia, Atlantic City and New York on the plate for the Richmond group. Atlanta, Miami, New Orleans, Houston and Dallas on the other end. At this point, Bolan and Brognola agreed there was no way any one terrorist would reach his destination, even if that meant a whole army of Feds and local cops shooting up the trucks, everything short of calling in an air strike on the nation's highways if the trucks managed to ram themselves through barricades and get that far.

Grim speculation. They were clearly faced with suicide armies in both cities, and people were going to die, no matter what. Say the trucks made the interstates, well, they weren't looking at any lonely desert highways to the east. The potential of more hazardous waste getting dumped on well-traveled roads, with the possibility of innocent people getting caught in some running gun battle between Brognola's forces and the bad guys... Or maybe the terrorists would just set the trucks off, rolling time bombs plowing on for some populated area... Bolan understood, and he didn't need to spell out his own sense of urgency to get to the next stop.

Bad news. Boston PD wanted Colonel Powers for questioning in the killings of more than twenty people in the Roxbury area. Commander Jeffries and Brognola had been in touch, Jeffries laying out his suspicions, but the big Fed told the man the Grevey-Powers situation was getting handled. Part of the problem was Grevey and Powers had gone to ground. Jeffries was on the warpath, thinking some great conspiracy had been played out under his nose, maybe even the Justice Department had duped him, vowed he would be in Atlanta ASAP, turning every stone, marshaling every resource he could to find Grevey and Powers, get to the bottom of what was going on. Brognola had a team watching the Leland airfield in Atlanta where a jet appeared fueled and ready to go. No one had bothered to log a flight plan for the jet in question. The soldier could already see Grevey and Powers slipping through the net.

"They're leaving the country, we both know that, Hal."

"So, what do I do, Striker? Say they show up. Have my guys put them under arrest when they try to board the jet?"

"No. Do whatever it takes to monitor that flight. AWACs, a squad of F-15s, I don't care. I want to know where they land."

"I think we've already got some idea. Part of what you and the team took from the Sudan? Bear traced three separate money wires from the late Omani sheikh's Swiss account to the Caymans.''

"Alert the Coast Guard, Customs, every military base you have to in Florida. Do not have your men approach Grevey and Powers. That'll just get them killed. They're running scared. They'll find out, if they don't already know, it's all going up in smoke. No telling what those two are capable of. If we can shut the operation down these next two stops, the world's not big enough to hide Grevey and Powers. I'll find them.''

"Why do I get the feeling this is going to get real ugly?''

"It's already real ugly.''

"One more thing. My Richmond team sent along some photos they took of a well-heeled mystery man who's been showing up at Leland trucking there, off and on, all day. He's been positively ID'd. Mohammed Amin. Syrian. The CIA had him under suspicion a few years back in Oman as a courier, a bagman for various terrorist organizations in the Middle East. He was more into recruiting new blood for the jihad, establishing weapons pipelines, shoring up the finer details, such as phony passports and visas. Interpol, the CIA, the FBI, Mossad have a sheet of charges on this guy reaches clear across the Atlantic. Guess who he was often seen being wined and dined by when he was a guest in Oman?''

A grim, weary smile stretched Bolan's lips. "And the first two guesses don't count?''

MOHAMMED AMIN was tired of waiting for the phone to ring. Something was wrong, and he needed to go to the contingency plan. One of the Americans came growling at him across the warehouse, his sarcasm only fueling the anger and fear Amin already felt gnawing his insides.

"Staring at it won't make it ring."

The American's name was Blake, the driver of the Richmond truck. Amin resisted the urge to take the Makarov pistol out and blast the fat right off his belly, aware he would need the American's demolitions expertise.

"We've got problems, and that phone call's just one of them."

Amin tried to ignore the American but knew it was pointless. The truck had been sitting in the loading bay for hours, its cargo of freedom fighters getting impatient, a few of them even having the audacity to bang on the walls, demand to know when they were leaving, when they could eat. He was beginning to doubt the courage and resolve of a few of the chosen, figured he had to do something drastic, even if that meant scaling down the number of attacks, cutting back distance to the closest cities or towns, anything, just to get it all launched somehow. A dead infidel anywhere was one less future enemy and oppressor of his people. Perhaps it didn't matter if they died in New York City or some small town in the Virginia countryside.

"We've got cops, looks like maybe FBI down the street, watching us."

The Syrian stared at the American. His mind was racing, wondering why the West Coast-bound unit hadn't called in at the appointed hour. Now cops were outside?

"How do you know?"

"Because I used to be one, that's how."

"Open the truck."

"What? Hey, we should be rolling. Should of left—"

"I want the detonators fixed to all the charges, one main radio frequency on a remote control box that I have! What are you waiting for?"

"You know how long that will take to prime all those charges? You're looking at maybe two hours at least before—"

"Just do it!"

"Hey, I'll do it, but you can get yourself another driver. I'm not here looking to commit suicide."

"Fine. Go!"

The American grumbled something, but Amin wasn't listening. He marched to a deep corner of the warehouse, opened a crate he had reserved for himself. He ignored the worried looks on the faces of his two men, shedding his jacket. Quickly, he dug out the vest with its C-4 bundles, wrapped it around his chest and fastened the Velcro straps on the front. He was forced to hang the shoulder holster at an awkward cant over his chest. He palmed the smaller remote box, dropped it in the left pocket of his suit coat.

"Abdullah, go out there, see if what the American says is true."

"And if it is the American FBI?"

Amin knew he had no choice. It was a shame, he thought, but he might never find himself walking into a throng of infidels on some crowded city street to the north. He might just end up forced to find enough satisfaction in taking out as many American lawmen as possible, clear the way for his truck to blow itself up somewhere in Richmond. "Then we will begin the jihad ourselves, here and now."

GREVEY LUGGED his bags across the tarmac, found Big Mike Leland waiting near the runway. The jet's engines, now cranked up, their pilot barely visible in the cockpit, were music to Grevey's ears. Still, he looked around at the darkness beyond the runway. The skyline of Atlanta to the north was too close for his liking, and paranoia wanted to warn him a million and one eyes were staring their way from the city. And with Powers marching beside him, that weird look in the colonel's eyes ever since he'd gunned down...

"Mike."

Leland, big, white-haired and decked out in his best Armani suit, aloha shirt flaming out a rainbow of color, held out his hand. Grevey pumped the hand, Leland offering the same gesture to Powers.

"Colonel. Glad you could make it."

"Was there ever any doubt?" Powers said, toting his bags, hefting them. "Going somewhere?"

"He's going with us," Grevey said.

Powers shot Grevey a look, then sported something

that struck Grevey as a sardonic grin. "That island's getting smaller all the time."

"Don't worry, Colonel. I'm only staying there a few days. I've made arrangements to get me somewhere else. Hey, retirement, guys, that's what this has been all about from the beginning. Our golden years. Thing is, don't look now, but there's an unmarked. Sitting east on the road, just beyond the office."

"I saw it on the way in," Powers said.

Grevey cursed. "Feds. Look, Mike, we had some trouble. We need to get in the air—"

"Not with those Feds we aren't."

The colonel was getting that look again.

"Sounds like just the sort of problem you can take care of, Colonel."

Grevey found Powers giving him a long, mean-eyed look.

"There's only two of them," Leland said. "From what I can tell, we're clear everywhere else. Just walk up and blow the bastards away, Colonel. No fuss, no muss."

"I trust you brought along an extra parachute?" Powers said.

"I'm not keen on the idea of drowning in the ocean, Colonel. Of course."

"Don't leave without me," Powers told Grevey. "If you close that door before I'm back..."

"Hey, hey, guys," Leland said. "What's with the hostility, all these tense vibes? Colonel, go take care of that problem. What are you drinking?"

"Heineken."

"Sorry, but I did have three cases boated in yesterday to paradise. Second choice."

"Wild Turkey and ginger. Light on the soda."

Grevey watched the colonel march off, angling in behind the office complex, already hauling out the sound-suppressed HK MP-5, depositing his bags on the ground. "He's got five minutes, Mike."

"He has less than that. If you're right about that Coast Guard and Customs time frame, the window's already closing. What's with you and the colonel anyway?"

"I don't know. But he's right about one thing. I don't mean you when I say this, but that island's feeling smaller by the minute."

THE BELL JetRanger soared in on the Richmond skyline from the southeast. Bolan had been in near constant radio contact with Special Agent Cowlins since his Stealth had touched down at Langley Air Base. From Norfolk Bolan felt each minute turn into an agonizing eternity. As promised a fresh blacksuit flight crew was on hand at Langley, and Brognola had delivered the necessary ammo to beef up the soldier's depleted supply of firepower.

The warehouse complex in question was a quarter-mile east of I-95. Poorly lit rows of redbrick and concrete buildings came into Bolan's sight as he stood in the rotor wash of the cabin doorway. Bolan's Justice contact informed him they'd been made, but for some reason, Cowlins stated, the terrorists had opened the back doors to the truck, disappearing inside for nearly the past two hours. Bolan now ordered them to fall back, hold their positions, no matter what.

Problems on the ground.

Bolan couldn't be sure, but something nagged him about the setup. If the enemy had made Cowlins and company, stalled around, delaying the pullout...

They were rigging the truck to blow. If they sent toxic or radioactive waste flying around...

The soldier had no choice but to risk exposure once again. The threat here was so deadly, with countless innocent lives hanging in the equation, if it meant the soldier was forced to give himself up before he took the enemy down...

Brognola would have to carry the torch from there on.

So be it.

Bolan moved to the cockpit, told his blacksuit crew to make a wide angle to the west, then come in from that direction, more or less on the blind side of the enemy. If little else, there was only one truck here to deal with, one SUV and a sedan making up the motor pool. From their surveillance position in an evacuated office building three blocks east, Cowlins filled Bolan in on the action.

The truck's doors were being shut. They were pulling out.

Bolan marched into the wind gusting through the open doorway. The Executioner looped the HK-33 around his shoulder, filled his hands with Little Bull- dozer.

AMIN WONDERED what the FBI or whoever they were was waiting for as Abdullah headed them out, rolling the sedan down between the long rows of darkened warehouses. The main gate was open, all clear, it looked, to the street beyond, which would take them to the interstate. More than two nerve-racking hours since the Americans had primed the loads of C-4 in the truck, Amin forced to malinger and calm the fears of his sixty-plus brothers in the cargo hold of that truck, and they were finally moving. Nothing, Amin thought, would stop him now. The larger of his two remote control boxes was in his right pocket. The smaller box he was hoping to use only as a last resort. If he was forced to, he wouldn't hesitate to blow the truck halfway across Richmond. He was wondering if there was enough explosive inside to take out at least a few square blocks—too bad the last of the toxic and radioactive waste had gone west—looking in his sideview mirror when something like a rocket came streaking down from the roof of the warehouse. He bellowed in rage and frustration at the sight of the truck's cab sheared apart by the explosion.

He was reaching into his right coat pocket when every single window around him seemed to blow a storm of glass in his face. It didn't take but a heartbeat for Amin to realize some of the slivers had gouged into his right eye, his screams of agony like some distant obscenity in his own ears. He couldn't believe the pain, white-hot needles lancing deep beyond his eyeball, something wet and sticky slapping his face. Then he heard the screams from Abdullah....

Amin knew it was finished, that they'd never reach the interstate. He bulled his shoulder into the door, somehow got it open, glimpsed Abdullah out of the stinging haze in his one good eye slumped over the wheel. The sedan was racing for the concrete wall of a loading dock.

Amin flung himself into the wind.

CHAPTER TWENTY-ONE

The Executioner didn't miss a beat, urged into overdrive at this point, suspecting the enemy had made some serious miscalculation for their pullout as far as his sudden appearance went.

Their mistake.

The chopper swinging away from the roof, the soldier drew a bead with the squat rocket launcher and began unloading as soon as he hit the edge. Not a second too soon, he found, but whatever the long delay, all the malingering here cost them their savage ambitions.

The cab went first, as Bolan pumped out the hell bombs from above, holding his ground, raining death and destruction before they knew what hit them. Decimated by two 40 mm rounds, the cab seemed to shear itself away from its cargo mounting, the housing behind it rearing up and through the fireball, bulling next like some rampaging leviathan through the flying engine wreckage, careening for its side, then slamming down on the asphalt. The Executioner already had the HK-33 in hand, running on, firing at the sedan, taking out passenger and back windows with a raking burst, then drilling 5.56 mm rounds through the roof, going for the driver.

He scored the wheelman, at least, as the sedan swerved, roaring on a collision course with a concrete dock. A figure was falling from the passenger door, tumbling up, rolling for a garbage bin, the trailing SUV clipping the lead luxury vehicle's back end, when Bolan caught the mixed bag of frantic English and Arabic shouting to clear the area below.

The way Bolan heard it, some kind of doomsday was seconds away for them if their fears panned out.

"Run!"

"That crazy bastard's got the remote!"

The back doors were flopping open, the cargo of savages disgorging, flailing about, most of them limping but all of them screaming that he—whoever "he" was, although Bolan had his suspicions—was going to blow the whole thing up.

There was a time to hold his ground and fire on, and there was a time to bolt for cover.

It was time for shelter from the coming storm.

The Executioner was racing across the roof when the sky lit up behind him in pure fire and rolling thunder. The door to the wooden housing that led to the stairwell looked flimsy enough but Bolan wasn't taking any chances. He hit the trigger on the M-203, blew the door away on the fly with a 40 mm blast. He could feel the superheated wind racing up from behind, heard it screaming like some living army of demons from across the roof as he hurled himself into the smoke. Bolan found himself tumbling down a short flight of steps, saw the glow of firelight framing a window as he rolled up on a landing. He felt and heard the volcanic eruption of the firestorm heading his way, could well imagine it taking out the warehouse facing, cleaving up the entire length of the roof.

The Executioner shielded his face with the HK-33 and launched himself through the window as rubble and fire poured into the stairwell above.

AMIN KNEW they were all dead down there, but they didn't matter anymore. The great scheme of jihad had gone with them, brothers in holy war to Paradise, the infidels to the fires of hell. He wasn't sure how long it was he'd stayed covered in the ring of garbage bins, but the sky stopped raining enough bricks and body parts at some point for him to stand without getting his skull caved in.

It was finished in Richmond, and he wanted to scream his outrage that luck hadn't been on his side, but instinct for self-preservation took hold, got him moving. At least if he could get somewhere, maybe a nearby restaurant, or grab a hostage off the streets...

It hurt his one good eye to look at the conflagration for any more than a second as he searched for survivors, staggering away from the hot wind, grimacing at the stink of toasted human remains hurled in his face. He checked his left pocket, took out the small box. It was in one piece. If the American law came after him now, he would threaten to blow them up, along with himself. Or perhaps he'd just run straight for them....

A brick ricocheted off his head, the lights nearly winking out as he toppled. When he found his legs again, he began staggering for the opening that would lead to the street. He couldn't be sure how many buildings the explosion had taken out, but the firestorm had been so tremendous he found the SUV that had carried four of the Americans crumpled on its roof, flung like some toy fifty yards ahead. He choked on his own blood, limped on, pain shooting up his legs. A figure moaned for help from the crushed debris. He fisted the blood out of his eye, drew the Makarov and shot the American in the face as he crawled out of the wreckage.

THE OPEN Dumpster garbage bin, heaped with boxes, broke Bolan's fall. After rolling over the lip, the soldier had hugged the face of the bin. It curved on an angle, up and out, and he found himself covered as the sky dumped loads of rubble for a full minute before the pounding subsided to a few flying bricks chinking off the alley floor.

The Executioner stood, marched off down the alley. If anything survived out front it would be a pure fluke. He found his handheld radio intact, raised Cowlins for a sitrep. The agent's voice sounded shaky. No casualties on their end, they'd hit the deck, but a few of them were good and dinged up from flying glass and debris. Cowlins asked for Bolan's position and the soldier told him. A note of urgency or disbelief broke through the ringing in Bolan's head when he heard Cowlins inform him one survivor with a pistol and holding something in his other hand was heading the soldier's way. Cowlins said he was looking through his field glasses, and a moment later he confirmed a Mohammed Amin sighting.

Bolan picked up the pace, HK-33 out front and sweeping the smoke ahead. The soldier ignored the debris still showering, a chunk winging off his back. A pall of smoke hung in the sky above the alley, the heavens above rippling from the firestorm beyond. The blast had been so powerful Bolan spotted entire sections of the back ends of the warehouse walls, here and there, knocked down. Bolan hacked out some of the grit and biting smoke, anxious to cut off Amin and end it. He slowed his pace, lifting the assault rifle when the shadow limped into sight.

"Amin!"

The shadow whirled toward Bolan, limped a few feet deeper into the mouth of the alley. The Syrian held something up in his left hand, shouted, "Do not come any closer! Even from here I can blow us both up!"

Halting, Bolan spied a hole in the wall, ten o'clock, a good three yards off.

"I know you Americans have no wish to die! You will let me go!"

"I don't think so."

"What?" He laughed. "You stupid fool! I'll kill us both! We both die!"

"You first."

And Bolan squeezed off a three-round burst, darting for cover. He nailed the Syrian in the chest, Amin screaming something in his native tongue, then Bolan hurtled himself through the dark maw just as the fireball roared downrange. Bolan grunted as his shoulders hammered into jagged rubble, the hot wall of fire blowing over the hole, shrieking past his point of shelter, taking whatever was left of Amin for the final ride.

THE LAST TERRORIST UNIT had turned a chunk of Atlanta into a flaming kill zone.

But he'd already gotten the worst of all possible news as soon as he was in the cockpit of the Stealth, southbound. Nothing but disaster was waiting on the other end of the quick ride from Norfolk to Atlanta.

The Executioner saw he was way too late.

Bolan found at least three or four blocks of the warehouse district was up in flames as his chopper lowered past the East expressway. He shook his head at the sight, anger and disgust wanting to control the warrior right then. Someone had jumped the gun, blown the call, and he could already see how many things had gone terribly wrong here. As if chewing some butt now and making sure heads rolled mattered.

It was winding down, according to his Justice contact on the ground. Bolan's impromptu LZ was lit up by so many flashing lights, with more local and state police cruisers, emergency medical vehicles, plus the raging pockets of flaming wreckage, he was forced to squint just to hold his bird's-eye view of the carnage.

Brognola had passed on the story of the disaster

here, and Bolan still couldn't believe it. It seemed a patrol car had been cruising past the Leland trucking warehouse, a uniformed officer calling in he'd spotted three men with assault rifles, watching two eighteen-wheelers getting loaded up with crates, the cop wondering why other armed men were moving into the cargo hold as if they were going into hiding, guarding contraband, announcing his own suspicions back to his precinct. Enter Luther Jeffries, SCTU monitoring all local and state police bands from their downtown post. Jeffries—in his feverish determination to track down Grevey and Powers—and SCTU had gone in, announcing themselves. The inevitable broke out, sixty-plus minutes of gun battle, the enemy cornered but having gone down to a man, and at a heavy cost to life on the other side. Armored SWAT vehicles rolling onto the premises. Terrorists, seeing the end of their jihad, made suicide charges for the police and SCTU and SWAT barricades, blowing themselves up.

Not even Brognola had a body count on friendlies taken out by the human time bombs or the hurled rockets and grenades or the thousands of rounds poured on lawmen and SCTU. And the word was Jeffries himself had gone down in a hail of gunfire. Eventually, as the terrorist numbers dwindled, they mined the Leland warehouse, it appeared. When SWAT and SCTU—no doubt squabbling over who was to head the charge and grab the brass ring, kick ass in the name of vengeance for their fallen comrades—finally moved in to storm the place, the whole warehouse went up, taking out at last count about ten police cruisers, two adjacent warehouses and a nearby office complex.

Fiasco was the understatement, Bolan knew, of the new century.

When the chopper touched down beyond the ring of fire, Bolan hopped out. The soldier's face was a bruised mask of cuts, scratches and dried blood. As he stood, handheld radios squawking all around, the flames reaching out to draw out the sweat and wash off some of the soot and grit plastered on him back in Richmond, he took it in. The HK-33 dropped by his side.

It was over.

Out there, he couldn't even begin to count up the number of dead, some covered with blankets, others just left to rot in the heat of the firestorm, presumably bits and pieces of bad guys. They were scurrying all around, checking bodies for a pulse, a few cops steered by medics through the open doors of EMVs. Somewhere high above the rising smoke clouds, Bolan spotted the police choppers. They hovered or dipped into crisscrossing patterns, searchlights fanning wide areas.

"Hey, I know you."

Bolan turned, saw a blacksuited shadow emerge from a swirling mist of smoke and light. It took a moment, but Bolan recognized the face of one of the SCTU commandos from the garage in Boston. The guy looked pissed, and Bolan could well understand his ire. The problem was, there was something accusatory in the commando's eyes, and the soldier wasn't sure how much patience he had left if he was going to stand there and face down some guy's temper tantrum.

"Justice guy, Special Agent Belasko, right?"

Bolan nodded, some point of utter weariness boiling out from deep inside. "Commander Jeffries? I heard he was hit."

The commando jabbed a finger toward a row of body bags laid out by a few meat wagons. "Pick one. Hey, real glad you could make it, Belasko. You know, I heard something. I heard Grevey and Powers maybe had a part in this massacre, that maybe you Justice people, if you'd spoken up and shared a little intel with us peasants, this might have been avoided."

What could he say to that? Bolan wondered. Sure, he could stand there and bounce around a dozen or more "maybe" scenarios. Maybe if he'd just shot Powers in that alley. Maybe if he'd had Brognola circle the wagons and send in the guns...

Skip it. He didn't think so. He was hardly going to stand there and pat himself on the back, but Bolan knew without his role in hunting down large tentacles of the hydra, a whole lot more innocent people would have perished. Then again, in the face of the guy's outrage, he could have stated that maybe if the forces here had held back and a solid plan had been put on the drawing board, instead of three or four different outfits bulling ahead, clogging up the machinery...

Instead Bolan held his tongue, maintaining a stony silence.

"Nice work, Belasko. Real interdepartmental cooperation. What the hell happened to you, anyway?'' the commando rasped, scouring Bolan's face. "You wreck the department's sedan on the way here or something?'' The guy stormed off, muttering something about how Belasko should stick to desk duty and sharpening pencils.

"THE COAST GUARD found the wreckage about an hour ago. Some point in what's called the Tongue of the Ocean, almost smack between Eleuthera and Andros. No bodies recovered.''

"Another smoke screen, Hal.''

After walking away from the hell zone near downtown Atlanta, Bolan had claimed a motel on the outskirts of the city as temporary haven to clean up, get rest, regroup and wait for word about Grevey and Powers. The only good news at the moment was that the dominoes on the edges of the conspiracy were toppling. Bolan's thoughts were somewhere else, down in the Caribbean to be exact, and he vaguely heard his friend go down the list of agencies and names found on confiscated disks who were right then getting snapped up by the Justice Department. He did, though, catch the note of cold anger in Brognola's voice when the big Fed informed him how either Grevey or Powers or both had just marched up to the agents he had placed at the airfield and mowed them down in cold blood where they sat.

"These guys, Striker, they're mad dogs. When I think about how many innocent people have died, how many agents and cops have been killed in the line of duty..."

Brognola let it trail off. Bolan felt his own anger. He wanted to be the one, though, to hunt them down, made that clear to the big Fed.

"I'm already on it. I've got all available resources doing round-the-clock surveillance of an area that reaches all the way from the Florida Keys to Venezuela and Colombia. CIA, DEA, we've got more aircraft in the sky, more boats in the water, the only chance they have of making it is if they're picked up by the Mothership and flown out of the galaxy. I still think it would be a good idea to freeze those bank accounts down there, Striker."

"No. When I find them, I don't want them to have the first clue I'm coming."

"We'll do it your way. Now, here's what I've been able to line up to get you moving again while we're on hold and waiting for a sighting of those two...."

CHAPTER TWENTY-TWO

"Enjoying your second day on the beach, Colonel?"

Powers smiled, an expression he felt even touch his heart, warming his insides just like the sunshine on his face. He adjusted the dark aviator shades, wiggled a little deeper into the lounge chair, then reached over and plucked an opened beer out of the cooler. "Indeed I am. Blue skies, green water, white sand. Cooler full of cold ones, a handful of Havanas in the shirt pocket, bottle of rum. Money in the bank, money buried in the sand. Already sampled some of the local flavor down here in the Bahamas, and I have to tell you, it's nice to know this old warhorse can still put a grin on a young girl's face. What more could a man ask for?" He saw the shadow falling over him, peered over the top of his shades at Grevey, the man dressed in white pants, holstered Glock jutting out over his aloha shirt, dark Blues Brothers shades, Jimmy Buffett shark hat rounding out the picture of a guy on vacation in island paradise—except for the dark scowl on his face, all that tension knotting up his shoulders. Man needed to learn how to relax. "Hey, you're blocking out my sun."

Grevey didn't move. "For some reason, I never quite pictured you in a pair of Speedos."

"Hey, like they say, if you've got it..."

"It never went down, Colonel. Put that in your nut huggers and give it a squeeze."

"I was beginning to think it never would anyway. Too many people were involved. I said that from the beginning, but like I've been telling you lately—you've got all the answers, I'm just along for the joy ride. Made my decision way back when, remember? When you showed me those pictures, told me how bad you needed my gun, my expertise, my military connections, some of my clout on the Hill to get the whole SCTU snow job rolling."

"True enough. That was then. Now, what I'm saying—" the colonel sipped his beer, stretching his legs, working his toes a little when he felt bathtub warm water rolling up under his feet "—maybe you need to start thinking about something else other than your tan."

Powers smiled again, but this time he felt his insides harden, a cold edge moving through his heart. The tone in the guy's voice was grating on his nerves more by the passing hour. Suddenly, he felt the weight of the Beretta on his stomach, hidden beneath a copy of some porn rag he'd found aboard the boat of the late Pablo Ramirez. "You're right," he said, and enjoyed the shadow of confusion on Grevey's face, then added the punch line. "We need to have those girls from the Turks over more often. Have to tell you, Paul, that was quite the party we threw ourselves last night.''

"There's not going to be any more parties like that, Colonel, not anytime soon."

"Shame." He felt the sun gathering heat as the anger mounted, his back dripping with cold sweat, the stink of all the beer and booze and the tangy juices of Lola, his little island girl, oozing from every pore, serving only to remind him he was on permanent vacation and didn't have time for Grevey's whining. "I may just have to borrow one of those cigarette boats, maybe that cabin cruiser, and head out one night."

"Not as long as I'm here."

"You'd still have transportation, what's the problem. What are you getting all pissy about anyway? Here I was, going to say, nice touch, the way you shot up Pablo and his two amigos the other night. Shark bait. I mean you just started whacking them with Pablo's own machete, and chumming the waters, an expert, like you've been with Jacques Cousteau or something all these years. That little display even made me nervous. I didn't think you had that in you. I was beginning to worry about you, Paul. You've been crying about our lack of security around here since we docked. I was about ready to remind you, I'm all the security you need, since I've been the one pretty much up to the other night to do most of the killing."

"Security's just a small part of it."

"You're watching too much CNN you're getting piped in by satellite. Keep it up, and the colonel may restrict your TV hours, send you to your room without dinner. All six of them, which, reminds me, I'll be damned before I give up my quarters. This island's getting smaller by the hour. Someone needs to go, and I hope Leland's got other plans like he said.''

"For some reason, Colonel, I don't find you very amusing.''

"So sue me.''

"We—Leland and myself—have been busy picking up a whole lot of air and boat traffic around this island the last twelve hours while you catch a buzz and watch the waves of your golden years.''

"In case you didn't read the DEA's last intelligence report, we're sitting in the middle of a tidal wave of drugs. It's the Indy Five Hundred out here of speedboats, seaplanes and low-flying UFOs stuffed with bales of coke, heroin and pot. They tell you it all goes through Mexico these days, but that's like the last president swearing to tell the truth about getting a hummer. Speaking of which, all the action last night has left me,'' Powers said, and yawned, "in need of some beauty sleep.''

"Colonel, here it is. The operation, from the Sudan to ConU.S., was terminated, shut down, eighty-sixed. By who or what I don't know. You getting a picture of our problem here, Colonel? I understand some people who helped us along the way, like the INS, a few CIA types, just to name the short list, have been busted by the Justice Department.''

"Justice Department, huh? Next thing you're going to tell me, I suppose, Belasko's going to come swim-

ming ashore, pointing a speargun at us, telling us
we're under arrest.''

"This isn't some joke. I'd tighten up. As for Leland, don't worry, he'll be making room for you come
tomorrow."

"Where's he so hot to get off to?"

"Someplace in South America. The man didn't
quite say."

"Yeah, down south. You know, I was sitting here
thinking anyway. Soon enough I'm going to get
bored, most likely I'll R and R myself right off this
island. I'm thinking you'll have the whole place to
yourself soon enough. Could be it's best that way.
You know how far our Yankee dollars will go, say,
in Caracas, Bogotá, Buenos Aires, Rio?"

"I've got to imagine the exchange rate..."

"Turns even a piddly ten grand gringo into fifty
easy. Live like a king the rest of my life, instead of
seeing you standing there in my sun, fucking with my
head, wringing your hands like some little snot-nosed
punk." Powers slipped his finger around the trigger
of the Beretta, Grevey tensing. Powers grinned as the
man relaxed. "There you are. Relax. Take it easy.
Put on some trunks, take a dip. The hard part's over.
It's easy street, mister, from here on."

"Okay, Colonel. Fine. Enjoy the sun. Go on, take
your nap."

"Why is it I get the feeling here I should be reading
between the lines?"

"No, you don't have to. I mean it. I mean I'm only
the guy who set up this whole operation, landed us

this little slice of heaven. Radar, sat dish, all the electronic surveillance and scanning gear. And don't sit there and tell me I shelled out a bargain basement price just to get some drug dealer down here out of a jam.''

"Listen to yourself. Now you want to tell me, I suppose, I haven't kicked in my fair share.''

"Do what you want. You're going to anyway.''

Grevey moved out, the sun blazing back full in the colonel's face. He turned in his chair, watched as Mr. Killjoy tromped up the sand, marching an arrow straight course for their stone-walled, thatched-roof compound. Back to CNN or watching the radar screens or whatever. Powers felt his blood racing, silently cursed Grevey for pissing on paradise.

Powers killed two quick beers, forcing himself to relax, listen to the waves, the birds in the jungle vegetation near the beach flapping and cawing, soothing his nerves some more with their sounds. How could there be noise in paradise anyway?

Everything was beautiful.

He put Grevey and all his fears out of mind, felt the warm envelope of much-needed sleep calling him down. He figured some music, turned up to a decent volume, would help put him under. He slipped on the headphones, opened his CD box behind the cooler. What the hell, he figured, some classic rock. One more beer, the CD player cranking out the good old stuff, back when they used to write songs and not bellowing anthems of rage and hate, and he felt his eyes grow heavy, the smile twisting one corner of his mouth, the sun beating on his face like a lover's touch as he drifted off. A long nap was all he wanted, one that came filled, of course, with dreams of Lola.

"WE'VE GOT THEM."

It was late in the morning of his second day on Great Exuma when the Commanding DEA Section Chief of Bahama Sector One-Midway made the announcement. Bolan was pivoting away from the computer-enhanced digital wall map of the Bahamas to South America, a number of cays and islands already flashing red where known pirates and drug runners used them as way stations or hideouts.

Once again, Bolan had Brognola to thank for getting him down here, the big Fed wielding Justice Department clout, backed by a presidential directive, to see the soldier track down the last traitors of the terrorist conspiracy with all the help of the DEA at his disposal. Bolan had pored over more aerial photos, map grids, even flying along for hours on end with the DEA when he had started to have some doubts. Bahamas. An archipelago of roughly seven hundred islands, almost twenty-five hundred islets and cays, stretching northwest to southeast for some 760 miles. Bolan was beginning to give up hope the combined resources of the DEA, CIA, the U.S. Navy, Customs and Coast Guard could pin down his quarry from a mere air search alone. It helped to have some eyes in the sky, but Bolan had been forced to wait for the necessary satellite passover of the Bahamas.

It was done. Almost.

Commanding Special Agent Brockton rolled through the doorway of the prefab corrugated outpost, marched up to the wall map and stabbed an area due west of the Caicos. He handed Bolan an eight-by-eleven color blowup, and the soldier felt the tension tighten his fingers into steel pipes. The expression on his face must have been all too easy to read.

"Right. There's your guy, this bastard, Colonel Powers. Just came through in my office. Sitting on the beach, working on his tan, this little island of theirs, not much more than a sand spit really. Word is some businessman bought it from a crooked cop in New Providence a while back, said businessman bringing snow to the islands—fancy that—who turned around and dumped it off about a year ago to two Americans, way a source of ours tells it. For once, I tip my hat to a few Congressmen back home. The latest budget for our war on drugs landed my people down here a Raven EF-111A. It primarily detects what I'll call hostile radar, and their radar is lighting up my Raven's screens to new levels. It also has long-range heat-seeking, scanning, infrared photo equipment... I'll spare you the particulars, I know you're anxious to be on your way. This other sheaf of pics details every square inch of their little nest down there."

Bolan looked at the map, gauging distance, travel time by chopper and eventually boat, putting together an attack strategy when Commander Brockton rushed to assist once again.

"This little piece of info should help you out,

Agent Belasko. I took the liberty to mark off a point
of penetration on the northwest edge of the island.
Little cove, plenty of rocks there to conceal you
should you decide to swim in. My new bird tells me
there's only two pieces of electronic surveillance in
the trees from that point in—yeah, my Raven's that
good. I marked them off, too, on a grid map. One
heat, one laser sensor. A little trail that cuts to what
looks like the big hut, couple hundred yards to the
south. Somebody got cheap on the north side maybe,
I don't know, maybe they figured the rocks and lack
of white sandy beach would discourage a landing.
What do you need?''

Bolan appreciated the commander's thoroughness,
efficiency, and the look of grim determination to get
him underway. Brockton asked no questions, even
though he could venture a guess this wasn't some day
at the beach the soldier had planned. ''A wet suit,
rebreather, a fast boat and a fast chopper, and a wa-
terproof bag to stow my weapons and gear.''

Brockton appeared to size up Bolan, something in
the man's eyes telling the soldier the man had deep
suspicions Agent Belasko was something far more
than a special agent from the Justice Department. He
looked ready to pursue a line of questioning but said,
''Look, I've got an outpost right on the edge of North
Caicos. I can have you choppered there, a cigarette
boat some drug dealer no longer has any use for on
standby. Save you a whole lot of time, if you were
planning on taking a boat ride from here.''

Bolan smiled from the heart for the first time in

what felt like a hundred years and offered his hand. They shook. "I appreciate all of your help, Commander."

"Yeah, well, the scuttlebutt I've heard, this Colonel Powers pulled a dirty stunt involving a couple of CIA guys down in Panama, you know, during that little war to grab up Noriega. The rumor mill has it he and a couple of spooks helped themselves to a small planeload of coke back then after a failed hostage-rescue attempt to free some Americans. My gut's telling me the reason you're here has something to do with what has happened in America involving some terrorists. I'm thinking the good colonel is something like, uh, shaving the stripes off that tiger. You still have a tiger."

It wasn't quite the way Bolan would put it, but the commander was close enough. It hadn't been that long ago when Bolan had come closer than he cared to man-eating crocodiles, left thinking of them as cold-blooded killing beasts, devouring life just to sate their primordial savage hunger. As he left, Bolan formed a brief mental picture of Grevey and Powers as more croc than tiger. They had devoured life, left behind a legacy of murder and mayhem, and now they were down here stretching out in the sun, leaving it all behind, the dead, the wounded and the living who would have to go on with shattered lives, grieving over lost family, friends, co-workers.

Bolan couldn't wait to help them along in their retirement. Their golden years should last forever, as far as he was concerned. In fact, the Executioner set out to put them both on permanent vacation.

GREVEY TRIED to keep the panic off his face, but Leland was squawking about the object on their radar screen, coming in low and hard, aimed right for the northwest end of their island like it was full of some deadly unknown purpose.

A quick head count, wishing there were a few more guns than what they'd brought. Grevey pulled up the bamboo door in the floor of the living room, growling at someone to give him a hand. An extra pair of hands slipped into the narrow space, and, grunting, Grevey hauled the large steamer trunk out of the floor, dumped it at his feet. He opened it, took an M-16 with an M-203 grenade launcher for himself. No way would he would get caught short on firepower. If it was a Coast Guard plane, a DEA chopper even, he would blow it out of the sky, run and hop one of the cigarette boats on the other side of the island, be in Caracas by nightfall.

Leland was snatching an HK MP-5 subgun, wanting to know about the colonel.

"All right, everybody calm down a second," Grevey said, walking for the open doorway, peering past the palm fronds hanging from the front porch. "Everyone take a deep breath. It could be nothing."

"Not the way that blip on our screen was flying in," Leland said. "Where's the colonel?"

Grevey stepped across the porch. At a time like this it would have been helpful to have the colonel's services, all that so-called military expertise, killing gusto, just in case a problem was, in fact, landing in paradise. But Grevey found the colonel slumped in his chair, one arm hanging over the side, head lolling, mouth open. At first he would have sworn the colonel was dead, then he heard the sonic boom of the man's snoring.

"Screw him," Grevey said. "If it is nothing, I'll just have to listen to more of his crap how he's the only one here with a real pair. If it is something then we'll handle it, come back and I get to do some chuckling."

Leland pinned Grevey with an incredulous stare. "This isn't some pissing contest between you and the colonel...."

"Settle down, Mike. It is just that. You don't know what I've been through with that guy. Come on, there's a main trail that leads to that part of beach. Let's roll, gentlemen. Smart money says it's just some doper looking for a place to lay low. That's the case, well, he can park it for a small fee."

Grevey found he was the only one laughing, a hollow sound, trailing off for the wall of jungle vegetation, swallowed up by the cawing of wild birds.

As SOON AS the soldier was hunkered down in a narrow clearing off the trail, but hidden from any extended probing looks by giant palm fronds and other vegetation that looked as if it predated the days of the dinosaurs, he tapped the button on his com link. A vibrating signal was bounced back, telling him the crew of the Sea Stallion was on the way to get the enemy nervous and running.

Bolan waited, scouring the trail in both directions, finally holding a long search for any sign of movement south beyond the rainbow of light knifing through the canopy above. From the direction of his penetration, he heard the hard chop of water spraying against the boulder-strewn inlet. Nothing the other way.

He took a few moments to search the forest, quietly draw in long intakes of air after his hard swim, and before that feeling the adrenaline while choppered to the Caicos, geared up the whole time for his piece of Grevey and Powers. From the DEA dock at North Caicos, donning wet suit, Bolan had ridden in by a cigarette boat to a predetermined drop-off point two miles out to sea, then gone over the portside after a check of the shoreline through his field glasses, the cigarette speeder never slowing. It was a hard dunk into the water, but Bolan wanted it to look like nothing more than some speed jockey or maybe a drug runner out there in case eyes were watching from shore. Coming ashore next, climbing deeper into the rocky inlet, he shed flippers, mask, the tank, then wet suit, his skintight blacksuit worn underneath. A watertight nylon bag had brought in the same combat harness and weapons he'd so far used to scythe down the enemy on this campaign. The commander had been right about them either being cheap or overconfident, perhaps, that this end of the island didn't warrant serious surveillance. So far Bolan hadn't detected anything other than the two surveillance boxes, hidden by some foliage in the trees, right where Brockton Xed the spots.

If Bolan had anything to say about it, this was the enemy's last error in judgment.

The soldier heard the bleat of rotor blades, saw the foliage obscuring the shoreline shimmy as the Sea Stallion went into its decoy maneuver. It came to a hovering point at the end of the trail leading out to the beach.

HK-33 in hand, the Executioner lowered the assault rifle when he thought he heard the rustle of clothes on leaves up the trail. He definitely heard someone grunting, maybe nearly tripping as he sensed the enemy picking up the pace. Reaching for the sound-suppressed Beretta, he expected them to send out one, maybe two hardmen to check out the blip on their screens.

He didn't count on finding damn near a full squad marching past his point of hiding.

"Slow it down."

Bolan held his breath, the shadows creeping by one by one. Five, six, then he glanced up and found that it was Grevey who was growling out the orders. Bolan crouched lower in the frond leaves as Grevey started to turn in his direction, eyes wild and looking around. The man slowly walked on.

"What is it?"

"I can't quite see from here. It's a big chopper, that much I know."

The soldier waited as they kept moving past.

HK-33 in hand, he reared up, glancing back down the trail, found it clear in that direction, and opened up on their blind side, full-auto and blazing on. He managed to drop four right off, his line of slugs chewing through the heart of their ranks, up spines, shattering skulls, screams rending the air. But at least three hardmen were already looking to get off the trail, moving with the desperation of doomed men who still believed they had life left worth fighting for. Bolan winged two of them, small comfort when ragged bits flew from their shoulders, since he had the full and raging attention of survivors.

The soldier was plowing ahead through vegetation, filling his hands with Little Bulldozer as a locust storm of steel-jacketed lead ate up the vegetation behind him. No time to accurately sight and seek out clear targets, the soldier began pumping out 40 mm grenades. They started bellowing in pain and shock, close by, ragged bloody things lost in the smoke and fireballs as Bolan marched a line of thundering doom from front to rear, side to side of the trail, a mental target range of the runners and survivors he'd seen moments ago guiding the pealing death knell.

Bolan dropped the spent rocket launcher, rammed a fresh magazine into the assault rifle and stepped out onto the trail. Right then his eyes would have to do, since the in-close detonations left his bell ringing. He hadn't gotten a clean look at every face, but as he rolled over the dead with the toe of his boot or the smoking muzzle of his assault rifle, he didn't find Powers.

Something wriggled in the dense brush ahead. The bloody thing rolled out, and somewhere in the bloody face Bolan saw the eyes widen in recognition. He couldn't be sure if it was anger or bewilderment he saw, but Bolan didn't care.

Grevey stared at Bolan, spent his last breath on earth looking as if he'd been cheated out of something, then the Executioner hit him with a quick burst of permanent vacation.

PRIMED FOR ANYTHING, the soldier fanned the HK-33 down the side of what appeared an upgraded, sprawling Quonset hut. Somehow this picture of paradise, with its allure of peace and serenity, the birds, beach and coconuts, didn't jibe with the kind of men the warrior had left strewed down the trail in a hundred-plus torn pieces.

Speaking of savages, he began to wonder if Powers was even on the island. Of course, the colonel could be heading out to sea right then in one of three boats the commander's Raven had picked up....

The Executioner spotted the figure in the lounge chair just as he made the front steps to the big hut. The sun was on a waning arc by now, but the glassy-smooth waters beyond the white carpet of beach still winked like countless glittering diamonds as they mirrored dying daylight. Why wasn't the colonel moving? he wondered, working his way, slow and cautious, down the beach. Closing, half of the soldier's grim focus was fixed on the wall of tropical paradise to his side, wondering if a few gunmen were poised to let it rip. There was no itch, though, between his shoulder blades.

Advancing, Bolan noted the headphones attached to a CD player, heard the snores rumbling all of a sudden from the man's chest, rattling out of his gaping mouth like a buzz saw.

The colonel had slept right through mop-up. But this killer had put in a few big days, the soldier knew, busy holding his world together, setting up the innocent for the slaughter, and the six empty bottles, going down real smooth, no doubt, had certainly helped put the bastard under. Whatever worked to get him there, up and over the man, the soldier decided, and kept the grim smile off his lips as he walked up behind Powers. Spotting the Beretta under the dirty magazine, he hooked a finger through the headphones, tugged them off the colonel's head, tossed the whole thing out to sea. Bolan had the HK-33's muzzle up and aimed at Powers's face as the man jerked awake.

"You'll never make it," Bolan warned him.

The warrior saw about six different expressions sweeping the colonel's face, the man's head most likely buzzing with a slew of questions, eyes behind the aviator shades searching for some exit, mind digging around for reasons or rationales to change it all—there had to be some mistake here.

"Caught napping," the soldier said, backing two steps into the surf. "But, hey, what's to worry? This isn't Roxbury, right?"

Powers chuckled. Bolan didn't bother with any demand to see his hands.

"Belasko. I bet that's not your real name. I bet you're no G-man, either."

"It's over, Colonel."

"Is it?"

Pulling it together, smiling, a shark in human skin.

"You want a beer, Belasko? I've got some cigars, some of Fidel's finest, right there."

"Maybe later."

"Couldn't just kill me in cold blood, huh? Kind of like Roxbury. I see you standing there, wondering what the hell, where did I go wrong, why a war hero would sell out, grab the brass ring. Maybe thinking," he went on, everything but his mouth frozen solid before the unwavering muzzle of the soldier's weapon, "if you'd gunned me down in Boston a whole lot of lives would have been spared."

Bolan wasn't there to spill his guts to this traitor. He did, though, silently admit he'd perhaps made the wrong call in Boston. It was rare when the Executioner second-guessed himself, but had it not been for Sudan... He caught himself, aware this journey through hell had carved a big piece out of him somewhere deep inside, bearing witness from start to finish to new extremes of man's inhumanity to man, seeing animal man sink to new lows where greed and desire for only self were concerned, and everyone else could go to hell.

Truth was, they had.

It would have been enough to make any soul pose a few big questions, and Bolan chalked it up to that.

"Okay, Belasko. I take it Grevey and Leland and

their vaunted security have been AWOLed for good to the great unknown.''

''One way of putting it.''

''I'd offer you money to let me go my way, make sure I turn up at the next party, but looking at you I think I'll just hear something about how you're not for sale.''

''Could have made it big on one of those psychic hot lines, Colonel.''

Powers chuckled, but something subtle changed in the man's voice. ''I was getting tired of Grevey and the others anyway. This island was getting real small.''

''It was just never meant to be.''

''I guess so. Now what, Belasko?''

Bolan let the muzzle drift a few inches off the mark. ''I think you know.''

''Paradise lost, that's the way it has to be?''

Whatever beast raged inside the man roared just enough to the surface to tip Bolan off, the colonel going for it. The Executioner cut loose, the HK-33 snarling at near point-blank range as the Beretta flew up, tracking.

The Executioner let the spent clip fall. The surf rolled past Bolan, absorbing the crimson run-off, taking the blood of the savage out to sea.

On the way past the sprawled body, which flopped once and rolled into the surf, Bolan helped himself to one of the colonel's Havanas. He might smoke it later, but right then he just wanted off that island. No matter how many versions of paradise on earth were offered up his way, looking to entice him into something else than what he was, the Executioner could take some small comfort he'd never become what the surf was now picking up to carry out to sea.

It wouldn't be long now, and the hungry predators out there would give one of their own a fitting burial.

TAKE 'EM FREE
2 action-packed novels plus a mystery bonus
NO RISK
NO OBLIGATION TO BUY

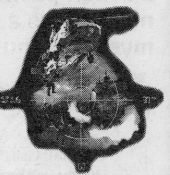